Contemporary

Ecuadorian
Short Stories

Translation by Mary Ellen Fieweger

La Cantidad Hechizada VII

PARADISO EDITORES

Eloy Alfaro 20-13 y Suiza, edificio Suiza

Teléfonos: 2445278, 2445279

Fax: 2445276

Email: paradisoeditores@porta.net

Quito, Ecuador

ISBN: 9978-23-008-4

Printing: Génesis Ediciones

FIRST EDITION

Contemporary Ecuadorian Short Stories

Selection, prologue, and notes by
Vladimiro Rivas Iturralde

Paradiso editores

PROLOGUE

Until the mid-twentieth century, Ecuadorian narrative was characterized by a high degree of uncertainty, as evidenced by suspect signs of identity. It was clearly the mestizo narrator, educated to a greater or lesser degree, who provided indirect testimony of social life. Between the thirties and the forties, these narrators had written about the Indian, about the *montuvio**, about the mestizo of the sierra and the coast, about the black, about the fisherman—in the singular and from above—reducing the complexity of the literary experience to something approaching gross over-simplification. Within this monolithic tradition of social realism, writer Pablo Palacio (1906-1947) was one of the few who dared swim against the current, becoming a fore-runner of Latin American's fantastic literature.

But rather than its monolithic character, what is surprising, and shocking, about this tradition is its longevity. Those who created works of social realism, including Jorge Icaza, José de la Cuadra, Pareja Diezcanseco, Gil Gilbert, Aguilera-Malta, Gallegos Lara, Adalberto Ortiz, and Angel F. Rojas, are certainly not to blame for the fact that Ecuadorian narrative stagnated during those years. They did what they had to do. It is their successors who are responsible for this situation, those who, fearful of unleashing the mad

---

*Term used to refer to rural inhabitants of coastal areas in Ecuador

woman of the house (the imagination, Ruiz de Alarcón *dixit*), allowed themselves to be guided by a moral (and even moralistic) prudishness, which was, in fact, a form of self-censorship, and cultivated a literature of the epigone, worn-out and insipid, a veritable monument to tedium.

This panorama remain unchanged for a generation, relieved only by poets Jorge Enrique Adoum and César Dávila Andrade, until the sixties and seventies, when new and original writers burst on the scene. The appearance of these writers, whose works form the bulk of this anthology, was not a matter of chance. The evolution of the socio-cultural structures of Ecuador, the growth of cities and the deepening of contradictions, the distance from, and the re-reading of, writers from the generation of the thirties, and, above all, the explosion that was the Latin American literary boom, made possible the works presented in this volume.

The birth of these new writers was not an easy process. Ecuador has evolved much more slowly than most other Latin American countries. Until the mid-twentieth century, literary tendencies and tastes leaned toward a recalcitrant *indigenismo* and the social realism developed by the narrators of the thirties. There was no other tradition. Geographically and culturally isolated, virtually at the margins of Latin American history, we had nothing to tell, in political terms, except for the tiresome repetition of military coups, nothing to describe, except for the repression of Indians, *montuvios*, and blacks of the Sierra and the Coast. Ecuador's writers seemed determined to turn their gaze outward; no one was looking within him- or herself. In an eminently rural society, with indigenous groups accounting for

45% of the population, mestizos (perhaps the only potential creators of literary culture in a country divided between indigenous illiteracy and the social and cultural irresponsibility of the dominant class) learned to present, in their most lucid moments, their own contradictions, their own class and racial divisions. Jorge Icaza managed this feat, in exemplary form, in his best novel, *El chulla Romero y Flores* (1958). So, too, did Alfredo Pareja Diezcanseco in a series of novels of tremendous vitality and testimonial force.

The oil era, which began in the early seventies, transformed the country. In Ecuador's cities, especially Quito and Guayaquil, it sped the delayed process of urbanization, a phenomenon that in other Latin American metropolises, such as Mexico, Lima, Buenos Aires, Santiago, Bogota, and Caracas, had produced great migratory waves after World War II. Only then did Ecuador's three major cities begin to think about themselves in narrative terms, which is not to suggest that prior to that time good novels and stories were not being written. However, it was with the oil boom that the bureaucracy and consumerism grew, along with the foreign debt and the gap between rich and poor. A new social class came into being, an upper middle class tied to monopoly capital, but also to the culture being produced in the centers of power. This relationship was beneficial in a number of ways: The educated classes became more familiar with European and North American literature, more influenced by film, jazz, rock, and modern communication media. The Cuban revolution had already provoked, in the sixties, a vague Latin Americanist dream in the consciousness of these groups, a dream from which they would take some time to awaken. The Spanish American literary boom was a tradition that would be legitimately appropriated, but it also became an impediment. A number of idols were dethroned—the writers of the thirties— and others were erected—those of the Latin American boom—who no doubt enjoyed more literary glamour than did their predecessors. But this was a phenomenon not only of the boom writers, but also of the enormous wave of literature that accompanied them. The writers of the thirties had created under the light cast by Zola, Baroja, Barbusse. The new writers, under that of Faulkner and Onetti, Conrad and James, García Márquez, Carpentier, Lezama, Cortázar, and Borges. In the sixties in Quito, the *tzántzicos* (head shrinkers) flourished, a group of young writers who created a cultural and political movement much like that of the Colombian *nadaístas*. Its members hoped not only to demystify but to destroy an elitist, traditional culture rooted in social acts, good manners, and polite speech. They proposed to take poetry, theater, and narrative to the masses. But it may be that in their emphasis on the political, they sacrificed the artistic. With a doctrine based on intellectual patricide, they produced, in the long run, interesting narrative works—though only after the movement turned critical and eventually disappeared—including the short stories of Abdón Ubidia, Francisco Proaño, and Iván Eguez, and the essays of Fernando Tinajero and Agustín Cueva. Critic Juan Valdano notes the existence of a

> generation of 1944 divided into two currents: those born between 1914 and 1929 who, while not cutting themselves off completely from the tradition established in stories from the preceding period (social realism and protest), attempt to

rejuvenate that tradition by adopting the new techniques of psychological realism (Pedro Jorge Vera, Alejandro Carrión, Adalberto Ortiz, Arturo Montesinos Malo, César Dávila Andrade, Nelson Estupiñán Bass, and Rafael Díaz Ycaza, among others). During the sixties and seventies, we already discover a different type of narrative in the works of writers who belong to the second current of the generation of 1944 (born between 1929 and 1944).

Adoum belongs to the first group, while in the second we find Miguel Donoso Pareja (1931), Carlos Béjar Portilla (1938), Marco Antonio Rodríguez (1941), Raúl Pérez Torres (1941), and, those more closely related in terms of date of birth, including Carlos Carrión (1944), Iván Eguez (1944), Francisco Proaño Arandy (1944), Vladimiro Rivas (1944), Abdón Ubidia (1944), Juan Andrade Heymann (1945), Javier Vásconez (1946), Jorge Dávila Vásquez (1947), Iván Oñate (1948), Jorge Velasco Mackenzie (1949), and Eliécer Cárdenas (1950).

The members of this second current are the creators and the protagonists of the new Ecuadorian short story, who will be followed by an explosion of notable writers, especially in Guayaquil.

But the growth of the generation of 1944 has not been smooth. It should be remembered that its members have required a long time to discover themselves and the world around them. Laboriously, and with a great deal of sacrifice, this generation has come to literary maturity, that is, an understanding of what a story or a novel is, and how one lives the writing of these works. These writers participated in the political, social, and economic backwardness of the country, the horrendous national dispersion, the historical disillusion rooted in the defeat in 1941 in the war with Peru and prolonged through the administrations of five-

time chief of state José María Velasco Ibarra and the
military dictatorships of the sixties and seventies. The
insularity of the nation was accentuated and reflected in
the works of young writers who continued to cultivate a
sort of literary populism, a linguistic *costumbrismo*, and
an urban colloquialism, none of which did our narrative much good; many of these texts were practically
unreadable beyond the borders of Ecuador. The "tech-
nical" problems, on the other hand, had a hypnotic and
limiting influence for some time. Writers experiment-
ed in a void for the purpose of experimenting. They
attempted interior monologues, for example, whether
or not the technique was justified. On the other hand,
the response of those who were conscious of the depths
of the nation's spiritual depression, drowning in a
hemispheric situation with no exit in sight, was to display a literary world appropriate to what they were living internally, a world enveloped in a rarified, almost
mummified air: the stories of Francisco Proaño Arandy,
for example, with their gloved atmosphere and pensive
prose; the absurd life projects, impossible in the end, of
Ubidia's solitary characters; the agonizing, decadent (at
the beginning) worlds of Javier Vásconez, which he
later transformed into sagas peopled by dark characters.

Both in this generation and in that which follows—
until Leonardo Valencia (1969)—we find a healthy cos-
mopolitanism, an air of freedom for so long absent
from Ecuadorian narrative. Action can be situated in
any part of the world and in any period. Vásconez,
Oñate, Rivas, and Valencia have set their stories not
only in their native land but also in Prague, Barcelona,
Italy, Madrid, the Basque Country, Paris, the

Caribbean, Cuba, China, modern-day Rome, and even Imperial Rome. The erotic world, explored so effectively by Iván Eguez and Miguel Donoso Pareja, has become one of the pillars of our modern narrative. The exploration of the socially and sexually marginal (Velasco Mackenzie, Raúl Vallejo, Javier Vásconez) has revealed, with audacity, unknown facets of our national reality and, above all, has become literature. The novel of the anti-hero has been a healthy development, as witnessed by the works of Ubidia and Vásconez. The techniques and resources used are no longer the "technicisms" of yore—a too visible and immediate heritage of the boom narrators—but, rather, are tied to, and blended with, ethical proposals. Now the important is what matters: not so much the solipsistic scaffolding of the text but the purpose of that scaffolding in the ethics of the story, its role in questioning the world. Because without questioning the world, true art is impossible. Vásconez, for example, one of our finest writers, has undertaken the grand adventure involved in searching for the absolute narrative: that place in which character and author, dream and reality become one, with no need for explanations as regards their fusing. Thus, there are reasons for optimism about the future of the Ecuadorian story. Vásconez, along with others of his and succeeding generations, knows that there is still much to be done in Ecuador, that writers must continue to verbalize, to found, or, better yet, to re-found, a tradition.

And here I offer a truism: The individual who puts together an anthology is making a bet, undertaking an adventure. This volume is no exception. I assume responsibility for its successes and its failings. Only years from now will readers know whether the authors whose works are included in these pages had something to say and knew how to say it with literary dignity. Nevertheless, I have selected writers whose work is solid, that is, published and sustained over time, and with meaning for the time period in which the works were produced. The twenty-seven authors included go from César Dávila Andrade (1914-1967) to Leonardo Valencia (1969), preceded by a portal composed of two columns: José de la Cuadra (1903-1941) and Pablo Palacio (1906-1947), our founding fathers, the former, precursor of magical realism, and the latter, grand representative of the Latin American vanguard of the twenties and thirties. I have omitted from this selection other writers from the thirties and their successors (Pedro Jorge Vera, Alejandro Carrión, Cuesta y Cuesta, Montesinos Malo), not because they do not merit inclusion, but because they figure prominently in the anthologies of their time, for example, that of Benjamín Carrión.

The works of many contemporary narrators have been translated into English, French, German, Italian, Russian, Bulgarian, and Portuguese. The prestigious German publisher dtv (deutscher tashenbuch verlag), for example, has released four editions, beginning in 1992, of a bilingual anthology of Ecuadorian short stories.

The reader will find the remarks in this prologue amplified, with additional specific information on the writers, in the brief comments preceding each work.

Finally, I would like to thank Hernán Lara Zavala, who encouraged me in this project in Mexico; his successors, Ignacio Solares and Felipe Garrido, who took up the post and knew how to wait; and Javier Vásconez who, in the course of wonderful conversations, helped me to see the panorama more clearly.   The essential critical anthology, *Cuento ecuatoriano de finales del siglo XX* by Raúl Vallejo (Quito, 1999), has been an indispensable resource in putting together this work, as have the equally marvelous *Antología de narradoras ecuatorianas* by Miguel Donoso Pareja (Quito, 1997) and *Así en la tierra como en los sueños* (Quito, 1991) by Mario Campaña, and the bilingual anthologies published by Librimundi as well as those by Cecilia Ansaldo, Eugenia Viteri, and Hernán Rodríguez Castelo.

JOSÉ DE LA CUADRA
(Guayaquil, 1903-1941)

Lawyer, teacher and government employee, José de la Cuadra's professional obligations often took him to rural areas on the coast of Ecuador, and these visits provided inspiration for the characters and themes he would use in his stories. With Joaquín Gallegos Lara, Alfredo Pareja Diezcanseco, Demetrio Aguilera-Malta, and Enrique Gil-Gilbert, he was a member of the "Guayaquil Group," whose works would become the basis for writers working in the social realism vein in Ecuador.

De la Cuadra's short story collections include *El amor que dormía* (1930), *Repisas* (1931), *Horno* (1932), and *Guásinton* (1938). He also published a novel, *Los Sangurimas* (1934) and was at work on another, *Los monos enloquecidos*, when he died in Guayaquil, in 1941. Finally, he published *Los montuvios* (1937), an essay on the *montuvio*, or backwoodsman, the term used to describe the rural inhabitants who dwell in areas along the coast and in the foothills of the Ecuadorian Andes. *Obras completas*, the complete works of de la Cuadra, was published in 1958. The volume includes chronicles, portraits, articles, and uncollected stories.

In describing the customs and denouncing the conditions in which Ecuador's *montuvios* lived, de la Cuadro elevated the craft of the short story to a fine art. Myth plays a leading role in his works. *Los Sangurimas* prefigured the works of magical realism which would come to flower during the boom years of Latin American literature. In the novel, his characters and their complex family relationships are interwoven with myth. His style, influenced by that of Barojo, is rapid-fire, with short, sometimes incomplete, phrases. A number of his stories are, at one and the same time, intimate celebrations of human solidarity and veritable prose poems.

GUÁSINTON
THE STORY OF A BACKWOODS ALLIGATOR*

I've found the *lagarteros*, the gator hunters, in places so diverse and unexpected that some turn out to be extraordinary in the extreme, unless you consider the nomadic nature of those men and their roving habits that lead them to wander far from the aupicious rivers and swamps, moved, perhaps, by an unconscious desire to forget the tremendous dangers associated with their trade. I ran into them one time when I was traveling on horseback from Garaycoa to Yaguachi. There were two of them then. One, already old and slight of figure, was a cripple; at one time, in who knows what distant pit, he lost forever to the jaws of the gators his right leg, cut off above the knee joint. The unfortunate man had a pitiful limp, and he leaned on a crutch of yellow wood, rough and out of proportion, that elevated his shoulder and obliged him to twist his trunk to the left. He was thus a curious sight, held at an oblique angle to the ground, which, contrary to all human sentiment, made you want to smile a little. I didn't exchange words with him beyond the required greetings, but from my hired man, who knew him, I

*From the collection *Guásinton*, 1938.

found out that, not withstanding his advanced years, he was still dedicated to the high-risk practice and that he was reputed to be a very skilled harpooner.

The other hunter, much younger than the first, looked to be his son or nephew. He treated the cripple with the unmistakable air of family. He was a strong young man, with a thick neck and rough complexion. Nevertheless, beneath his coppery skin there was the pallor of malaria or ankylostomiasis. But he didn't display any visible trace of his dealings with the green savage. His body remained whole. Up to then, at least, the saurians had respected him.

When the hunters had passed, I asked my traveling companion, "What's the old man's name?"

"Celestino Rosado," he replied. "You haven't heard folks talk about him?"

"No. Who is he?"

"Well…Celestino Rosado…I believe he's from around Balzar or Congo."

My long-legged hired man related what he knew about the hunter, which wasn't much.

He ended with, "He was one of them that killed Guásinton."

"Guásinton? And who was Guásinton?"

"Guásinton was, well, he was Guásinton… A gator this big…."

The hired man made a sweeping gesture with his hand that took in meters of the path.

"Real big!"

Unfortunately, at that very moment the cross on the church of Yaguachi, under whose sway Saint Hyacinth performed his famous miracles, appeared on the horizon.

My guide pointed at it. "We'll be getting there soon."

And I don't know how he got himself tangled up in a complicated speech about how the rice harvest had been so good and why, therefore, the price of the grain was so high in Guayaquil.

"It's because of the factories, naturally! There's nothing worse..."

The "factories" were the mills.

And that was the first time in my life I heard talk of Guásinton.

I didn't really know, not yet, who you were, Guásinton, man-eating alligator...

I didn't suspect that your ten yards of savage beast in water would plague my dreams on sultry nights when I lay down to sleep in the stern of the mountain canoes plying the backwoods rivers.

And I also didn't know that your right hand was mutilated and that you were without the most powerful of your claws... Guásinton, illustrious cripple.

I remember that I met up with the gator hunters again in Samborondón.

It was at night. The following day was the town's major fiesta, in honor of its patron, Saint Ann, and everybody was in the streets.

Samborondón was a fantastic sight, lit up by Chinese lanterns and jolted by the explosions of firecrackers.

We were drinking at Victoriano Acosta'a saloon that's on, or used to be on, a corner of the square. I was at a table near the bar, with other traveling salesmen. Back then money flowed in rivers in Samborondón;

and during fiestas we sold great quantities of our cheap merchandise. On that occasion, I had a huge shipment of gingham, and I'd sold the lot for a healthy profit. So I was satisfied and in the mood for a good time.

There had been a great afternoon of cockfights, and between one fight and another I'd downed shots of cane liquor so that by the time night came I must have been a little drunk. I don't remember that detail very well.

My neighbor at the table, a traveling salesman for the Beer Company, said to me, "How about it, Concha, let's hire some musicians to play for us."

(Because that's my name, Valerio Concha, and, as I've already insinuated, I move around the countryside engaged in the lucrative and honest profession of traveling salesman.)

I accepted my colleague's invitation, and thus, after overcoming a thousand setbacks because musicians were scarce in the partying town packed with tourists from the city who had them giving serenades hither and yon, we got an orchestra reduced to its basic parts, namely, a guitar and a tiple.

With our improvised orchestra, the salesman from the Beer Company and I, along with some other salesmen who joined us, went to the house of the widow Vargas who, in addition to being one of the most solid businesses in town, had a collection of samples made up of pretty daughters and their partying friends.

The dance we threw was merry and ardent, but I didn't participate much. I was tired and so I looked for a quiet corner in the dining room, next to the bar. Those who hated the foolish noise and loved alcohol gathered there, among them, Don Macario Arriaga, a backwoods landowner, a character well on in years and learned, and, as I found out much later, another of those who killed Guásinton.

Yes, by then I'd know for some time: Guásinton was a gigantic man-eating alligator, the center of whose misdeeds was the area around Babahoyo, from the lowlands of Samborondón to the backwaters of the tiny port of Alfaro, just across from Guayaquil. I had also learned, not long before, that like one of those legendary pirates who during the boardings lost their hands to the axes of the ship's defenders, he was bizarrely maimed. But I didn't know that that had happened in a heroic episode, and that his lost paw thus represented a sort of medal for bravery.

Don Macario Arriaga told me about Guásinton's bold feat, the time he was maimed.

"Guásinton was in heat, and he came downriver, with a female, on an embankment. A paddle steamer (I believe it was the *Sangay*; yes, it was the *Sangay*) crashed into the embankment. Guásinton was enraged: Just imagine, they had interrupted him in his conversations; he was enraged and went for the boat. Of course, one of the wheels dragged him in its wake and I don't know why it didn't destroy him, but the tip of a vane cut off his right hand. Blood streaming, Guásinton swung around and tried to attack again, but the pilot skillfully maneuvered the *Sangay* on its side and got away from him. Those who witnessed the scene say that it was something oddly moving. No one in the boat dared to fire his weapon at Guásinton, think about that, they could have killed him then and there, easily, he was two meters away, but the courage of the animal paralyzed them, because nothing is as moving, sir, as courage. So they let Guásinton escape, and he went back to his female on the bank.

Two individuals I had never seen before approached. They were guests, like Don Macario himself, of the widow Vargas.

Don Macario introduced them, "Jerónimo Pita... Sebastián Vizuete... The gentleman... Look, sir, at the coincidence we have here: They were also involved in the hunt for Guásinton, when we put an end to him... with Celestino Rosado, with Manuelón Torres, with... There were fourteen of us; were you aware of that? The hunting party. And we were lucky: There was only one dead and one wounded. That's it. We were lucky, indeed.

Pita and Vizuete were professional gator hunters. They loved their trade like a cult, bloody and savage, but generous with the faithful.

For them, the green beast of the rivers, the alligator of the hot tropical waters, wasn't just any old prey, but an enemy, in spite of its reputation for clumsiness, in fact astute, and brave, besides. The hunt for the alligator was for them what the contest with the beast is for the bullfighter: an art they judged noble and dignified, and one that, moreover, provided something to eat.

Pita and Vizuete, with confirmation on occasion from Don Macario, recounted that night isolated feats of the fluvial hero, who somebody, no one knew who or why, christened with a backwoods version of the North American general's surname. (It wouldn't have been for reasons of toothlessness, of course, since the backwoods monster possessed a formidable set of teeth.)

One could fill a large volume with Guásinton's singular feats, and I harbor the hope that this tome will be written. There wouldn't be anything strange about that, especially today when people have acquired the knack for writing biographies of just about every Tom, Dick, and Harry, and even biographies of rivers. Apart from that, Guásinton deserves a biography.

It was an original spirit that animated that dark green giant, armored like a battle ship or like a medieval knight, and who measured ten yards from the tip of his snout to the tip of his tail.

They say he was generous, like a benevolent god. Between a horse grazing on the bank and a woman washing clothes on the shore, Guásinton preferred to devour the horse. The housewives insisted that it was compassion rather than gluttony that moved him to choose the beast rather than the loudmouthed female.

It was only during periods of great famine that Guásinton went after people. Normally he swam with those who were bathing, serene, powerful, aware of his power, without bothering them, without even letting them know he was there, apparently. So he satisfied himself with the tribute he collected from the herdsmen: Whenever they had to drive a herd from one side of a river to the other, Guásinton was there, attracted by who knows what mysterious information, to demand his rights as feudal lord of the backwoods waters. He claimed a cow, just one cow, no more, but the largest one, always the largest. Guásinton chose well. And he didn't do anything to the rest of the cattle, nor to the herdsmen. They knew the custom of the saurian, and set aside his cow in the negotiations:

"Bring the price down a little," they said to the cattle sellers, "so that Guásinton's cow won't cost us so much."

The cow they had to pay for permission to cross the river…

A safe river, when all is said and done, since Guásinton did not consent to have a single competitor about: When some silly little alligator dared to slip into the Babahoyo after a long siesta in the quaking bogs, Guásinton knew at once.

On the riverbanks his fame was almost mythical. There was a kind of veneration for him, very like a religion. It all began with frightening the children with his terrible name, and later the fright spread to the adults. As tends to happen, from that fear a superstition was born, and from that, something like a cult.

When, entertained by amorous enterprises, perhaps, of which he was particularly fond, or simply sleeping the long sleep of his species, he was late in appearing in the usual area, people asked, vaguely troubled, "What's Guásinton done with himself?"

And they added, now fearful, "A bad sign! The river is going to dry up this year."

Because according to popular belief, Guásinton, lord of the waters, brought the water with him.

Sometimes Guásinton altered his old habits. This happened during the hungry times. Then he climbed up to the pastures along the riverbanks and dragged away his prey. He attacked the canoes, upending them with a slap of his tail and devouring the occupants. He turned into a sinister force, a fury unleashed.

But that soon passed, and Guásinton returned to his usual placid ways. He developed an ear for the sad music of the backwoodsmen; because even if one believes that alligators are practically deaf and guided only by smell, it seems that Guásinton's hearing was very sharp and that he even found in that sense a special delight.

They say that at night, when the fishermen played their guitars while taking their catch to market, Guásinton, like a faithful guardian, followed the canoes, and if one of them made a misstep and fell into the water, Guásinton moved away at full speed, no doubt to avoid the temptation to eat the man.

Thirteen experienced *largarteros*, armed with repeating rifles and aboard two iron canoes, were needed to kill Guásinton.

And even then it wasn't easy; because the animal defended himself tenaciously, and on dying he took with him one of his killers and seriously wounded another.

It was Don Macario Arriaga who mounted the expedition and directed it. A curious thing: Don Macario never haggled with Guásinton over his cattle tribute; but one day Guásinton devoured Don Macario's favorite dog, and that made him decide to put an end to the alligator. Here's where that saying about small beginnings applies…

They had to proceed in great secrecy on forming the expedition, so that the people along the rivers who took Guásinton for a being almost supernatural wouldn't find out.

Bait didn't work with the old saurian. He followed from a distance the pigs tied to the canoes or rafts, behind which the watchful gunners shielded themselves. He made fun of the little hat trick. As is well known, this ruse involves a hunter who, bare-chested and armed with a knife, submerges himself in the water, letting his hat float on the surface. The alligator is fooled and takes off for the hat, believing that the man is there, while from below, swimming fast, he emerges and stabs the beast in the belly with the knife once, twice, three times, until he gets to the breathing apparatus and the animal bleeds to death. Very dangerous, the little hat trick! If the first knife wound is not decisively mortal, the bold attacker perishes without fail in the jaws of the gator.

With Guásinton, they had to use methods more subtle than the ordinary. They watched him for a number of days, until they found out that he generally rested in a certain pool, small and calm, but deep. He went there one morning, and the hunters quickly blocked the mouth of the pool with a floodgate, prepared beforehand, of boards and barbed wire.

José Carriel, the most courageous *lagartero* of all time in Guayas, dived into the water, dagger in hand, to defy the beast.

Guásinton refused to fight at first. He would have known that he was trapped and tried to force his way out, breaking the lower part of the floodgate, without coming to the surface. He must have been wounded by the wire because at the mouth of the pool the water was stained with blood. And when he doubtlessly failed, he turned, furious, against the man.

Carriel was waiting for him, alert, tracking his movements by the swirling mud. He dived and managed to stab him, but the gator was quicker: With a formidable slap of his tail, he brought him to the bottom, with his spine broke and his head smashed.

At that point, Don Macario Arriaga ordered the hunters to take up positions on both banks of the pool and to fire their rifles into the water.

"One of the bullets will get him," he said.

And an amazing thing happened: Guásinton—who under water was invulnerable within his armor of shell and in light of the scant force of the bullets fired from up close—jumped to land; and mad, monstrously mad, he attacked the men. They were disconcerted by this unexpected turn of events, and the beast took advantage to carry away with a single bite half of Sofronio Morán's leg, which was what was closest to his jaws.

But the men recovered. Instead of taking care of the wounded man, they moved back, and a shower of bullets fell on Guásinton.

He turned over to die, belly to the sky. His legs flailed about as though trying to grab onto something. He opened and closed his enormous jaws and emitted a deafening roar, still threatening.

Don Macario Arriaga approached to finish him off. He didn't have a chance to plunge the dagger as intended: At that very moment the indomitable spirit of Guásinton departed to become one with the great all…

The ten yards of his body shook violently and the gaze of his bloodshot eyes was fixed on the void:

Guásinton, feudal lord of the backwoods waters, was now, and forever more, invincible…

PABLO PALACIO
(Loja, 1906-1947)

Before his death, syphilitic and insane, in Guayaquil in 1947, Pablo Palacio published one collection of short stories, *Un hombre muerto a puntapiés* (1927), and two novels: *Débora* (1927), and *La vida del ahorcado* (1932)

Three books were sufficient to earn for Palacio his reputation as the father of the Ecuadorian short story, and one of the greatest writers among the Latin American vanguard of the twenties. He is a narrator of the strange rather than the fantastic. His is a literature of limits. From the scathing social criticism to the self-absorption of his characters, from the humor to the terror, from the abrupt phrase to the most surprising digression, from the watchful lucidity to the demented outburst and the delirious image, from the straightforward prose to the poetic tremor, his texts are an experience in limits. Palacio was, above all, a magician of reality, that is, a humorist—a rare species in a period of combative, severe builders of realist literature and of a nation. His humor requires victims, and Palacio chose to sacrifice his creatures, diminishing them, turning them into midgets on the altar of his discourse.

A MAN KICKED TO DEATH*

At approximately twelve-thirty last night, Police Constable no. 451, the officer on duty in the area, found an individual by the name of Ramírez in a state of nearly complete prostration on Escobedo and García streets. The poor wretch bled profusely from the nose, and interrogated as he was by the Constable, said he had been the victim of an attack by a number of individuals whom he did not know, simply for having asked them for a cigarette. The Constable invited the victim to accompany him to the police station in order to provide the necessary statement so that the matter might be cleared up, which Ramírez categorically refused to do. Thus, the former, in compliance with his duty, requested the aid of one of the drivers from the nearest station and took the wounded man to the police where, in spite of the medical treatment provided by Dr. Ciro Benavides, he died within a few hours.

This morning the Commissioner of the 6th, having complied with the procedures prescribed, has been unable to

---

*From the collection *Un hombre muerto a puntapiés*, 1927.

discover anything regarding the murderers or the background of Ramírez. All that was learned, through information come upon by chance, is that the deceased was
depraved. We will do our best to keep our readers informed
of all that is learned about this mysterious event.

The *Diario de la Tarde*'s crime section said nothing
more.

I don't know what my state of mind was then. The
fact is, I laughed with glee. A man kicked to death! It
was the funniest, the most hilarious of occurrences
imaginable, to my way of thinking.

I waited until the next day when I leafed anxiously
through the Diario, but about my man there was not a
line. Nor the following day. I believe that after ten
days nobody remembered what had transpired on
Escobedo and García.

But I became obsessed with the matter. Wherever I
went, that hilarious phrase followed me. A man kicked
to death! And all the letters danced so gaily before my
eyes that I finally decided to reconstruct the street
scene, or to penetrate, at least, the mystery of why a citizen had been killed in such a ridiculous fashion. By
Jove, I would have liked to undertake an experimental
study; but I've seen in books that such studies propose
to investigate merely the how of things; and between
my first idea, which was that one, reconstruction, and
the second, to inquire into the reasons that motivate
certain individuals to attack another with their feet, the
latter seemed to me the more original and beneficial for
mankind. Of course, the why of things, they claim,
falls within the realm of philosophy and, in truth, I
never found out what, if anything, philosophical my
investigations were going to have, besides which, any-

thing containing even a hint of that word thoroughly depresses me. In any event, between fearful and discouraged, I lit my pipe—that is essential, very essential.

The first question that arises for those who dirty their hands with these little jobs is that of method. This is something that students at the University, the teacher colleges, the high schools, and, in general, all those taken to be educated, know by heart. There are two methods: deduction and induction. (See Aristotle and Bacon.)

The first, deduction, would be of little interest, it seemed to me. I've heard that deduction is a method of research that goes from what is best known to what is least known. A good method, I confess. But I knew very little about the matter and would have to move on.

Induction is marvelous. It goes from what it least known to what is best known... (How does it go? I don't really remember... Anyway, who does know about these things?) If I've got it right, this is the method *par excellence.* When one knows little, it is necessary to induce. Induce, young man.

The matter resolved, the pipe lit, and the formidable arm of induction at hand, I hesitated, not knowing what to do.

"Well then, and how do I apply this marvelous method?" I asked myself.

This is the result of not having made a careful study of logic! I was going to remain ignorant as regards the famous incident on Escobedo and García streets simply for my damned laziness as a youth.

Discouraged, I picked up the *Diario de la Tarde* for January 13—that fateful *Diario* had never once left my table—and sucking vigorously at my lit, big-assed pipe, I read again the crime report reproduced above. I had to furrow my brow as is a studious man's wont, a deep line between the eyebrows being an unmistakable sign of concentration.

Reading, reading, there was a moment during which I was nearly dazzled.

I was particularly struck by the second to last paragraph, that part about "This morning, the Commissioner of the 6th…" The last phrase put a gleam in my eye: "All that was learned, through information come upon by chance, is that the deceased was depraved." And I, by means of a secret intuitive force that you wouldn't be able to understand, read it thus: *Was depraved*, in prodigiously large letters.

I believe that it was a revelation from Astarte. The only point that had any importance for me from then on was to prove what sort of depravation the dead man Ramírez had. Intuitively, I had discovered that it was… No, I won't say it, lest the memory of the man offend the ladies…

And it was essential to verify through reasoning what I knew intuitively and also, if possible, with proof.

For that purpose, I set out for the Commissioner of the 6th, who could provide the relevant facts. The police authority hadn't succeeded in clearing up anything. He was very nearly unable to understand what I wanted. After long explanations, he said to me, scratching his forehead:

"Ah, yes… The matter of one Ramírez… Look, we haven't a clue… The thing was so obscure! But take a seat; why don't you sit down, sir… As you may already know, they brought him in at around one and about two hours later he died… Poor man. Two photos were taken, just in case… a relative… Are you related to Mr. Ramírez? You have my condolences… my most sincere…"

"No, sir," I said, indignant. "I didn't even know him. I am a man who is interested for reasons for justice and nothing more…"

And I smiled ever so slightly. What an intentional phrase, eh? "I am a man who is interested for reasons of justice." How that pained the Commissioner! In order not to distress him further, I quickly added:

"You've said that you have two photographs. If I may see them…"

The esteemed functionary pulled open one of the drawers in his desk and rummaged through some papers. Then he opened another and rummaged through some more papers. In the third, now in a frenzy, he finally found them.

And he behaved in a very courteous fashion:

"You are interested in the matter. Taken them, then, sir… You are obliged, of course, to return them," he said to me, moving his head up and down while pronouncing those last words and delightedly displaying his yellow teeth.

As I put the photographs away, I expressed my endless gratitude.

"And tell me, Commissioner, sir, you wouldn't remember any particular distinguishing mark the deceased might have had, any detail that might reveal something?"

"A distinguishing mark… a detail… No, no, he was an absolutely ordinary man, of course. Like that, my height, more or less (the Commissioner was somewhat tall), stocky and flabby.   But a distinguishing mark...no...at least not that I recall..."

Since the Commissioner could think of nothing more to say, I left, thanking him again.

I went home in haste; I closed myself up in the study; I lit my pipe and took out the photographs, which, along with the note in the newspaper, were precious documents.

I was convinced that I would come upon no others and resolved to work with what fortune had put within reach.

The first step is to study the man, I said to myself. And immediately got to work.

I looked, and looked again, at the photographs, one by one, making a complete study of them. I brought them close to my eyes; I held them at arm's length; I attempted to discover their mysteries.

Until finally, having looked at them for so long, I managed to memorize his most recondite features.

That savage protuberance that was his forehead; that long, strange nose so like the crystal stopper on the water bottle at the restaurant I frequent; that long moustache curving downward at either end; that pointed chin; that lank, tangled hair.

I took a piece of paper and sketched the lines of which the face of the deceased Ramírez was composed. Then, when the drawing was finished, I noted that something was missing; that what I had before my eyes was not he; that I had left out a complementary and indispensable detail...

There! I again took up the pen and completed the portrait, a magnificent portrait that were it cast in plaster would not be out of place in an Academy. A bust whose chest had something of a woman's.

Then… then I became enraged with him. I gave him a halo! A halo that is fixed to the skull with a little nail, like those fixed to the images of saints in churches.

The deceased Ramírez cut a magnificent figure!

But, where is this going? I tried…tried to find out why they killed him…

Then I came up with the following logical conclusions:

The deceased Ramírez was called Octavio Ramírez (an individual with a nose like that of the deceased can by called by no other name); Octavio Ramírez was forty-two years old; Octavio Ramírez was badly dressed; and, finally, our deceased was a foreigner.

With those precious data, his personality was completely reconstructed.

All that remained, then, was the bit about the motive, which, for me, gradually took on more elements of evidence. Intuition revealed all to me. All I needed to do, a small point of honor, was to eliminate the other possibilities. The first, the question of the cigarette, according to his statement, merited no consideration whatsoever. It is absolutely absurd that an individual would be so vilely victimized for such a trivial thing. He had lied, he had disguised the truth; worse, he had killed the truth, and he had done so because he would not, he could not, reveal that other matter.

Would the deceased Ramírez have been drunk? No, that cannot be because they would have noticed immediately at the police station and that fact would have been so clearly stated in the newspaper as to leave no doubt, or, if it hadn't been included due to the reporter's carelessness, the Commissioner would have revealed it to me without hesitation.

What other vice might the unfortunate victim have had? Because, as for being depraved, that he was, a matter nobody will dispute. The proof is his obstinacy in not wanting to declare the reasons for the attack. Any other motive could have been stated without embarrassment. For example, what would have been shameful about these confessions:

"An individual deceived my daughter; I ran into him tonight in the street; I was blinded by rage; I told him he was a swine; I went for his throat, and he, aided by *his friends*, has done this to me;" or:

"My wife betrayed me with another man I tried to kill; but he, stronger than I, began to kick at me furiously;" or:

"I got mixed up with a woman, and her husband, by way of revenge, attacked me in a cowardly manner with *his friends*."

If he had said something like any of this, the incident would have surprised no one.

It would also have been very easy to declare:

"We had a row."

But I'm wasting time, these hypotheses are without foundation: In the first two cases, the relatives of the unfortunate man would have come forward; in the third, the confession would have been unacceptable because it would have been too honorable; in the fourth, we also would have known about it by now since, inspired by revenge, he would have revealed the names of the aggressors.

None of what had come to me via the deep line between the eyebrows was what was evidently true.

There is no need for further reasoning. Consequently, bringing together all of the conclusions arrived at, I have reconstructed, in summary, the incident that occurred on Escobedo and García in these terms:

Octavio Ramírez, an individual of unknown nationality, forty-two years of age and of ordinary appearance, lived in a modest hotel on the outskirts of town until January 12 of this year.

It seems that this Ramírez lived off his income, very modest to be sure, which did not allow for excessive, and certainly not extraordinary, expenditures, especially on women. From a very young age, his instincts had deviated and they corrupted him in succeeding years, until, due to a fatal impulse, he would end in the tragic fashion we so lament.

In the interest of greater clarity, let it be known that this individual had arrived only a few days earlier to the city, theater of the incident.

The night of January 12, as he dined in some dark eatery, he felt an already familiar uneasiness that troubled him more and more. At eight, when he left, he was shaken by all the torments of desire. Given the unfamiliarity of his surroundings in a city foreign to him, the difficulty of finding satisfaction incited him powerfully. He wandered, almost desperate, for two hours through the streets of the center, longingly fixing his blazing eyes on the backs of the men he came upon; he followed them, very close, attempting to take advantage of any opportunity, though fearful of suffering a rebuff.

Around eleven, he felt a tremendous torture. His body shook and he felt in his eyes a painful void.

Considering it futile to trot along the busy streets, he

slowly turned off toward the outskirts, always looking back at pedestrians, greeting them with a quavering voice, stopping periodically without knowing what to do, like a beggar.

On coming to Escobedo Street, he could bear it no longer. He wanted to throw himself at the first man who passed by. To weep, to lament piteously, to speak of his tortures…

He heard leisurely footsteps in the distance; his heart palpitated with violence; he moved close to the wall of a house and waited. A few moments later, the robust body of a worker almost filled the sidewalk. Ramírez turned pale; nevertheless, when the man was near, he reached out and touched his elbow. The worker turned abruptly and looked at him. Ramírez attempted a honeyed smile, like that of a hungry procuress abandoned by the wayside. The man snorted with laughter and swore; then he went on, walking slowly, bringing the wide heels of his shoes down hard on the cobblestones. A half an hour later, another man appeared. The wretch, trembling from head to toe, dared to direct an endearment his way, to which the pedestrian responded with a vigorous shove. Ramírez was frightened and moved quickly away.

Then, after walking two blocks, he found himself on García Street. Weak, his mouth dry, he looked first one way and then the other. A short distance away and with hurried step, a fourteen-year-old boy walked. He followed him.

"Psst! Psst!"

The boy stopped.

"Hello, dear… What are you doing around here so late?"

"I'm going home. What do you want?"

"Nothing, nothing… But don't go so soon, my lovely…" And he grabbed him by the arm.

The boy struggled to free himself.

"Let me go! I've told you I'm going home."

He began to run. But Ramírez ran after him and caught up. Then the rascal, frightened, yelled:

"Papa! Papa!"

Almost at that same instant, a few yards away, a square shaft of light was suddenly cast on the street. A tall man appeared. He was the worker who had been walking earlier along Escobedo.

On seeing Ramírez, he rushed for him. Our poor man stood there, looking at the worker, his eyes as large and fixed as plates, trembling and mute.

"What do you want, you filthy pig?"

And he landed a furious kick in his stomach. Octavio collapsed, with a long, painful hiccup.

Epaminondas, that must have been the worker's name, on seeing the scoundrel on the ground, decided that a single kick was too light a punishment, and he give him two more, splendid and marvelous in their genre, on the long nose that provoked him like a sausage.

What must those marvelous kicks have sounded like!

Like the squishing of an orange when it's hurled forcefully against a wall; like the falling of an umbrella whose ribs crash all aquiver; like the cracking of a nut between the fingers; or better yet, like the meeting of another hard sole with another nose!

Like this:

Chah! ⎫
        ⎬ with a great, delicious interval.
Chah! ⎭

And then: How Epaminondas would have glutted his fury, worked up by the perverse instinct that brings murderers to riddle their victims with knife wounds! That instinct that tightens innocent fingers with increasing force, purely for the enjoyment it brings, around the necks of their friends until they turn purple and their eyes glow.

How the sole of Epaminondas's shoe must have battered the nose of Octavio Ramírez!

Chah! ⎫
Chah! ⎬ vigorously
Chah! ⎭

While a thousand tiny lights, like needles, pricked the darkness.

CÉSAR DÁVILA ANDRADE
(Cuenca, 1918-1967)

César Dávila Andrade lived in Cuenca, Guayaquil, Quito, and Caracas, committing suicide in the Venezuelan capital in 1967. Before his death, he regularly contributed articles, stories, and poems to two periodicals, *El Nacional* and *Zona Franca*, and, from Venezuela, to *Letras del Ecuador*, a publication of the Casa de la Cultura Ecuatoriana then at its height in terms of the quality of the works published in its pages.

The writer published seven poetry collections: *Espacio, me has vencido* (Quito, 1946), *Catedral salvaje* (Caracas, 1951), *Arco de instantes* (Quito, 1959), *Boletín y elegía de las mitas* (Quito, 1959), *En un lugar no identificado* (Merida, Venezuela, 1960), *Conexiones de tierra* (Caracas, 1964), *and Materia real* (published posthumously, Caracas, 1970).

His published story collections are entitled: *Abandonados en la tierra* (Quito, 1952), *Trece relatos* (Quito, 1955), and *Cabeza de gallo* (Caracas, 1966).

Dávila Andrade's character was a complex one. He left a body of work uneven in quality, but which, at its finest (*Catedral salvaje, Boletín y elegía de las mitas*) achieved heights seldom seen in the work of other Latin American poets. Rather than becoming a follower of the regional, indianist school of his contemporaries, he risked creating his own world open to transcendence. He brought to his narrative an exalted realism, characterized by signs and symbols of agony and death: coffins, illnesses, a great deal of suffering, rites of destruction. While other Latin American writers went beyond realism by means of the techniques of fantastic, and marvelous and magical, realism, Dávila attempted to do so through the esoteric and the hermetic.

A SENTINEL SEES LIFE APPEAR*

I watched the first condor through the window of the wagon. We had left at three-thirty in the morning from the Saxadumbay station in a black storm rumbling with thunder that seemed to swell the bulky cargo of sheaves and bales of tobacco and crocodile skins.

We were at an altitude approaching four thousand meters. The radiant day of the peaks was like a star sliced into a thousand streams of glitter.

And now, between two waterfalls of splendor, the condor flew, drowsy but tense, nevertheless. He stretched his neck, as red as a beacon, and then withdrew into his ruff and watched the convoy with cold, skeptical eyes.

Suddenly, a splinter of ice the size of a razor smashed against the window. It disintegrated like a kind of semi-liquid iguana and finally unraveled in rivulets.

From my seat lined with wiry straw—the second to the last in that old third–class wagon—I watched my traveling companions.

All had boarded in Saxadumbay that indescribable

---

*From the collection *Cabeza de gallo,* 1966.

morning. There were eight of us in total, brought together for the journey by chance. An immigrant couple, Poles or Finns, two narrow blond heads and very long skinny legs wrapped in a blanket of gray wool. An Indian, half petrified within his thick, stiff poncho, red with black stripes. A nun, pink and fleshy, wrapped in her black and white habit. An extraordinary leper with the face of a hairless lion; his guard, a mestizo policeman with Indian-like eyes and with a rifle. And, finally, a young black woman wearing a raspberry colored dress who traveled with a basket of watermelons.

To the right gleamed the cone of a volcano carved in rock crystal. It seemed to turn at an unheard of speed. Over its slightly flattened peak there floated a cloud of immobile vapor, almost inconceivable. Behind, a sooty mass extended, shot through with translucent streaks. Masses of granulated metal rose up suddenly at intervals, and their peaks winked as though they were devouring light.

At times, streams of fine sand broke away from the rails and took on arborescent shapes.

As the convoy advanced, the domes of the mountains rose and fell. Immense swellings, half-ruined cupolas, crests and humps in the extremely slow boil of centuries. The plateaus shone like ferruginous mirrors crisscrossed with cracks. At the bottom, the valleys slept, wrapped in their own emanations.

A wall of black lava advanced to the right and the sky in the background reverberated like a beveled edge. At the base of the cut, over a shelf twisted like a kidney, the rails wound, joining and disappearing. The curve glistened like the rim of a goblet recently washed.

Just then, I lowered my gaze toward the terrain that made the machine vibrate. There, a few meters away, was the skeleton of a pack llama. The bones retained the attitude of the animal kneeling on its forelegs with its snout nailed between them. The engine sounded a high whistle that bounced off the peaks, and the vibration shook the bony sculpture, breaking it into pieces.

With the convoy of wagons aligned once again, we headed for the outline of the peak. On both sides of the cumbersome hulk, the flanks of stone licked by the wind slid away.

At some point, the conductor managed to enter. He did so almost oozing through the door at the back of the wagon, which closed again with a bang. He came to my side and pulled off his woolen scarf. He was gasping for air, ashen, and perspiring frozen drops. He let himself fall like a bundle. Blood trickled from his left nostril. I took out my bottle of cane liquor and offered it to him. He gulped several times as though it were pure water. "There's no air outside," he panted. The immigrants watched us, breathing with their mouths open. The others had their heads thrown against the backrests. The Indian turned with a spark of curiosity in the corner of his eye. He had smelled the cane liquor.

The previous afternoon, when I bought the bottle from some muleteers under the lean-to of the only inn at the station and the rain storm seemed bent upon destroying the metal sheets of the shed, I had been surprised for the first time by that direct though fleeting look contemplating my purchase. At the time I had assumed sadness in those eyes. He had lowered his eyelids. I saw him again an hour later. With his eyes downcast, he was as though hypnotized by the rain, watching the drops of water fall.

"Father," I said, leaning toward his seat. He turned at once, his thick woolen hat slipping back on his head. "Have a drink."

I passed the bottle to him. He hesitated for a moment, staring at me. He took a swallow, wiped the mouth of the bottle with the edge of his poncho, and gave it back to me.

He cleared his throat loudly in order to demonstrate the quality of the drink.

The solitary condor stood out against the side of the volcano and was submerged in space striated with ether. A little later he reappeared at the head of a formation of his fellow beings who formed themselves into a spiral. Behind them, there appeared another line of small condors flanked by a number of females who propelled the young ones forward with gusts of wind from their arched wings.

The Indian turned toward me. The males, their necks rigid, opened into two symmetrical pincers and surrounded those who were ascending. The Indian looked at me again and with his eyes guided mine. I saw a very high peak in the form of an altar.

The first condor glided now above this refuge-like formation. He shot over it and posed with his wings high, fanning his race.

The squadron followed the direction of the guide. And all alighted at the same level, disappearing into the coloration of the rocks.

The Indian half-raised himself from his seat and, taking off his hat, moved close to the window. He continued observing from an oblique angle, looking down.

Then he turned to me again, wanting to tell me something.

"What's going on?" I shouted to him.

"Condor does not want to die," he replied and took his seat, remaining motionless.

I understood that the condors were taking refuge from something that threatened them. I was having difficulty breathing again and got up. The conductor had fallen asleep with his scarf up to his eyes and didn't notice me passing.

There, in the emptiness of the peaks, almost all the conductors sleep, and they can also die.

The black woman saw me stumble and smiled in an impish way. She was unscathed. The immigrant woman slept with her head on the shoulder of her companion.

I had gotten up to do something to relieve the difficulty I had breathing, but no longer remembered what it was I intended to do.

I looked at the hands of the leper tied with a piece of twine. The policeman slept at his side with his cap falling over his nose and his rifle between his knees. I woke him up with a thump that sounded as though it had been administered with a paper tube. In a flash of lightening, I saw the nun. Her previously sanguine and healthy face looked like a ball of yellow fat. She had vomited into her lap and the bones beads of her great rosary were tangled in the mess.

The policeman woke up suddenly, he looked at me, smiling, bewildered, without knowing what to do. I indicated with surprise the leper's bound hands, the right one of which was missing a thumb. And I must have pulled back because something like a film of crystallized honey exploded around my mouth, and he began to loosen the ties binding the hands of Lion-face. He held out the cord to me as though it were a worm. He most surely didn't realize what he was doing. Next, he handed me his rifle as well.

Before falling, I managed to drop the weapon on a seat. I was perspiring ice.

With a look curiously vacant and disinterested, I gazed at the leper's smile. His wrinkled face, shaped like the snout of a rabid dog, contracted even more when he smiled and seemed to contradict itself. He put his deformed hand on the policeman's shoulder and shoved him. The man obeyed and moved to the seat ahead. Relieved suddenly of his authority, he took off his cap and let his head drop against the backrest. That's when I noticed that the leper's nose, having curled up, came to a point with the nostrils at his forehead.

The black woman had been observing me. She pressed her face to the glass and I imitated her.

Over a large expanse, an immense white flock came flying. They were doves. City birds violently torn from their former way of life. What had happened to them?

With their feet drawn up, they displayed thousands of crops spotted with red dots. (I said to myself, "To this place come only those birds that have no need for eaves nor care and that can do without human affection.")

I pressed the mouth of the bottle against my lips and sipped its fleeting and savage clarity, flavorless. It was now metaphysical cane liquor.

I became lighter in a new notion of myself. An infinite, detached happiness was moving beyond us, with no need of our agency.

Disconcerted, I looked out the window again.

Three snow-covered volcanoes floated, rootless, over a plain of polished material. An enormous bubble the size of a lake moved below, like the eye of a layer of water gone mad.

The black woman became frightened and shouted something to me that I didn't understand. At that very moment, an enormous and ill-assorted spurt of wings irrupted into the mirage.

Thousands of birds of all kinds were thrown, or had escaped, from their habitual worlds. Some fell shortly after appearing. Those that managed to remain aloft at that altitude headed in desperation toward the flanks of the massif over which the convoy dragged itself and we didn't see them again.

("They are saved from their past, undoubtedly, and want only what they have accumulated within their sheaths as slight as the dawn. They come to live their brief memories during the time of their last warble.")

The Indian touched my shoulder.

"What's going on?" I said.

And I followed him to the other end of the wagon

"Look, master!" he exclaimed.

Huge flocks descended toward the hidden jungle after a pause in the strata of the clouds.

"What's going on?" I asked again.

The Indian blinked, confused. The effort darkened his brow.

"The earth is leaving…," he said.

A tear glittered in his right eye, which closed quickly, reabsorbing the liquid.

"I think about my little horse…and about my wife!"

He had turned ashen. I heard him sobbing softly.

The leper watched the spectacle with delight. The conductor and the policeman slept in their seats. The nun and the immigrants whispered, leaning toward the first window, and they made the Sign of the Cross together. They had a foreboding of something dreadful. But none of them had heard the Indian's disturbing words.

The parrots, the macaws, the parakeets flew in a great red, yellow, emerald cloud. I imagined their frightened chatter over those skies recently invented for their eyes.

Over the narrow bed of steam, a slight, pallid shadow began to grow, like ash made of light. An unspeakable melancholy pierced the vanquished beauty.

The black woman approached us. She had her hands pressed against her breast.

"The Lord's little creatures! Where are they flying to?" she asked.

I heard a growl and turned my head.

The leper had pressed his enormous noseless face against the glass. The coming together was like a monstrous kiss. The breath emanating from his forehead had spread a serous stain with two transparent holes. The leprosy seemed to have infected the glass.

"Is it possible to know what is happening?" said the nun in anguish, and on receiving no reply, exclaimed, "My God, my strength!"

"A hurricane," I shouted.

The Indian stood. He remained ashen and did not speak. With his eyes, he followed in the air the wake of the word "hurricane," as though he were following the edge of a peacock's tail. And with a shake of his head, disproved my words.

The immigrant woman, coming completely undone, her eyes wild, dragged her husband to their seat and broke into sobs.

The engine whistled again, a long whistle. I looked out the window. The flocks had disappeared.

Now the narrow pass of Guamanchaca appeared. It was the highest stretch of the cordillera. It had been etched, little by little, into the live rock along the edge of the apse. No window could remain open over that stretch and nobody ever crossed it without succumbing to great fainting spells.

Suddenly all the windows on the left side turned black. We moved very close to the wall of the pass. The windows of the right side glistened, alone.

The policeman and the conductor—asleep or dead—didn't move from their seats. The rest of us understood that it wasn't necessary to confirm their state. The immensity rendered each of us equally insignificant.

The Indian approached me with an enigmatic air.

"Do you hear, master?" he asked.

"Hear what?" I asked.

"You don't hear?"

And he shook his head with a despondent air. Then his hands went to his abdomen and he bent over as though he had received a blow.

And suddenly I heard. I heard it. It was like a great dark, conquering sound that climbed.

"It is a roar from the earth!" I shouted

Everyone turned to me. They were ashen.

"My God, my strength!" shrieked the nun and fell

back against her seat, her face turned toward the window. "Our Father, which art in…"

An immense bellow went through the wagon and resounded like an "M," closed, muffled, concave. The vibration broke and a brilliant flash washed over, blinding us. The voice of the black woman rose in a scream of animal fear. Then, silence. We listened to the silence for I don't know how long.

When we opened our eyes, the sky shown with an intense sulfurous light.

Before we could comprehend our situation, the roar sounded again and our faculties were split from one another. A primitive beatitude, with no moral sense, invaded us for a moment. Then we felt the cord that ran through the planet snap. And, paralyzed with terror, we heard the cosmic wave ascend like the desperate race of an infinite herd of rocks.

The doors at both ends opened violently. A frozen gust entered.

The wooden walls came together in a simultaneous stampede. We were flung within the wagon and each one of us fell without a sound into his own misery as into a hole. I found myself sitting at an angle and had the impression—extremely sharp—that all was over, dead.

There was another contraction. The stone mass over which the train traveled reeled on. All of the other wagons and the engine lurched forward, but our wagon, pressed to the slope like a drunken man, returned to its place.

The black woman let out another scream. She was desperate. Then, a faded, cold peace of beings resuscitated wrapped itself around us all.

We felt that we were finished.

The leper, who was the first to get up, directed me with a grunt to the nun. "Ummmm." She was stretched out on the floor of the wagon. Almost naked, with her blond hair cut like that of a boy sticking up from her head, she seemed, oddly, both infantile and obscene. The immigrants looked like a strange, grotesque ball. Their embrace was so strong that they must have died with the same breath. The bodies of the conductor and the policeman lay across one another at the door to the latrine. I went toward the Indian. He was cowering under his poncho. I touched him and he stuck his head out.

"The little earth!" he exclaimed as though in a dream, and went toward the window, half-staggering. The black woman stretched in her seat.

"Good God, the snake bit you!" she exclaimed with her incurable innocence. She raised her eyelashes to the sky and the light flashed in her large obsidian and coconut eyes.

I looked again—incredulous—at the wagon that had been saved. I was drunk with an exalted feeling foreign to me. I felt an urge to say or do something, at any price.

"You've been completely freed," I shouted at the leper.

"They weren't taking me away because of the skin..." he answered, insolent.

In a flash, I imagined him with a nose, and there appeared before me the face of the old renegade Castañeda for whom the police had been searching the jungle for years.

"Of course," I replied. "Above and beyond anything else, you are Castañeda. Servando Castañeda!" I proclaimed.

"I was…the man you mention!" he answered firmly.

"Yes, because now there is no blood to spill!"

He smiled in silence, stroking with a splayed hand his hairless chin.

"Nobody can begin to divide up the world," he announced with malice, as though talking to himself.

"But we can begin to decide about ourselves."

"No longer. You are mistaken. We are no more than ghosts now… Don't you realize that? No more than ghosts…!"

"You, ghost: Stand in the corner," I ordered, pointing the rifle.

He obeyed and went to lie down there, spitting in disdain. The black woman turned toward the nun and covered her, the tender gesture touched with impishness.

High above, the sky cleared.

From the edges of the canyon misty clouds ascended. The wagon had remained on a kind of natural shelf, next to an unexpected terrestrial scene.

At dusk, the air outside became tinged with green, and then it suddenly turned dark. And it rained hard for hours.

When the rain stopped, an immense moon of gnawed white stone appeared through the windows. I resolved to spend the night in my seat with the rifle in my hands.

Soon, the steady breathing of the black woman was heard. I understood that the Indian stayed awake, but that he didn't dare to speak.

It started to rain again, and I was overcome with sleep.

When I awoke, a tenuous light was distributed on either side of the windows. The corners were still dark. A distant phosphorescence glided across the horizon. The odor of death, sweetish and cold, floated in the enclosed wagon.

When, with the first light of dawn, I was able to recognize the hard paleness of the windows, I approached the Indian. His head came out through the opening in his poncho. I asked for help and he came with me in silence. We threw the bodies out with no ceremony. The two immigrants rolled down, joined in their tight embrace.

The leper observed, silent. A half hour later, he got up with inexplicable urgency, and grunting something, he walked between us. Before getting to the door, he bent over solemnly and picked up a black umbrella that had belonged to one of the immigrants. He hung it by the handle over his forearm; he coughed deliberately and proudly directed himself to the ceiling: "I'm leaving before they do away with me!" he exclaimed. (It was clear that he wanted to be theatrical.)

He threw open the door and disappeared, on his way to the great beyond.

Only a few minutes later did I understand his words and his insolent outburst of laughter a little earlier. We were, in fact, ghosts. Ghosts! There was no longer anything in us to kill.

Knowing that only the void awaited me, I asked the Indian, "And…you? What do you think you will do?"

"Return to the Earth," he answered, impassive.

The black woman woke with the sun.   She burbled something like a canary and went to the window. Her long, black fingers were joined on one of her knees, and her eyes were lost in contemplation.

She jumped from her seat suddenly, and we saw her dig in the basket she had brought. A little later she approached with three slices of watermelon and offered them to us, laughing with her entire body, as though she were offering us the loveliest of organs. I didn't know what to do with that bit of freshness belonging to a world that had disappeared.

The last mists from the depths drifted away. At the bottom, very close to the chain of volcanoes, the polished ocean glittered.   Islands, recently polished, had appeared.   The immense and ferocious shores that I knew had been devoured. There, at some point among the submerged ruins, one would find, perhaps, the ancient Judicial Statute that we had respected and obeyed.

The Indian took off his poncho and folded it meticulously on his seat. From a knapsack of red wool, he took a tiny basket and he felt it carefully as the contents sounded mysteriously.

We moved closer to him. They were rare stones. Four of these he placed in the form of a cross, arranging them according to the cardinal points. They represented an iguana, a cow, a condor, and a leopard. In the center he placed the fifth stone, flat and round with the figure of the sun. On this, a steel needle pointed north.

And he knelt, sitting back on his heels, with his hands pressed against his thighs. Seated thus, he waited a moment with his eyes closed. After a few minutes, the small strip of steel began to move of its own accord. It vibrated toward the left and toward the right, and at last it stopped. It pointed to the condor. The Indian came to. He smiled shyly.

"We will go that way," he announced, directing his words to the black woman, and he took her hand in a natural way. For the first time, the black woman seemed worried. But he, without looking at her, began to put his stones into the little red bag.

"When will you go?" I asked.

"Tomorrow, with the sun," the Indian answered.

The black woman smiled in silence and bit the tip of her tongue.

"And…you, master?" the Indian asked me, his face expressionless.

"I will stay here," I said, feigning naturalness. And without knowing what I was doing, I pointed to the rifle that hung from the ring over my seat. I don't know what he was thinking, but he smiled in a strange way. I understood that, for him, I was a hopeless case. And I fell silent.

He, for his part, kept busy throughout the day scanning the horizon. He searched and he chose.

I slept heavily that afternoon in the strange atmosphere of the wagon. The cold of the moon, now high over the ocean, woke me. The expanse trembled and moved in an endless coming and going of phosphorescent strings. They reverberated their fans of liquid gold and their bubbling trails trickled among the new islands.

I awoke with the light of dawn.

The Indian and the black woman, sitting up now, waited, looking from time to time at the earth they would receive with the arrival of the sun.

I sat up decisively, forcing myself to appear steadfast.

The Indian stood and the black woman followed suit. Then they went toward the door, walking slowly, a little sad.

"*Adiós*, master. This was meant to be!"

I lowered my gaze.

I listened as they opened the door and as they closed it again, delicately. Then I watched them descend.

She, behind, looked back from time to time. With great care, his head bowed, he tested the earth with his toes.

They disappeared like two small waves of dust.

I collapsed in the seat and lit my last cigarette.

All that had nurtured me was fodder for the abyss. There no longer existed even the possibility of the former vices. The virginity of the new world terrified my blood, weakened by the excesses of the world that had disappeared.

What sensations, except for the most profound humility, could I offer in the face of that immense conflageration?

I took the rifle. I put the strap over my shoulder and began to walk from one end of the wagon to the other. I wanted to dream as I once had, when walks stimulated my imagination. But one dreams only when one is still able to lie in some way.

I hung up the weapon and sat down again.

A cloud, low and heavy, moved from north to south. When I was about to contemplate it, a shard of ice crashed against the window. I followed it with my eyes.

A ray of sun—disappearing within—illuminated the shard and began to melt it. It took on an oval shape and acquired a gelatinous, milky-toned consistency, with cloudy granules that truly absorbed the light and grouped themselves into an elongated shape. A little later, a tiny fiber of nervous substance solidified in the center and ramified rapidly, intertwining with small bloody channels that emerged from the palpitating center similar to a heart. At the same time, in the upper part there took shape a small mass much like a brain. Immediately after, flesh and bone formed and darkened. The abdominal part sticking to the glass took on a greenish gray color, while the back and the extremities were covered with a bright, wrinkled epidermis. The chin began to beat, stretching toward the sides. At last, the tiny beast raised its head toward the world with the first surprise of the sun. I saw its little eyes: They were two globules of slime, with a spark of light in each. It looked at me and its skin suddenly bristled.

The extremities contracted, moving the body forward. It moved its tail, went over the window frame, and fell from the side of the wagon. Almost immediately, I saw it reappear on the embankment and reach the rocky ramp in search of the country that the sun had established within the small profundity of its brain on creating its eyes…

Now I remained there, with an old, yellowing memory in my mind. And with a useless rifle.

Because solitary sentinels, when they stand out in their remote, inaccessible sentry boxes, wrapped in the unreal desolation of the dawn, and visions of their shattered lives torment them, cling to their irrevocable arm, take between their teeth the mouth of the barrel, set the butt on the pavement, and pull the trigger with the right foot. But, I…

In my stupor, I looked down. There wasn't a trace of the Indian, nor of his companion.

With no definite purpose in mind, I opened the door and suddenly found myself facing the immensity of the rubble. Among the rails twisted like vine shoots, the spikes stood out against the limpid sky.

I began to descend.

I heard, then, in the most profound interior silence, a voice that said to me, "Your guides are gone. You alone, Sentinel, choose!"

MIGUEL DONOSO PAREJA

(Guayaquil, 1931)

Sailor, puppeteer, guerrilla, political exile, journalist, editor, director of literary workshops, and even government bureaucrat, Miguel Donoso Pareja's career has been characterized by extraordinary variety. He lived for eighteen years in Mexico, where he became a veritable legend as a result of his literary workshops. On returning to Ecuador, where he has lived in Quito and Guayaquil, he continued directing the successful workshops. In 1994, he received a Guggenheim fellowship to write *Hoy empiezo a acordarme*.

He has published four story collections: *Kelko y otros cuentos* (1962), *El hombre que mataba a sus hijos* (1968), *Lo mismo que el olvido* (1986), *Todo lo que inventamos es cierto* (1990), and *El otro lado del espejo* (personal anthology, 1996).

Donoso Pareja's poetry collections include *Primera canción del exiliado, Cantos para celebrar una muerte,* and *Ultima canción del exiliado* (1994).

Finally, the writer has published five novels: *Henry Black* (1969), *Día tras día* (1976), *Nunca más el mar* (1981), *Hoy empiezo a acordarme* (1994), and *La muerte de Tyrone Power en el Monumental del Barcelona* (2001).

Donoso Pareja's is a literature of literature, of woman, eroticism, death, exile, the word's anguish, reaching at its finest a sensuality rare in Ecuadorian literature. With the exception of *La muerte de Tyrone Power*, in his reiterative novels he ignores structure and plot, whose death warrent he vanely attempts to sign. His most recent stories are his finest.

THE MUTILATION*

Nothing matters more than a letter to someone who is absent. Thus, N is there every day, lying in wait, resting his elbows on the small balcony, watching. To the right the street begins a sharp curve and rises slightly, straightens in front of him, and then falls in the direction of the sea which can be seen, sometimes rough, sometimes smooth, as the wind blows with greater or lesser intensity. A triangular sail is visible in the distance, almost at the point where the Mediterranean turns deep blue, leaving behind that emerald green that begins on the beach made by Dutch engineers specifically for the summer that is ending, transforming the Maresme from Montgat to Premiá del Mar.

Across from him, on the second floor of the house on the sidewalk opposite, a sign says "For sale," and the young woman talks to a child, probably her son, in a slightly shrill voice. The woman is interesting, slender, and always wears her hair, an extremely pale blond, pulled back. If one looks carefully, it becomes clear that a part of her left arm is missing, that about fifteen centimeters from the elbow she has only a stump. This

*From the collection *El otro lado del espejo*, 1996.

detail makes her extremely sensual, as though there is a caress pending in the hand she lacks, an unbearable tenderness, a kind of provocative absence.

N remains there, lying in wait, immersed in his own absence that identifies him with that hand the woman lacks like an offering. And below, in the street where the garbage bags accumulate in the afternoon, the cats, their faces round and soft like the woman's stump, electrifying him.

Toward eleven in the morning, the boy passes by. He emerges from the right side of the street and has no doubt come down from Turó del Mar, the highest part of the town. Thin and awkward, he walks very fast, as though he were being pursued. N pretends he doesn't see him, though his attention is fixed on him, on the long rhythmic stride that takes him from door to door, zigzagging from one sidewalk to the other. The boy, as though he feared him, never looks at N, while the mutilated woman is busy with the child playing on the balcony, she pampers him with that shrill voice that, or so the absent one supposes, pronounces tender things, as does the arrival of the boy at the doors he knocks at and disappears through, to emerge later, always in a hurry and looking downward, avoiding him who rests his elbows on the low red iron railing, feigning indifference, mutilated because the boy goes on, always absent with that absence that he is over there, where he is not, with that absence that he is here, where he acts as though he were.

The absent one doesn't know, in reality, in what or where his absence is rooted, and he also doesn't know what he hopes for here, on the balcony. Maybe he hopes for a smile from the woman, the approach of that stump that seems to him so sweet, painfully tactile, as though the fingers were multiplied with the promise of an awful caress. Or maybe he hopes that the boy will knock one day at his door, will stop being that mutilation fleeing from house to house, zigzagging in the street, disappearing always in the direction of the sea, turning to the right and leaving, against the green of the Mediterranean, that other distant absence that is the sail bobbing in the water, floating like an indecipherable corpse.

N looks at the time and sees that it's just a few minutes before the morning ritual begins, before the boy appears at the far right of the street and climbs with long strides while the woman forgets for a moment the child playing on the balcony, and he watches them, because the boy is there now, head bowed, fearful of the absent one to whom he cannot offer that which, in and of himself, he comes offering day after day in the months during which he has seen him, lying in wait, waiting for him on the balcony, anxious, disturbed by the woman's stump that marks again a distant caress, a tenderness that now will never belong to him, and that he, with his entire load of promises, his daily offering, cannot give to him.

The boy passes by yet again and the ritual ends desanctified, with no magic. N sees him disappear and his gaze stops at the sea, he bathes in that green where a journey is almost a burial, a sign of death.

Now all that's left to the absent one is to hope for rain, until in the night the illusion of the woman across the street, her truncated arm, is renewed for the following day, the promise of an impossible embrace, and the boy comes by yet again, perhaps he stops, he stops being that zigzagging mutilation, but all he sees is the garbage truck picking up the bags accumulated on the sidewalks, the cats returning to their corners, sinuously malignant, indifferent, cold, their small eyes gleaming in the dark, laughing at him, anticipating and hoping for something as well.

A few minutes before, the absent one is already resting on his elbows in the window, watching as though from the other side of a great chasm, lying in wait. The wind is blowing now, and it rained for a few hours at dawn. At around five in the morning, the rain began to fall, urged on by a rough, cold wind. N woke up and knew that the eyes of the cats had not lied to him, that something was going to happen at last. He inspected the apartment, saw the books, the typewriter abandoned so long ago, the dirty dishes in the sink. He walked through the hall to the other room and stepped on to the lonely, solitary platform. From the terrace, he saw the sea in the distance as he soaked in the rain, cold now due to the beginning of that late autumn.

He returned to the house and dried himself, rubbing vigorously. Since he couldn't go back to sleep, he went to the window. The rain had kept the cats away, but he knew that they were there, that from somewhere they amused themselves watching him with their heads round like stumps filled with a malign phosphorescence. He thought about the woman: She probably slept, resting on her truncated arm.

When he saw him appear, he knew that the ritual that day would be different. He looked at the woman playing with her son and the mutilated arm was no longer the promise of a caress but the confirmation of an implacable absence. The triangle of the sail had disappeared in the Mediterranean, which strangely displayed the certainty, for him, of an imminent shipwreck, the postponement of a threat.

Now the boy looks at him in triumph without the slightest anxiety, without a drop of fear. He takes several long strides and heads for the door. N trembles on hearing the bell and goes down, not without first looking at the woman who greets him with her raised stump, painfully tender.

The absent one returns the greeting and knows that he is saying goodbye, that the longing for that caress is definitively impossible, that it is perpetuated like a dream.

When he gets downstairs he takes the key to open the small box on the wall. The boy is already moving toward the sea, with long, rhythmic strides. The water of the Mediterranean is a deep, gloomy blue. The cats are there, surrounding him, lying in wait, unmoving, like oh-so-sweet stumps with eyes, blind, without a caress to comfort him, absolutely without mercy.

N removes the envelope.

He doesn't need to open it to know that everything has ended.

LUPE RUMAZO
(Quito, 1935)

Lupe Rumazo was born into a distinguished family of writers. She studied in Colombia, Uruguay, and the United States. She currently resides in Venezuela.

The writer has published three collections of essays: *El en lagar* (1962), *Yunques y crisoles americanos* (1967), and *Rol beligerante* (1974), a work praised by Ernesto Sábato. She has also written two long, ambitious novels, *Carta larga sin final* (1978) and *Peste blanca, peste negra* (1988).

Her single short story collection, *Sílabas de la tierra* (1964), contains seven works. Her only other story, "La marcha de los batracion," included in the essay collection *Rol beligerante,* is notable for many reasons: its complex structure, clean style, and cultural references which function as characters in the narration.

THE MARCH OF THE BATRACIANS*

> *Que le monde es un défaut*
> *Dans la pureté du non-etre*
> PAUL VALERY

THE NEWS

The body of internationally renowned novelist Rubén Alado was found yesterday, two days after he is presumed to have committed suicide. His remains were discovered by a cleaning woman at the Motel Trilco where the writer lived for a number of years. Because Sr. Alado had not answered the door for several days, the maid, Genoveva Pereira, decided to go in to clean the room. There, on the bed, she found the lifeless body of Alado who had resorted to a form of hara-kiri, stabbing himself in the heart. The short dagger was still in the body; the dead man could not, or did not, wish to remove it. Rubén Alado has no immediate family, but he has left a considerable body of work. He is the author of…

He didn't flee from his house because his house was little more than a hotel room; it had been a hotel room for many years now. Hotels afforded freedom and they

---

*From the collection *Rol beligerante*, 1974.

afforded solitude, including the solitude and the freedom to kill oneself. But he acted as though he did, in fact, have a house, a home, that is, and he fled; it was part of the plan. A predetermined plan was essential to a good story, even if when one sat down to write the mind bolted and the words raced, crashing into one another, leaping and galloping, and it was then thought that it had come about through an extraordinary force, unknown and magical, unrevealed and impenetrable. That marked and real force that in life's design also led to certain unexpected actions, the twisting of a course, like this one now, the decision to kill oneself. A force that the stars marked with a specific day and a time and that necessarily corresponded to an orbit almost impossible to break out of. The orbit turned and he had entered into it. The orbit had a path, the orbit had its stages. In the first he had to arrange the desk, not leaving his papers piled up or scattered about, or his files in disarray. Everything corresponded to an order that tomorrow, when he was gone, would be examined. So that they wouldn't think that the first pages of his unpublished novel, *La marcha de los batracios*, nor the rough drafts of letters constituted his diary. One wrote fundamentally for posterity. One also had to leave a kind of farewell, never an explanation, never a clarification of the mystery. A bad writer would be he who became explanatory and argumentative; pity the poor man who boasts of his expository burden. To hell with dogma; to hell with orthodoxy. And he wrote, on a sheet of paper he placed on his desk, in full view: "Misery is not alone; the fourth power has taken up lodgings on the Earth." The idiots, those who believe that one writes exactly what one thinks, would conclude that hunger had driven him to kill himself; for them, the four shirts and the few changes of underwear in his closet, and the old suit and the extra pair of shoes; for them the odor of his body still present in the clothes, a body of struggle and sweat, a body of exhaustion and defeat. For those less stupid, the legacy of the fourth power. The fourth power that would permit him, tense but willing, to annihilate himself. For the initiates, the particles of his astral body and of his ethereal body which would begin to come together and unite until forming the double of his self at the moment in which the dagger, long and sharp, opened the amphora of his heart. He closed the door to his room with a bang. The unreal witnesses would confirm his flight, the real—the poor old man in reception or Genoveva—never amazed or appalled, would be delighted that he, a customer—and a customer is he who pays and for that very reason has rights—had shut the old door with a bang, the door alien to their miserable boss. One last detail: He had acted like a phantom. Phantoms appear and disappear, they are free. He was free from the moment he decided to kill himself. Phantoms pirouette. This was one of his last pirouettes.

THE OMENS

I have never enjoyed anything more pleasurable than that early morning when I dreamed in color. I don't know if others dream in color, and if in their dreams they even have entire conversations in English or French, or see complete pages of a chapter of a book, for example, with the words divided at the end of the line and all, and with page numbers. Yes, there was the placid quality of a mattress in my spirit, that is, the mattress was within me and I felt it; I was the mattress, rather than resting on a mattress. And a half-circle appeared, like a rainbow, except that it was of a single compact shade of orange, or rather, lighter below and more intense above, at the far edge—am I making myself clear?—and in that circle, just as the news items appear letter by letter in Picadilly Circus, a name was revealed, and the name was in bright lights, and the letters weren't made of light bulbs but of neon gas, instead—I knew then that neon gas was also good for dreams—they took shape little by little, until I could read that they clearly said RUBÉN ALADO, I'm certain of that, absolutely certain. Then, standing above the half-circle, but without a head and therefore without a face, was a man and that man was Rubén Alado, dressed in black, with his hands forward, clasped almost at the level of his legs, and though he said nothing to me—how could he say anything to me?—I knew that he wanted to let me know that he wasn't angry and that we were at peace, even though I hadn't yet thanked him for the favor he did for me on arranging the connection I needed. Then I slept peacefully, because I had been extremely tormented by my own ingratitude, even though it was most disagreeable to have to thank someone for something as that was a way of saying that I was inferior and that only thanks to him, or that in any event I was in debt and debts had to be paid, or better yet, that he had acceded, maybe because of pressure from me and not of his own accord.

So, I've said that this was a dream, but thinking about it further, perhaps it wasn't a dream, but something I really saw and that now seems to me uncertain, the outlines unclear, because it may be that he did appear to me or that I believed that he had appeared to me.

I'm not the sort of person who dreams frequently; rather, dreams terrify me because dreams are omens and true omens, regardless of what they say. I dreamed that I was lying down and that suddenly black water began to flood the room, almost like the black water of latrines, divided like that, white in one spot and oily black in another, and that the current was rising, I don't know how far because now I wasn't thinking about the water that enveloped me and that stained my arms, smearing them with mud, but about the worms that started to emerge and to crawl on my arms hanging down outside the sheet and even on my legs, which were covered. And then I screamed and I dug my nails into my wife, and she woke up and said that I had had a nightmare and that to break the spell I had to talk to her about it. But I didn't say anything because it was useless and I already knew that worms and death are the same and that it was entirely possible that I was the dead person, or that she was, or that any one of us, maybe the children, and it was better to remain silent. The following morning, I read the newspaper and learned that our friend, Rubén Alado, had killed himself.

He went straight to the Municipal Library, the city's small library, not the National Library, because he had to work in secrecy. They might follow his trail, not today, but tomorrow, and it would not do for anyone to know that before killing himself he had found it necessary to look something up, something insignificant. He already knew, as did everyone else, that the fiftieth anniversary of the death of Rubén Darío had just been celebrated, his Rubén, the Rubén of the same name, who had been born under the same sign; Darío and Alado, conquest and flight, royalty and Pegasus, resplendent dominion, footprint of fire on the earth, immense wings in the sky. Darío, surrender, but surrender on high, not dragging yourself below, that of yesterday continued today, in him, Rubén Alado, so that Rubén Darío would be Rubén Darío Alado. Born together, died almost together, with a difference of only fifteen days but always under the same astral sign, no other, and thus the reincarnation would be fulfilled and would not fail. Darío in poetry, so that he, Alado, could be thus in the novel, another form of poetry. But more firmly tied to the earth, like a flying vessel with weights on either end. Weights to get to the center of things, to the humus of the earth and of beings; wings to go forward, without crawling. Had Darío been born on the eighteenth of January, as he was almost certain, or on the thirty-first?

THE BURIAL

We got to the funeral home to see a bird resting in a box. One shouldn't say things like that, but it's true. His face a sparrow's, the round eye sockets of a larger bird and the head resting to one side, on his left shoulder, in that gesture of the biped that asks for tenderness and hoards it, whose very rounded shape speaks of the need for a roof over its head. They had filled in his face and that made me feel better. I had always seen him as more than lacking in flesh, gaunt, emaciated, as though he had some windows inside that sucked him out or some absurd bellows that absorbed his flesh rather than inflating it. I didn't realize then that death inflated many things and did indeed have the lungs of a real bellows. I looked at his round, domed forehead and his thin lips, closed, but not pressed together, nor smiling but, rather, precisely formed by the outline of an artist's brush. I wanted to see the hole of the dagger, there in the very center of his heart. But I would have had to raise his shirt to be able to see it. The shirts of the dead are not to be raised, but I didn't think that he was dead then. In spite of the coffin and the flowers and the black dress of those who had gathered. Death seems to come after the burial, in the days that follow; it's a horse that drags its hearse, except that the hearse can be far away. Maybe for that reason, as at every burial, I heard talk of many things, more of the details of the death than of the dead man himself, more of the matters that each one had to attend to that day than of the grand matter of accompanying the deceased. The deceased was in fact absent, not because he was dead, but because there are dead persons who in their very gestures seem to be present.

But not this one; he was a bird, yes, maybe because his name was Alado, or because his head was bent or because of the eyes, but a bird that had already flown far away. Then the intellectuals arrived, those who had never gone to see him when he was alive; he had gone to see them, yes, but they had never gone to see him. One of them tossed his card from a distance onto the high table where the other cards were, I thought that his aim was stupendous, the same aim that kept him in the adjacent parlor and not close to the corpse. There one could converse and make contacts, because it is a well known fact that to be a famous intellectual is to have contacts. His Bohemian acquaintances also arrived. They didn't seem to me to be any better than the rest, though they were indeed better disguised. They struck this pose and that pose, which ended finally in the matter of poor Alado. Not that they all or even a single one of them had to commit suicide, but to die, yes, which is the same as handing over command. Life was a succession of powers, death the giving up of credentials. Because once dead, how could one even sustain, with the infallibility that is incumbent upon the intellectual, all those half-truths and half-lies, discoverers of gun powder or, better yet, of ice, in the words of Aureliano Buendía; that bit about how "inspiration doesn't exist, but rather a long period of training," or "I believe that all new writers proceed from Joyce." Of course, the written word remained, but on those words other words would be superimposed, and others, until "the library of Babel" was formed. I didn't see them take the body out, nor who went to the cemetery. Those who wanted to see their pictures in the paper the next day would have gone, I suppose, or those who used the occasion, yet again, to pontificate. To stand up and speak brings great happiness; to stand up, it goes without saying, while one is able to and there is an audience present and not when one is already condemned, like Alado, to the horizontal position. The coffin, about this there is no doubt, was taken out horizontally, and was carried horizontally, and was buried horizontally. I forgot to say that I didn't see who cried at the funeral; but I did see a lot of dark glasses, handkerchiefs scented with lemon having gone out of style.

The farewells that he had to extend were of little importance to him now; they simply brought to a close a season of spectacle, which was in the past. Had he been true to himself, he would have burst into Monsalve's office—he never got up to receive anyone, not even ladies—and landed a punch in the very center of his face. Thus he would have returned the offenses, that hoo-hoo especially with which he assented to questions. But no, I'm very interested in his next book, I'll write about it; there is no chitchat, no crumbs, that is, in his prose, unlike that of Bulmes, who if he was once great, is no longer. Nor pseudo-erudition, taking a bit from here, a bit from there, creating the appearance of an inflated balloon of wisdom, as in Mahler. And Mahler's family waiting for him with a great dinner, chicken, and he, I'm not anthropophagous, that's why I don't kill animals in my works. And the wife, laughing at the witty remark, if only we'd known about your aversion; but there are so many other things that we've prepared for you, and he, enigmatic, his voice hoarse, I prefer not to eat anything, just to watch you; you are mine, of my blood, even though certain intellectuals don't like Mahler, just like that, to their faces and maybe to disconcert them. And she, furious, but hiding that fact, wanting to know at the same time what they say about her husband. And he, one day I'll tell you about that, like the opinion they have at the Association, especially the poet Cortez, a dead man, liquidated, in his poetry of bright beads like Indian necklaces, but distant from that which is his, from the pain of the American man and from his confusion and his desolation. He asks for a whiskey and they hand one to him, he begins to pound on the wooden chair in which he is seated and simply by pounding, tun-tun tan, a an, an, he beats time to a wordless narration, detached from language, as must be that which emerges from the depths of the earth, that which takes shape at the deepest levels, that only he and a few others hear, the story of the ancestors that seemed to drag a chain, tun, tun, he pounds a link, silence, the connection was broken, tan, he found it again. And Mahler's eyes and those of his wife fastened on him, astonished by his magic, by that power he had to create mystery, so strange, so unique. And the legs of the woman stiff, fixed to the floor, but a little behind the legs of the chair, and the hands also supported, but on the cushion, also rigid, her entire body, the body of a spring, in short, ready to jump if he were to say anything more inappropriate than what he has already said, and he, because he hates them with all his heart, and it's impossible to hate except with the heart, I also visited your enemy, the one who now has an official post, and they told me that there were many who repudiated you. And they pour him another glass of whiskey to keep him talking, but he's already leaving, though it wouldn't be right to leave without reading at least a few lines of the first chapter of his novel, *La marcha de los batracios*, and "the great procession left, moving against the river's course," because, he explains, if it had moved with the river, it would have meant that those who participated in it had something clean about them, of pure water, but it wasn't like that, but rather all were a single human channel that deposited its filth in the clear flow, the carrier of the loveliest of round river stones, of the city. And the grass that on either bank extended down to the river, always hanging, like an endless green sheet, and the sky always higher than the spire of any church, or than the sublime voices that emerged from those same temples, and you are at bottom a poetic spirit, we greatly admire you, but from her mouth, that might be sincere. And Mahler, silent, as so often, not even looking at him, his pupils whirling, stopping finally at that amorphous painting, by Boticelli, I believe it's *The Birth of Venus*, or by Simonetta, or *The Three Graces*, I don't know, the face of a woman that says nothing, unless it's her hair, disproportionately spread to one side, as though it were windy, or because it's supposed to suggest that she can fly, that being more important to him, in short, than my words, and suddenly realizing that he has acted badly, but go on with what you were reading, but the desire had now left him, so he told them maybe another time, I'm getting up now, I'm leaving now, he said I'm off, or I'm going, and they, stopping him, wouldn't you like to eat a piece of cake, at least. Shoot, it's almost time, they exchange glances, time for what?, they don't say it but they think that he's mad, the time when we will surprise the world, the time when everything will rattle and collapse and explode. We have to be prepared for the grand upheaval, all the signs are announcing its coming, as in the *Apocalypse*. A revolution in values will begin, and those who are below will be above, and the great cloud of dust of the many necessary dead will sweep away, because dust also sweeps, it also cleans the great filth of this life. He's not mad, he's being theatrical, that's all, Mahler later says, you should hear him when we're alone, he speaks normally then, in simple, ordinary, maybe even common language. And the hypocrites and those who exploit will be left in the cold, and the cause will triumph, that one, yes, the maker of an admirable campaign, not Bolivar's or that which Rubio made when he praised you.

THE WRITERS' ARTICLES

And he wrote THIS, the sometime revolutionary:
"He's died on us, and by his own hand, a complete man of letters. Symptom of the decadence of a society which knows no values beyond the monetary and that sympathizes, if indeed it ever does, with the visible misfortunes but not with the profound, lacerating misfortunes of a creator. If there is guilt, it is not the novelist's but the capitalist government's, blind in the face of the drama of an existence it could not value, that even less attempts to interpret, and that never—it must be said—managed to stimulate. By free lance work one does not live, by books one barely eats, make a request and watch how they reject it or tell you to come back tomorrow. A beggar's toil is that of every artist, a base pilgrimage is what they impose on him, from one place to another place, a miserable stipend that which falls to him, almost amusingly, on which he barely subsists. It is time to assign new value to concepts, to demand transformations, to ask that structures be changed."
And he wrote THAT, in a very spiritual liqueur:
"A faded outline, his, being of fine lines, almost a contemptible smudge, thus he appeared to us in order to leave and in his passing left us impregnated, almost saturated, with that dense mist that accompanied him, an enveloping heap like a veiled Limean woman. And one saw in the man the ghosts of Goya, the very blackest of them, those which overwhelm on sight, which because they are so dramatic, mysteriously blood-curdling, are kept in the basement, and never on any other floor, in the Museo del Prado. He was a live well, or the innermost recesses of a roaring cave, into which one had to enter for better or for worse, such was his power. And once inside, to feel the deafening pulse of the profound footsteps, those that mark the earth or those that are fleeting, lugubrious but true."

And he wrote THAT OTHER piece, the grandiloquent:

"A holocaust worthy of the moving Greek tragedies has just been consummated. And the victim? The essence of modesty, of rare and incredible gifts, a heart open to justice, an immeasurable talent that now burrows into the inaccessible and mysterious vaults of immortality. He wrote in blood, he unleashed explosions, he burned himself like the martyrs in the sacred fire of truth. An authentic genius, he knew how to hide his greatness; sincerity and composure were his norms. America loses something of the grandest it possessed: a pure heart from among its rare pure hearts; an incomparable novelist from among its irreplaceable, incomparable novelists."

And they, THOSE WRITERS, their teeth clenched, said:

"Maybe it was necessary to die in order to grow, or perhaps one also had to live in a shameless fashion in order to grow. 'If you haven't received my book, I beg you, let me know and I'll send you another copy. Comments, please.' 'Don't forget the pseudonym I've used for the short story contest.' 'I'm counting on your vote for Club President.' And if shamelessness didn't suffice, by all means, kill oneself, especially if one were shameless and alone, independent, backed by no party."

There remained the telephone, and there remained above all the hidden powers. He phoned his most intimate friends and said to them only: "As always, I hope you will save me; just a bit of aid…"

He hung up and ordered another beer at the bar. He drank it down in great, vulgar gulps and wiped his mouth on the sleeve of his jacket. He ran to the bus stop, jumped on a red one. He got off and walked two blocks, slowly, glancing alternately to the left and to the right. He positioned himself behind a flower stand; the stand was green and he was very pale; one might think it was a case of mimicry. He waited; he put his hands in his pockets; he seemed to be freezing and it was twelve noon on a tropical day. He realized that the moment had arrived; the sun fell in a perpendicular line. She, one of the women that he loved, came out of the building where she lived. She walked to the street; she felt as though she were surrounded by a polar wind or that someone had brushed her with the sharp blade of a knife. He had left the knife, a short dagger, in the hotel. She looked toward the stand, approximately ten meters from where she stood. She believed that he was there. She saw him and didn't see him because he had already managed to hide again. The uncertainty remained, but even more there remained the unpleasant sensation of having been cut and of the hair on her arms standing on end. Later she completely forgot about it. For him, on the other hand, that had been a way of saying goodbye to her: He had approached her without speaking, almost throwing himself at her, with only the tiniest effort at concentration. Would he have achieved, maybe by meditating more deeply, a mental marriage of blood. An aerial coupling...

THE VISITS TO THE HOTEL ROOM

Leave him alone, don't go near, don't touch him, the open mouth is full of germs, you already know that he's ice cold why touch him or do you think that the cold of this corpse is colder than that of other corpses. The room stinks. The room doesn't stink, the corpse doesn't even stink, it's the cologne that Genoveva sprayed all over the place. When did she come in? Before we did, she's the one who found him. Could she be the one who killed him? There's no sign of that, her fingerprints aren't on the dagger. So he committed suicide, then? That's the initial version. And what are those candles lit for? Genoveva brought them. She's very stupid that woman and you're even stupider for letting her light them. We're screwed with you and with her; screwed with heat and odors. You're the one who's screwed, I'm not; you don't understand a thing; she believes that that's the way to hold a wake for him, because nobody else is going to hold a wake for him. Stupid, his friends and his enemies are going to hold a wake for him today. You are always so practical, so practical it's nauseating, so that now to be practical is to be realistic, to know about life. Yes, you always know what's in your interests and what's not, what's happening and what's not, you would never have committed suicide. Do you think I'm an idiot, that that's a great act of heroism? The time for romanticism is past. You don't even know what romanticism is; romanticism is having a conscience. Now you're going to start up with your grand explanations; the truth is that the dead stay dead and that's all there is to it. Why don't you shut up; by talking we're showing disrespect for him and for this entire setting of tragic ceremony. I don't want to hear anything more from you, you're in the habit of preaching, of weaving webs around everything, of not simply seeing the facts but of twisting them; that's why you have such a hard time with life. And you, what difference does my life make to you? None, of course, but your handkerchief interests me. You are an animal. Animals don't sweat.

There was a time when he thought that his novel, the last one which he still hadn't written, might have created a sensation. To have written it would have been like shutting the mouths of Mahler and Bulmes and Lince. Because I, the narrator, was at the end of the last street to which the procession led, almost at the edge of the river, or maybe in it. Or better yet, above it, poised in the air, like a large angel, to describe the circular conversations, without forgetting the other bits, someone scratched himself and someone else stared, and this one sneezed, and that one coughed, and that one over there was silent, and there were no scripts, nor quotation marks sprinkled about the dialogue, nor were the descriptions separated from the narration and everything spun round like a whirlpool, dizzyingly. Of course, this would have been more evident if the scene unfolded in the river, since there in fact they sailed and whirled, but on land one could follow the same procedure, given that life was round, and speaking in literary terms, there was no shape better than the circle, as is the triangle in a painting, and then the line that followed the procession was the diameter of the circle, from top to bottom, drawn in a straight line, rigid, though spilling over at either end in the many waves of people who moved and swayed, always following a rhythm, a poetic rhythm, and to provide in that way the sensation of the motion of waves. And the windows of one house and another house opened, and one face and another face appeared and I spoke of each face and of each past, in order to minutely analyze the entire town in that way and to unfold in confusing but transparent and clear placards, for anyone who knew how to read, the infamy and the ruin of those people. And though Mahler were to say that *La marcha de los batracios* was precisely the same as the painting of the Final Judgment that he had seen in some church, in which there were more toads and serpents than people, and more fire than purification, and that to write about this was no different than vomiting animals. To act like a magician who unleashes a dance of death, a dance without music, that is, with no basis nor transcendence, and thus in the end no more than a gesture, contortion and dislocation, not thesis, which is what one had to achieve in writing. Because it was better to say but without saying, in other words, make the characters pirouette but without showing that they were pirouetting, leave realism in the background while always hanging on to it, and without going to the other extreme either, of vacuous chatter or airy characters. Mahler, know-it-all Mahler, always ready with a refutation, just like Javert, the new Boss, imagining himself a Saint Beuve resuscitated and acting like a self-taught expert of the Sartre of the posters plastered one over another, and I also write because he has a poem; and the reciter who believes himself an artist because he rattles off some verses by Vallejo and Neruda, as a result now better Neruda and better Vallejo, and the ladies of the Societies, so spiritual and so mystical, that their entire lives are an incense burner that exhales perfume and if they hear the word vesicle they excuse themselves and go off to vomit, and if they make a child they do it the way Bulmes wrote, with a vial; and the poetess who says to the other you're a genius, I've always praised you; and the other, as far as I'm concerned, you are America's greatest gift, I've always said that, and the guilds, and the associations, and the speeches. And the flower arrangements and the little medals that they exchange, identical to the ones they distribute in convent schools, with diplomas and all; and the tropical orchid, and the carnation, and the rose, and the floripondio, all in gold, for the sagging breasts of the forty-ish lady writers. He was fed up. Yes, at one time he had thought that his novel would create a sensation. The novel done, finished in three hundred pages, one hundred thousand copies printed and distributed. Not the two-page novel that he had and that ended at the moment with that magnificent phrase that said: "And they carried something that was not an idol, though it looked like one, but that in any event weighed so much that they couldn't keep it steady."

Because it had to be explained that this procession was not religious, but of another order; that's why it was called a march. A revolutionary march? A march of insects? A march of blacks with demands, and who go from New Orleans to Washington? That would have to be specified, though it would never be known. The novel never managed to get beyond those two pages, although it was entire in his head; it was a novel about a march that, paradoxically, wasn't going anywhere. The arrested novel, just as the existence of the author had to be arrested today, and no later. Thus did the novel die with him, but in him and within him. Volatilized in his astral body, that body that would begin to take shape with the descent of his carnal being, it would surely come to be an obsession and a reality for the new man which, beginning with himself, would be created. From Darío came Alado, from Alado would come another; from the germ of *La marcha de los batracios* a great novel would be born, perhaps with another name. The novel that would supplant those of Fuentes and Cortázar, because none of them had such a marvelous and strange origin, of blood and death in a pierced heart.

THE SUPPOSITION OF A GOOD MAN

I don't know why he killed himself but, of necessity, he did it conscientiously. Introducing a dagger into oneself is an act less impulsive than swallowing a box of pills. In any case, it has us distressed, hurt, sad. He was a strange man, chaotic and maybe defeated by life. There are destinies that cannot be avoided and that demand defeat and annihilation; they are the destinies of the gluttonous jaws. And he was cut off, but first he went through a slow process of demolition. Life can sometimes seem to be a hardship. I helped him a lot, I drove him and I believe that I contributed to his choosing narration; he wanted to do theater, or poetry. A phenomenon of intelligence has been born to us in you, I told him, and we are captivated by it. But he began to have a certain mistrust in my actions; unexpectedly, he began to push me away. He was an evasive being, impossible to pin down. One day he sent two thugs to beat me up. They didn't find me, I'm weak, they could have killed me. Then he attacked me directly in an article.

THE SUPPOSITION OF THE PSYCHOLOGIST

Suicide falls within the clear process of alienation. It is an illness whose clinical manifestations are directly related to psychiatry. It begins with an evident process of melancholy and ends with violent masochism unleashed again the self. The act of vengeance, which was initially to be exercised against the environment, is inverted into a punishment against the self, given that society or the environment are, for the suicide victim, powerful enemies, impossible to defeat.

THE SUPPOSITION OF AN INTELLIGENT CHILD

"Son, don't read those stories about dead people in the paper. You now see how one must be good and take care of oneself. Death is dangerous and comes when least expected."

"How can it be dangerous if the dangerous part is over when one dies? Mama, you don't know anything."

So why don't you just die, Rubén Alado, right now and not later? Why don't you holywater bless with a bullet, or with a dagger, or with whatever, all the evil you have within you? Why don't you demonstrate with your death that it's still possible to hope for some sort of purification in life? What are you waiting for, Rubén Alado, what's stopping you, what do you care about a few more hours, a few more years? You are already killing me Rubén Alado with your living presence in this world; I could even grant you the miracle of dreaming that you were alive as long as you were dead. Rubén Alado I have followed you today to the library, and to the strange visit to the woman you love, and I have heard you call your friends and I have believed that maybe all of that was an indication that you wanted to kill yourself. I'm in the small foyer of your hotel, I've picked up a magazine and I've sat down to wait. I'm near your room, maybe five meters away. I would be the first to hear the gunshot, and also the first to know if you killed yourself some other way. A spasm, a rope suddenly breaking inside me would announce it. But there is no sound, absolutely nothing, Rubén Alado, Rubén, what are you doing there inside? You're writing, you're sleeping, you're thinking, maybe, about how you might best kill me. You already threatened me once, with a toy gun, it's true, but it could have been a real one; Rubén, from that moment you've had me terrified, from that moment and long before when I began to suspect you. You haven't been my shadow, Rubén, because shadows walk with one, but below, cowering; they are the least of one, not the most; one almost never turns around to look at them if they are behind, and one also doesn't look down at them when they are ahead. No, Rubén, you haven't been my shadow, but, rather, my tragic destiny. I must follow you, as I'm following you now to prevent you from killing me, to keep the evil in its nest. Thus cared for, wrapped up, maybe evil won't explode, maybe it won't blow up. Have you noticed Rubén that I'm one of the few who is nice to you? Even after your threat and the scene you made in front of everybody in the middle of the office. Rubén, I almost never talk to you or seek you out, and when I do it's with the least offensive of words, the least compromising, the most delicate, the most innocent. I praise your novels, I get excited when you begin to read to me the only two pages you have of *La march de los batracios*. Maybe I'm not being very explicit, but you understand me. Rubén, if you like I can also study esoteric science and that part, which I don't understand, about the fourth power. But do calm down, don't kill me.

DEAD TODAY AND FOREVER

For your work and for your glory, kill me Rubén. I've dreamed that I died and one feels no more than the strong anguish of not being able to breath, of the throat being closed. But that's before Rubén, a few seconds before that instant, yes, it's only an instant or a fraction of an instant, in which one understands, grasps, feels, thinks, ascertains, convinces oneself, affirms, in short, all the verbs, that there is no longer a solution, that there is no appeal, that everything has ended, that a bomb is exploding within, yes, truly exploding and one sees oneself flying to pieces, and gazes at the rays of light, and hears the explosion and then screams: mama, mama, don't laugh, Rubén, one always screams mama, yes, mama, and I'm sure that you, too, would scream mama. Rubén I want you to scream mama, but don't want it to be I who screams mama.

DEAD TODAY AND FOREVER

I will go to your funeral Rubén, I will do not one but three articles. I know how to write like a pseudo-revolutionary, a spiritual, and a grandiloquent writer would write. I guarantee that you would like the three, even though you were to say that they're not literature. You would like them, Rubén, because they speak well of you. And after your death, according to your beliefs, Rubén, nothing would have happened because you would be reincarnated. And if those beliefs were theater that you performed to convince or a ruse to live, at least you still have the bronze bust though it be hollow in the style of Henry Moore.

DEAD TODAY AND FOREVER

You suspect that I suspect that you want to kill me. We are playing cards. I don't play my card if you don't play yours first. My card is only to ask that you die; your card perhaps is to kill me. I say perhaps, though I am certain, because that perhaps saves me from desperation. Perhaps you will never decide, perhaps it's more important to you to leave that line blank. But that's normal, exactly normal, that you want to leave one like that. A reputation, do you know Rubén how much a reputation is worth? It's worth less than a corpse, if one has no money and you have no money, Rubén Alado.

DEAD TODAY AND FOREVER

Are you going to take your afternoon walk today Rubén? You will be seen walking up the streets that go up the hill, on the way to Avila. Your hands will rest in your pockets and since your arms are long and your jacket short, your shoulders will be raised. From behind and against the evening light you will look like a black silhouette that climbs the steps of the rainbow. I believe that your head will gradually disappear and that only your body will remain. Perhaps for that reason you will be seen headless in someone's omen.

DEAD TODAY AND FOREVER

I'm going now, Rubén. I've waited for a long time. There is no sound in your room; I'll come back tomorrow and the day after, just as I came yesterday and the day before. I'm like that strange man who's at the post office everyday. Have you seen him? They say he's a former employee and that's why he's always there. Sometimes he does calisthenics in front of everybody, and nobody laughs and nobody asks him anything. They don't ask me anything either at this hotel. Ruben I hear your typewriter now, as though you now live so that I will begin to die. What are you writing? You're writing my name.

CARLOS BÉJAR PORTILLA
(Ambato, 1938)

Born in Ambato, Carlos Béjar Portilla has lived his entire life in Guayaquil. He studied law but abandoned the profession almost immediately after graduating and dedicated himself to literature.

He has written four short story collection, *Simón el Mago* (winner of the José de la Cuadro Literary Prize, 1970), *Osa mayor* (1970), *Samballah* (1971), and *Puerto de Luna* (1986), as well as three novels: *Tribu sí* (1981, finalist in the Barral Literary Contest in 1976), *La rosa de Singapur* (1990), and *Mar abierto* (1997, first prize in a national literary contest sponsored by *El Universo*, one of Guayaquil's major dailies).

Béjar Portilla has also published two poetry collections: *Los ángeles también envejecen* and *Plumas* (1997).

Stories by Béjar Portilla have been translated into French and German, and included in a number of anthologies.

Béjar Portilla introduced science fiction into Ecuadoria literature. However, his most authentic, sincere, and most finely crafted works are his recent, evocative minimalist narrations purged of all that is even slightly extraneous, featuring scenes in ports and on docks and ships.

PUERTO DE LUNA*

In the ill-assorted collection of cabins, there at the top of the hill, flashing lights and music dance. Lanes that descend to the beach. Street-lamps. Somber piles and sea walls upholstered in algae and mollusks. Phosphorescences. It smells of the sea, of salt, of a simple, enormous whale.

Dozens of ships, skiffs, brigs lick with their listing gunwales the peace of the still water. Their captains and assistants, followed by noisy, rowdy crews, abandoned the ships long ago and, now, in the cabarets of the port at the top of the hill that overlooks the bay, rehearse outlandish poses, unforeseen weighings of anchors, leeward tacks.

The brothels are lined up one after another and from the road the sailors take stock of the possibilities. El Cangrejo Cojo, La Gallinita del Mar, and La Esponja Beoda competed for customers, but it was always Puerto de Luna, the dancehall, that won hands down. Hundreds of officers and cabin boys fought to get in. Its fame is greater than that of any other on the south

---

*From the collection *Puerto de luna*, 1999.

Pacific coast. It's an obligatory stop for privateers and ship owners from around the world, it can't cope with the extraordinary demand posed by the entire navy. It's there that famous sea captains drink and make love: Morgan and Dampierre, Alvez, El Portugués, the romantic slave trader invented by Salgari, who when traffic on the Benin-Rio route falls, finds a way through the Straits of Magellan and sails up to Valparaiso and Puerto de Luna. He rests then from the English gunboats that hound him on the Atlantic. Von Hollock, the Bloody Dutchman, is also there. The locals claim that he's the only one who has a gigantic white shark astern. It follows his ship through the seas of the world and it seems that his master provides succulent banquets daily.

I go there myself, every hundred years, to visit my lady love, the perfect Dolly, as soon as the drift of my solitary ship takes me to that landfall, with the indisputable honor of being one of the few phantom ship captains remaining in the world.

Dolly, Dolly, my love, so long imprisoned between the mist and the Sargasso, contemplating in you the song of perfect happiness, separated by the curse of that limitless hope.

Instead of the ship's course, I have in the binnacle a detailed list of longings. And in the bilge, instead of the human ebony that Alvez transports, the blue pearls of Java and Timor with which the Dutchman pays his bills, I bring sea cucumbers and jellyfish to buy your love. I hope, my blue-eyed, golden-haired doll, that we can dance at least till dawn. Let my arm encircle your waist, let flocks of frigate birds and boobies rise from among the fish of your breasts.

Because Dolly, we are, above all, fallen angels who come to exchange the grand coin of eternity for the shiny bauble of the here and now. Nevertheless, for as long as Montanez sounds, for as long as Willie unloads, may there be only gravy and coral, shipwreck and moans, tobacco and rum, in spite of the occasional sailors who transport puritans and those Nordic explorers with their red beards who understand no language more subtle than that of blood. I've seen them raise their colors of tepid crusades and skeletons.

Later, when the day dawns, we'll give to the innkeeper the sum agreed upon for the bed and then we will be alone.

Puerto de Luna will no longer be this, but a humble hut rising over the water of the rice fields, you a simple peasant woman toothless and full of children, my ship a flimsy little canoe tied to the shack on stilts, and only thus will the spell be broken.

RAÚL PÉREZ TORRES
(Quito, 1941)

This prolific writer has published seven story collections: *Da llavando* (1970), *Manual para mover las fichas* (1973), *Micaela y otros cuentos* (National Short Story Prize, 1976), *Ana la pelota humana* (1978), *Musiquero joven, musiquera viejo* (José de la Cuadra Prize, 1977), *En la noche y en la niebla* (Casa de las Américas Prize, 1980), and *Un saco de alacranes* (1989). In 1995, Pérez Torres won the Juan Rulfo Prize, sponsored by Radio France International for his story "Sólo cenizas hallarás". His stories have been translated into English, French, and German, and included in virtually all Ecuadorian short story anthologies. He has also published a novel, *Teoría del desencanto* (1985).

There is no mistaking Raúl Pérez's stories. The story itself is not what matters. His is a world of unabashed virile tenderness, of garrulous melancholy—the melancholy and intimacy of the *pasillo* and the *bolero*. His characters come together in order to confess, in the search for sincerity and the informality that exists among close friends, to remember, to evoke the past. The plaintive tone of his stories is tempered by narrative experimentation and a certain poetic touch.

ASHES ONLY WILL YOU FIND*

I swear with my hand on my heart, Patitas, that when I met her I was already bad but not to excess. God and the devil took me by the hand. Of course, I was twenty years old. The thing is, her eyes smelled like mint. Can you believe that? It's the only thing I remember. The smell of her eyes that came to me in gusts. Yeah, sure, it's not the only thing, but it's what I remember most. Disappointed eyes, like they'd been dulled by time.

You probably think I'm making this up, but you've got to remember that what we're talking about here is all mixed up with time, memory, and even culture to some extent.

I was always checking her out when she left the university. Yeah, the philosophy department, what else was I going to study since I wasn't interested in studying, period. She always came out covered with chalk dust and misery after teaching her classes. It sometimes seemed like first she came out, empty, vague, and then came the thousand years that got into her body at the bottom of the stairs. It was when she shook her

---

*From the collection *Sólo cenizas hallarás*, 1995.

blouse a little and smoothed her hair back with her hand and a movement of her neck so slight you almost didn't notice, that she gave me something for the rest of my life at that time in my life. No, are you crazy? I wasn't her student, no way. Guess what she taught. She taught a subject that doesn't exist: Cosmogony of the Seer. Imagine that. It was enough to make you laugh. I would have laughed if I hadn't been as lovesick as a dog.

There were only three students in the class, not real bright, who followed her around everywhere, like they were hypnotized, they lit her cigarettes, they surrounded her in the café, they pulled out her chair, they recited Oriental poems for her, but they especially protected her like a suit of armor so that the bad stuff wouldn't get to her, or the things people (like me) said about her, or the stupid music by Vangelis they played in the bar, with that "good to see you" over and over, or even my mind's impotent caress that got wasted in the smoke before it touched her.

Yeah, she had a name, but it was an ordinary name, a name that made it pretty obvious that her parents weren't real fond of her. Her name was Esthela. But I don't want to talk about her name, I want to talk about how there was this wake she created, dragging me along, because if it hadn't been for her I might have been a soccer star, or maybe a great leader, or at least a promising pederast, but there it is, Patitas, there has to be a pair of green eyes in the life of every soulless youth, and it was at a friend's show, Marcelo Aguirre's, where Esthela finally slowed down enough to notice me. Yeah, slow, man, like that, I'm going to spin this tale out a little at a time so it'll last longer over a beer than it did in real life. Marcelo Aguirre, namely, the painter who's taken a nosedive to hell, the one who opened a door for us that will lead to nobody knows where, yeah, yeah, but no, your readings are way off, superficial, it's got nothing to do with Dante, nothing to do with Beatriz, just the fox of intelligence devouring herself.

She was alone in one of the classrooms, in other words, I took her by surprise, alone, you get my meaning? Her three zombies were there, of course, but she was alone, alone, defenseless, without a tit to suck on, an orphan, her and the cadre, her and the tunnel of oil painting. Did I tell you, Patitas, that I was already bad but not to excess? Ok, so I got myself behind that loneliness that gave off a chill, behind but above, but inside, damn, that's the problem with words, they're like a shirt when what you want is skin. Ok, so I got behind that neck, in a position to pray to the god of that neck, so that that stubborn muscle could hear me, and standing at attention I asked Yahweh, Otum, Pachacamac, Jesus, old man Marcos, for a breeze of solidarity, energy so that the hands of my brain could reach out begging, like, and the miracle happened, she turned around, the look in her eyes full of gloomy colors and just like that she ran up against the great bird of happiness which was my youth.

It's ok, man, take it easy. Think hard and you'll get my meaning. What I'm saying has a lot to do with the beer and what they used to call tenacity. And so she came over to me right away, obsessed by my blazing love, pale, I'm here to tell you that pale is the color of the magnolia, like the song says, she came over pale, she came up to me gray and timid and kissed my black cheek while saying, so nervous she was almost embarrassed: "The dream is the greatest conquest of modern art." "No," I said to her, as she traveled searching for the gold of her old age, "modern art is the nightmare."

What else can I tell you? The rest is always the rest. The magic is the beginning, the rest is the end. It turns out that with her it was always the beginning. It was later when I found out about her chains, the phoniness of the sixties, the romantic gibberish that she lived and that left her in pieces like clay, without enough energy to deal with now, this very rich time of emptiness.

Then we were out of there (that's how fast it happened), we were out of there and on our way to Guápulo, alone, alone for the first time, to go over her life again, to get back those years. The night that night was real night. Sometimes it seemed like a black's smile, a night of spasms, in other words, a night that whitened at times, glowed, in other words, with her words.

She talked a lot, stumbling over her words, she yelled at me for my times, the roses lost, and sensuality, and the beautiful words, and the utopias. "What are you," she said to me, trying to lump everybody who's young together, "an ambiguous, ironic, soulless generation; you feed emptiness, you are 'monks' of emptiness, that's what you are, you live for today because thought doesn't take you to tomorrow. Do you think I haven't watched you, do you think that I haven't observed your sad poses of being beyond," and she put a lot of emphasis on that "beyond" that took her even further, "you've reached the point of intellectual nothingness" ("You haven't read Macedonia?" she asked while I swooned in the eye at her waist), "you look at life with a kind of tragic humor, centered exclusively on your emotions, on your moods, on irony, with no moral or political consciousness. Everything surprised us, we went from one surprise to another, from one discovery to another, from one search to another. Be surprised that you're alive, damn it!"

"Alive at the edge of a fetid river," I said, "a river of worn out words, of worn out attitudes." But I just said that to seem hard, to feed her words. I wanted her to do the talking, of course, to strip me of all knowledge, all reflection. I can honestly say that I almost didn't care what she thought. She didn't believe much in what she was saying, or, at most, she was feeding her guilt. But what did I care about her guilt when I had those phosphorescent bones there next to me…

Guápulo. I already knew all about the skulls, the readings, the acid, the paintings, the grass that had been consumed in honor of the new man, I'd even already got a look at her in my dreams (I've told you, right, that I dream first and then I live?), dressed in black or in some Hindu rag, sandals, a necklace of coral and shiny beads and her string bag filled with little quartz and amber stones, and a copy of Sartre, the whole thing underlined and stained with life's yellowing, circular liquor, rising agitated, boiling, full, maybe, of a communal happiness, the happiness of a communal work gang, because that's the kind of thing they did, communal works gangs to fix heads, fix the world, unfix order. Yeah, I watched her rising in my dream, with a triangular face that already predicted disappointment, and as she talked to me like from some grand distant place, like she was her own echo and not herself, I saw her rising, and rising, and rising, fifteen years before, always on the move, in a hurry, her heart filled with burning coals, and the Beatles, and Los Panchos, without thinking even for a second about the ashes that were falling by the wayside, ashes we were picking up that very night so that she could warm her heart a little.

Leaning against the railing on the stone wall, her back to me and to the church, she drank a small can of German beer, like a bird, taking little sips, making a soft sound in her throat, with a constant, tenacious *saudade* (they say there's no way to translate that word but all you have to know is that it means a ball of melancholy that chokes you when you're remembering) while I went to the car and played in her honor that real romantic song Luis Miguel's made famous again: "*You are the reason for all my anguish...*" That's right, Patitas, for all my anguish, except for one thing, except for the anguish of being right next to her and drinking the time of her body, because that wasn't anguish, but more like sky diving. No, I've never done it, but I've gone hang gliding, from Cruz Loma, it's got to be something like that because her body was an abyss and I was falling into it a little at a time, an abyss of magic charms and spells that were taking me into the air headed for the chasm of that time which I wished for her sake I could have lived in the flesh.

After the third Clausen, she told me she had to pee, that's how she said it. There had been a little shed there at one time, used for that purpose, but by then it was falling apart, empty, without the joys of a flush toilet; she walked over to it, taking along the bear of her melancholy. I was pulled in her wake which had the force of a hurricane, no, I didn't actually follow her, that´s gross; I waited for her to get back and, excusing myself, I flew to the spot. Her smell was still there, even sharper, more overbearing, and the grass was wet there with her pee, so I bent down and, real devout, I picked a little leaf she'd peed on, I still have it, I keep it between the pages of the *I Ching*, the Holy Book she gave me one day so that I would know who I was and where I was going. I get it out sometimes and sniff at it, yeah, the little leaf, it still tastes like her cunt, a special taste, sort of like tea but saltier. Yeah, tea, don't ask me, Patitas, I don't know, I've never tried coca tea, sort of like ammonia?, no, that's not what I'm getting at, here I am trying to cast a spell and you're trying to decipher. Of course, you're younger.

"You're beautiful," I told her, looking at her sharp profile, black against the wild purple of that night. "You look like one of Viver's women." "You're crazy," she told me, all motherly, stroking my face with the back of her cold hand, "but your craziness it too normal."

Ok, so since I was innocent and therefore not responsible for my actions, I begged her to come with me to my room, "I have some musical relics there," I said, not wanting to give offense, or I don't know, "Lucho Gatica and Led Zepellin, María Luisa Landín and Tina Turner, Elvis Presley and Daniel Santos, Leo Marini and Nat King Cole, they all sleep together there. And, of course, Julio, always Julio." Iglesias? What Iglesias, don't be a retard, Julio Jaramillo. "Let's go," she said, and I was kind of hurt because she didn't, like, resist.

But I ordered more beer, Patitas, I'll tell you the rest, if you want. But you already know the rest…

Ok, so, the first night I acted like a green midget. You're not going to believe me when I tell you what happened, but there it is. The first night I cried, she was so beautiful. When I looked at her naked I started to cry like a Korean, it was so moving, her nakedness broke my heart, all she still had on below the freckled sun of her shoulders was a black silk bra, a vaccination mark, why go on. Just because I felt so alone, I grasped her tired breasts, no, it wasn't nostalgia, what do you mean, Oedipus!, keep Oedipus out of it, it was just fear, fear of the marvelous. I kissed her breasts and she opened her eyes real wide, I felt my youth entering those eyes, all the nostalgia she felt for my youth. Anyway, it was a bust. The first time is almost always a bust, no, I'm not making excuses, what happens is that the bodies don't come together, they don't consti-tute, they look strange to one another, like animals.

Then, a few days later, the fluttering and the groan-ing came together, but that night I felt, I don't know why, like we were making love in front of a crowd, maybe it was because of her memories, they came into the room in a herd, taking over my tongue, my hands, my needs, and I even felt like they wanted to throw me out of the bed, like I was an undesirable.

When the tryout was over, she got real sad and start-ed to cry, she cried and cried, it was pitiful, her sobbing, a monotone, like the drizzle in Lima. The silence was a pool, full of toads. At dawn she got dressed and left. Esthela. So I got busy picking up the intelligence she forgot in my body, wanting to make it ordinary, to give it a simpler meaning, less frantic, but no way, because beginning that night I started to love her like I was autistic, like a lap dog following her everywhere, doing everything for her, on her behalf, I didn't want her to do anything domestic, nothing ordinary, nothing human, in fact, I brought her pure water from a sacred irrigation ditch on Mount Pichincha, I made herbal teas for her aches and pains, I rubbed her feet with my lips to get them warm, I collected jokes for when she was feeling panicky, I bought exotic fruits to perfume her skin, medlars, rose apples, mandarins, I hired jugglers for when she was lonely, in short, I was on this earth to serve her, so that her heart wouldn't suffer the petty things, or the stupid, or the evil that was everywhere. Not being with her tore me to pieces. A play, a book, a song, a movie we didn't see together made me feel sad, small, paralyzed, damn!, maybe I'm exaggerating like a bad choirboy but what do you want, we've had six already, and right now her shadow is everywhere, even the color of the beer reminds me of the butterfly of her smile. It was martyrdom, a torture not to be with her, imagine that, me, who'd always left girls so that I could miss them, so that I could love them a little.

I almost always woke up next to her because she had conceded the favor of letting me sleep at her house Mondays, Wednesdays, and Fridays, which didn't have any bad omens attached. But the mornings I woke up alone in my room, little by little I started becoming aware of something called reality; I put myself in her hands like she was a goddess, to help her deal every new day with the presence of the military, the loss of hair, the smell of the priests, the talks with the family. Then I got up and just about had enough energy to get to the shower and dream under the water about her liquid body.

Don't laugh, pimp, there's nothing funny about it, I

was close to going crazy with so much sensibility, like the faggots. Imagine, one day on the phone, she told me with that plush voice of hers, "I've been thinking about you," and I was as sad and lonely as a mop, because that meant there were times when she didn't do that, when she didn't think about me, so why couldn't I, dumb faggot, get her out of my damn head for even a second?

I was scribbling poetry at the time, yeah, it never went beyond that, show me the twenty-year-old who hasn't lined his vulgarities and his complaints up in columns, I scribbled poetry and tormented her daily with my poems and my flowers which she touched to her lips in a way that had something Japanese about it… Speaking of the Japanese, it was around that time that a German showed up, an anthropologist with raspberry eyes, he was renting a room at Esthela's place. My heart fell to my feet the first time I saw him talking to her, he was pretty, the pimp, as pretty as an altarpiece, like a god, like Marlon Brando's face when he dies in *The Fallen Gods*, have you seen that movie?, you're not serious, you haven't got beyond Pink Floyd, bro. Ok, so as I was saying, he was pretty and seeing him with Esthela tore me apart, better yet, turned me into a wreck because it was like somebody had put the missing halo back on the head of the young Christ, and then, later, I systematically tormented her with my absurd jealousy, and she didn't take me at all seriously, with her little face filled with love, with her wet lips lavishly exploring my whole body, a young body that every night she was inventing, for herself, inventing to the extent that once she said to me: "What I love most about your body is the perversion, it's a perversion that has nothing to do with you, like a child's," but I was always hoping for something from her gestures, hunting for something that would help me figure out what was wrong, something I couldn't put my finger on, not even in the long, clear nights, sleepless, that I spent like an amanuensis taking down her most insignificant words, her attitudes, her gaze lost like she was watching a different movie. I'd never before seen up close a face that switched expressions so fast, suddenly it was confusion, stupidity, sadness, seldom, real seldom, happiness. Her face was a Pisces, does that make sense?

Lots of times she'd go on and on about the past, it was real irritating, there I was, ready to make love, looking at her body already naked, open like a poppy, sitting on my chest, and I was having a hard time controlling my vulgar hands and tongue that wanted to taste the salty honey of her thighs, because I didn't want to listen to her, I wanted to drink her, to taste her, to sample her, so there I would be, real anxious, and she would stop dead and look at me with those eyes lost, distant, cold. "What's wrong," I asked her, embarrassed, the way you feel when you're naked and somebody's analyzing you, and she would say, "Nothing's wrong, age is what's wrong," and she would start talking about her damned sixties, about some guerrilla war or other and I don't know what mountains. "I remember," she said, "I remember those years, when we still loved one another, and we respected one another, and intelligence was like a fine wine that we shared again and again." But the way she said it was so distant, so vague, like she was talking about the Paleolithic. I went away from those sessions bored as an Eskimo because afterwards she jumped out of bed without any consideration at all for my manhood, and she started pulling those memories preserved in mothballs out of her little chests, yellowing photos of when she was queen of her high school, president of her class, valedictorian, debate champion, daddy's little girl, her fifteenth birthday, her twentieth on a boulder in Portovelo hugging Olimpo Cárdenas, and the issues of *Ecran* and Lana Turner and Ava Gardner and Rock Hudson, did you know he was a fag, Patitas?, and James Dean and Julieta Greco and she started to recite stupid poems by César Dávila, Vallejo, and baby-faced Adoum. I don't know why, now that we're drinking, my memories of her seem like widowhood, but it's no big thing, man, don't get bitter, you look like an Argentine, wait a second, I'll be back, I'm going to the bathroom, whenever I get lucid I want to vomit...

So, I'll keep talking. One night I dreamed that she was talking to me in foreign languages, think about that, shithead, she was talking to me in foreign languages, why did I dream that she was talking to me in foreign languages? I don't know, and I don't care anymore, but heavy and bitter and drunk as I was, the hurricane of that lightness I felt kept me awake and jumpy until the next day when I got up and went to her house with a serious hangover. I knocked on her door, that old wooden door I worshipped, that I'd fixed real carefully so the cold wouldn't get in. She opened the door a crack, sad, like a conspirator, her face filled with grief (let me say grief so my pain won't seem so bad), but no, no way!, she was just tired, exhausted, I can't lie to you, I can't lie to anyone.

Drink the last beer, Patitas, they're closing, but what

I'm about to tell you is worth one last brew, ok, it's nothing, nothing happened, or rather, what happened was nothing. It's just that against the light, in the space next to her messed up hair, I could make out, real clear, the naked, golden German. Imagine that: his scared eyes looking at me, and behind, lighting up the bed, the German's sun.

I started vomiting in the patio filled with geraniums. Out of my guts came a black, heavy mass like coagulated blood and an image or words I'd seen or read in some movie or book came to me. When a deer knows it's all over he lets himself die. He doesn't struggle. His heart bursts. That's it. His heart bursts.

That's what would have happened to me Patitas, if I hadn't met up with skinny Encalado at the corner, carrying my soccer bag. "I've been looking for you everywhere," he said, "we're in the finals and your mom told me to try the old woman's place."

We beat the team from Belisario that day, five to zero.

I made four goals.

MARCO ANTONIO RODRÍGUEZ
(Quito, 1941)

After studying philosophy and law, Marco Antonio Rodríguez began his literary career with the three volumes of essay: *Rostros en la actual poesía ecuatoriana* (1962), *Benjamín Carrión y Miguel Angel Zambrano* (1965), and *Isaac J. Barrera, el hombre y su obra* (1969).

This writer's short story collections include *Cuentos del rincón* (1972), *Historia de un intruso* (1976, winner of the prize for the best work in Spanish, sponsored by the International Book Fair of Leipzig, 1978), *Un delfín y la luna* (National José Mejía Lequerica Literary Prize, 1985), and *Jaula* (1995). His stories have been translated into English, French, and German, and included in various anthologies.

Raúl Vallejo writes that "Marco Antonio Rodríguez introduces himself firmly into the multiple aspects of daily life, sniffing about and uncovering the mechanisms of consumer society, revealing the lack of authenticity of ordinary people; his character are beings who, having decided to confront the world, end up suffering the consequence of that choice."

THE ROUND*

*The future defunct
happy as a knife.*
GEORGES BATAILLE

He goes into their bedroom to ask her, yet again, to be patient with him and his mother, to forget mama's crime, that second bowl of soup yesterday, Saturday. But she has her back turned to his plea, her head confined in a helmet of rollers, her hands covered with cream. In the light from the nightstand, he imagines the facial mask that leaves bare only a segment of her frivolous features and that makes her look like a fish under water. He doesn't know if he should lie down next to her, considering that he hasn't anything more to say other than what he's already said so many times, or leave and then come back an hour or two later, after deluding himself by pretending to read back issues of boxing magazines. On turning toward the hallway, he notices the almost astral odor of cosmetics and the

---

*From the collection *Un delfín y la luna,* 1985.

obscene crack in the mirror, exactly like hers.

He closes the door with the same troubled feeling he had when he opened it, but just then she waves her arm at the light as though it were a cloud of tiny moths, she coughs twice. He turns into a rag doll curved into the void, his right hand soldered to the doorknob, listening to the malignant murmur she spreads throughout the house. It's cold, and even colder on crossing the passageway that leads to his mother's room. Perplexed, he looks at the sad olive miracle of her closed eyes. Beyond, his trophies expire, subdued by dust.

Now in the street, he bends over to tie his shoes. The pale knit pullover leaves bare his neck taut with thick veins. Then he stretches his head and shakes his hands, inhales and exhales through his nose. He jogs down San Juan at an easy pace, annoyed by the dim lights in the shops, the boys in their street corner gangs who still recognize him and stand back to let him pass, the bars that exude their harsh odors. At La Merced, in the light of the church's farthest dome, he thinks he sees the vapid grin of Ceferino Congo, the black deaf mute who lived for a hundred years taking care of the friars' colossal clock. When Ceferino died, lay brother Valenzuela insisted in catechism class, there was no way to get the hands of the clock moving again. He crosses the plaza at the church of San Francisco and 24 de Mayo where illusions are for sale. He climbs the hill with the pawnshops and comes to Huascar. Weak, he hides from a pitiful shape, flattening himself against a door. He barely notices the bundles, picnic grounds over which cockroaches swarm, or their raspy razor sharp screeching that rips through the squid belly of the night. He breathes in rapid double time, bracing his head until the tendons in his neck jump like wet jackrabbits. (Punish his muscles and prove that they're still vigorous or wander among his scattered joys like a caged jaguar looking for the freedom he's misplaced, that generally brought him back to an acceptance of his routine lot in life, but now his resolve slipped away like the string of a broken toy.) He's worried that somebody might recognize him. Maybe if he were to go back home. Or look for his friends. Or lose himself in a whore from Lima and songs about love lost. A petty impulse, like the foul smell growing at his side, flashes through his nerves. Exasperated, he checks his pockets, putting together all the money he finds.

Two forces, both hazy, do battle in him: one compulsive but excessively soft, and the other like a rough, merciless mass in league with time. No matter how often he shuffles the dark deck of his brain, he finds no answer beyond the insufferable gloom, than that vengeance that in recent months ravages his blood announcing a death limply calculated.

At La Esperanza, he can taste the penetrating fumes of stale beer, tobacco smoke, and clandestine sweat. There are only a few people in the bar—the word Sunday comes to mind—all men, except for one brittle woman who drinks alone at the back table. The walls are covered with grime interrupted here and there with etchings of sex organs and hearts pierced with contrite phrases. Behind the bar, the bartender, disheveled, slides over to him. He's a man as nervous as a little lizard, his face stale from long nights, with a fuzzy cap bobbing on his head. He makes stupid little hops, shakes his apron, blinks like a simpleton. He shouts champ and his shout wades through the notes, hastily arranged, of a *cumbia* that booms from the jukebox. Nobody else notices him, but he feels a comforting euphoria and comes in flexing his muscles. When he gets to the bar, the little man with the cap dazes him with a cross fire of shots of cane liquor and infantile accolades. He drinks diligently, quieting the flattery of the bartender.

He's startled by a slap on the back. He turns on the revolving bar stool, steeling his jaw and widening his eyes dulled by the first drinks. It's Pup Cespedes, his old idol: a limping gray stew, his eyes almost invisible in rolls of fat, and a dirty tangle of hair at his neck. Champ, they say to one another, and surrender to an endless embrace, heavy with secret complicities. Still a champ?, the words bubble over to him. You bet, boy, the old man answers, caressing him with a fake jab to the jaw.

They sit down at a table near the woman's. Pup swears: It's One-Eyed Moncayo, Colonel Arcentales's daughter. In the old days we used to call her The Lobster, because she had the tasty part in the rear. The King knows the story just like everybody else in the barrio, but he laughs anyway and he looks at the little woman shamelessly. He's intimidated by the look in her damaged eye, the grimace of her red, toothless mouth, but he keeps looking at her. Pup distracts him, pretending to hit him with his meaty fists. It's like being at La Arenas, except without the fans, he jokes. Sure, the King laughs, rubbing himself like a champion against the back of the chair. The drunks turn around to watch, timid, without meaning to, and they start laughing too. Pup orders a bottle of cane liquor and cigarettes, the King that they play *Tormentos* and

Rebeldía on the jukebox. The bartender runs back and forth, accommodating them, his big butt jiggling. Pup settles himself in the chair, works on getting his eyes focused, curls his lips, lights the little candle in the attic, says: The good times, boy, are the ones that get your crotch hot, the punches, on the other hand, they toughen up the soul. Now he pushes his cut rye face toward the middle of the table, knocks over a glass with the left, puts it back where it was, roars: "You know what, King? Drink and I'll give it to you straight: A boxer is a Roman candle, he throws off some sparks, four or five years, after that he spends the rest assimilating the beatings, he spends the rest fighting with life, if they've left him a whole man." *Torments and grief tear ayayayayayay, through my chest, my shattered heart...* "The flies haven't settled on you yet, King, why don't you get back in the ring, or if not, set yourself up in business," the Pup goes on philosophizing, and his licked cork heart floats over the words, "I'm doing all right with the french fries, you gotta quit being a guard dog for the politicians, I know what I'm talking about, they're not our kind, King, whatever else they might be, they're not our kind." *Now I have someone to love, discrete and better than you, she doesn't know how to betray two...* The King's not listening to the well-meaning advice of the only man he's ever admired in his entire life, though he hides his indifference with an easy smile. He needs time to drink and think. He thinks about the sun-drenched days when she and his mother got his bag ready, shook out the plush cape, arranged his shoes, his socks, the bandages with ointment, and outside now, surrounded by kids chattering away like birds, fighting to get close to him, he calmly broke threw the protective wall thrown up by his assistants and anticipated the singular blush of glory, kissing her fresh and anxious lips, certain that he had the world in his fists. He thinks of the fights of his life, while the Potolos blaspheme in macho tones: *Lord, I'm not satisfied with my lot, nor with the hard law you've decreed...* Angel King Clonares vs. Dynamite Altamirano, Fugenio Rocky, Duke Olivares, Big-Mouth Lobato, Marvin Curry, Charlie Lee Hagler. *...because there's no good reason for why you've brought me down...* He, always coming from the side, tight-lipped, always on guard, his left up, the right at his waist, using his earth-shattering hook or his one-two, which his rivals knew were tickets to the hospital. *...And you haven't wanted to listen to me, or haven't been able to...* Now he's fixating on his dashing figure in the fight posters, more like a dance instructor than a boxer: the nappy hair, the serious forehead, the fine nose and jaw, the proud eyebrows, and the small, sly eyes. *...suspend your sentence and my condemnation...* He thinks of her light mulatto skin, the part around her breasts. *...And I'll pay my debts when I can...*, and as though a lamp were lighting her up from within, spreading a warm, fleshy whiteness. *...I'll give back the life you gave me.* And other hands possessing her.

They drink until dawn. Defeated, jubilant. Swearing eternal friendship, feigning swift combat, talking about the old days and about the stingy business of life, confiding in one another their darkest secrets, the Pup irritating the few cats who drank that night at La Esperanza, swaying his bulk the size of a triple-doored closet, mimicking the bartender, the King living up to his reputation as a hard drinker who never let the booze get to him, from time to time their gazes joining at some undefined point along the shelves, grinding their teeth, both letting the music penetrate, digging its sad claws into the spandrels of their hairy chests.

The King settles his friend on an improvised bed of newspapers in the back of the bar. He scribbles an IOU. He picks out the salvageable butts. He runs his fingers through his hair. As he leaves, he sees One-Eyed Moncayo nodding off in the doorway. A whore's luck, he mutters. In the semi-gloom of the street, his imagination begins to take pleasure in the details of his revenge. Then he heads back. When he first noticed the car it was harmless and distant, ready to disappear at any moment in the neighborhood's winding streets. Later, he noticed it a few blocks away, fearless, cunningly spying on the outlines of his house. Then he felt its existence like a vague but menacing reality, aggressive, pawing, its horn blowing Bertha's delay, and Bertha running harried, now I'm screwed, Angel, now I'm screwed, the boss just got here, running like the wind down the stairs, now I'm screwed, Angel, waving her just-polished nails. And he going to the window, gasping for air, pressing his depraved anguish to his heart, as though it were his wife's body.

At Cruz Verde, a bunch of drunks comes his way. He's pretty sure he knows who they are and tries to avoid them. Too late. The thugs pile up on him, slice the air with their commands, confuse him with their tragic party steps. I'm Angel the King Clonares, sonsabitches, he shouts and searches like a blind chicken for a vulnerable point, but he always crashes against a wall of rabid shoves. They grab his arms and check his pockets. He's clean, the pocket-checkers say. Pimp, howls an old hunchbacked man, aiming a kick to his stomach. Angel falls curled into a ball. I'm Angel the King Clonares, his lips pray.

He wakes up suffering an implacable pain in his bones, as though they'd ground him up in a press. With his right eye, which is the only one he can open to the size of a coin, he sees a meaningless horizon of furtive lights. Not a single thought can penetrate his mind. Behind him, everything has ended with no demands, but in his shred of time now remote and past due, there remains the body of a woman broken by his blows. That's all. Nevertheless, he's still cheered by his sinister decision. Little by little, in place of the pain a feeling of detachment takes root and he smiles, finally, in spite of the fact that in doing so he is reminded once more that he will never be the same again. He thinks about the Pink Panther broken up into dozens of small cubes. He stops at the cube that holds one of his eyes—maybe the right—and watches how, from there, the Panther weeps for the pieces of his body, lost in previous sequences. He gets halfway up. Leaning against the wall, he tries to move, managing the swaying of a decrepit animal. *And you, who thought you were the King of the world…*, the Panther, dressed like a Mexican cowboy, sings in his head.

She's in the same position she was when he left. He gets undressed with difficulty. Then he gets into bed, slowly. He raises his wife's bathrobe and pulls down the tiny silk panties, rolling them almost to her knees. She takes care of the rest without opening her eyes, her movements expert but listless, a grimace of boredom visible on her lips. He gets on top of her and says in her ear my queen, penetrating her and detecting the unmistakable scent of fear in his blood.

CARLOS CARRIÓN
(Loja, 1944)

Carlos Carrión was born in the town of Malacatos in the south of Ecuaor. He has published five short story collections: *Porque me da la gana* (1969), *Ella sigue moviendo las caderas* (1979), *Los potros desnudos* (1979), *El más hermoso animal nocturno* (1982, winner of the José de la Cuadra Prize in 1981 for the collection originally entitled Catalina sacándose una espina), and *El corazón es un animal en celo* (Joaquín Gallegos Lara National Literary Prize, 1995).

The writer has written three novels: *El deseo que lleva tu nombre* (1990, second place in the Bi-annual Ecuadorian Novel Contest, 1989), *Una niña adorada* (second place in the Bi-annual Ecuadorian Novel Contest, 1991), and *Una Guerra con nombre de mujer* (1995).

Some critics have characterized Carrión as a literary experimentalist, and this is not necessarily high praise. Nor is the colloquial speech of his characters always a virtue. Distracted by his experiments, his writing becomes superficial. Nevertheless, his recent narrative, exploring erotic love as a desire fated to die, suggests that he is capable of more profound texts. His novel *El deseo que lleva tu nombre* is without doubt his finest work.

APRIL AGAIN*

*They each brought a rose. And they left it behind.
Not a single one was missing. Then
they took us to the classrooms, and they
put us on the playground against the wall.*
with and without nostalgia
MARIO BENEDETTI.

The girl was surprised when she saw me. From behind the door, half open, uninviting, I felt the pure amazement in her black eyes on the bitter face with which I went to let her in after hearing the hurried knocks that had brought the building back to life with impunity, and I also felt, instantaneously, confused by the genuine blush of a petrified child, a sensation with which I was entirely unfamiliar. But I didn't see the danger yet, though it was already too late. The girl was alive and suffering on the gray tiles of the hall, beautiful and without a shadow, as though she had invented the day in the face of the very history of all my badly lived centuries. She held in both arms against her chest, as if by force, a little stack of school notebooks. Her gaze was busy, deeply besides, with an anxiety that would have

---

*From the collection *El más hermoso animal nocturno*, 1982.

seemed to be the cause of my own if I hadn't known
such a thing to be impossible. Are you Luis's father?,
she said, putting into the name her beauty, her tenderness, her immortal childhood, her melancholy that did-
n't wear daisies yet, and her anxiety. Which Luis? I
answered with the unbearable certainty that this was
one of my son's girlfriends whom I hadn't met, in
which case there was reason for the girl's surprise. We
were identical animals, the two of us, with the sole
exception of the unpardonable infidelities that were my
years, years made more than anything of the torturous
matter of long nights and lonelinesses carefully wasted
among sordid bottles and companions. And resolved
in what I called a simple compression of life and an old,
invisible cynicism applied in understanding it. Apart
from the white temples, which I judged a difference in
my favor, I could thus live the hallucination of having
the age and the face of my son, as well as the name.
Luis, Luis Morán. Yes, I said, and like a fool I opened
the door wide for her. When she walked by, almost
brushing against me, I felt that every tomorrow
remained outside in the street, splendid and useless,
and that since a minute ago I needed this girl forever,
independently of the cruel circumstance of son and
father. She walked ahead of me to the living room,
while I, behind her, suffered the humiliation of my dis-
astrous hair, my unshaven face, my old-fashioned
bathrobe, the heaviness of the air in the room, the hardness of the furniture, the horrible paint on the walls,
and the damned empty bottles. And wetting my fingers surreptitiously with saliva, I ran them through the
disorder on my experienced head and was an adolescent again that morning. The tiny black shoes stopped

next to the easy chairs, waiting for me, in spite of the fact that she had heard my invitation to sit. In that brief moment, two dreadful meters from the girl made of a pure, adorable substance, I saw that the anxious depression of her waist, the tender space that went from one hip bone to the other, the splendor of sacred pollen that shimmered in her hair, the solitary beauty of the flesh of her face in her eyelashes, her lips, her tiny freckles, her little nose, and, above all, that child´s time that stretched, taut and undulating, in her body, from head to foot, like a deadly and inevitable leopard, caused me an infinite helplessness and the hallucination with respect to my son, that served to sustain my crazy vanity, assuming the entire reality of his being because he was the only one who was twenty years old in this house, vis-a-vis that marvelous womanly girl who no longer mixed up the two men. It was nine in the morning. She took a seat after I did, in response to the offer I had to repeat. To one side of us, but more obvious than a cow three days dead, was the small table with the infamous bottles. Her legs, with school-girl socks and a short little skirt, adopted a lovely oblique pose, more pronounced because the easy chair was low, and she put her notebooks on her knees and above them, as though they were additional objects, her hands, her tiny bust, and her face. She didn't use the backrest, that much is certain, tense, tenuous. I did, distinctly and deliberately with my back to the window in order not to face the light and diminish that help-lessness, though neither managing nor desiring it from the bottom of my bones. The light, too bright at that hour, walked like the devil through the glass and the sheer curtains, revealing, unfortunately, the room's

desolate surroundings. But now it was an object hap-
pily soothed surrounding the child. Luckily, besides,
her eyes hadn't come to see the house. Then she began
on the edge of the chair the tale of the tragedy that had
brought her to miss class, swallow her pride, and come
to see me, with her beauty. My name is Lilia, she said,
and I love Luis very much. I saw that it was a name
invented for her body and that what she said was true.
She closed her eyes, turning bright red, as though she
suddenly forgot what she had to say next, in spite of
the ardent beginning, and found herself obliged to read
the part that followed. Or as though, on the other
hand, whatever she suffered was extremely grave. It
was beautiful and sad that this girl loved my son. In
some strange way, my fate as monstrous driller felt vin-
dicated, but it wasn't equal, damnit. My loneliness
continued intact and eternal as ever and paining me
more than life itself. My heart longed horribly and
deliriously to be twenty-five years younger and with
the same ability to produce the suffering in those black
eyes. A half a minute had gone by and her lips didn't
find anything, twisting, hurting themselves. Only her
eyes, the tears. I saw them grow between the lashes,
and the painful and tender force that crushed them,
and then stretch out dizzyingly and any minute now
fall maybe on top of her tightly clasped hands, or, no,
maybe here, on my soul. I couldn't talk at first, perhaps
because I wanted to savor her closed eyes and better
resist that adored face or because I couldn't find the
way either. That's wonderful, I said at last, holding
back the painful desire to go over and comfort her,
don't cry my adorable heaven. This kind of luck was-
n't meant for just any rambunctious kid. As though

offended by my words, she burst out crying and I was by now capable of abhorring any man and damning myself for the rest of my days, if my hands didn't knock the stupidity out of that brute of a son of mine. And, without a single transition between what she'd heard me say and the new heights of her brimming and gorgeous eyes, she said with a heartrending hardness what she had to say, and she sat there her very open face bearing up under my old stupor, my conviction, and my dreadful indignation, three consecutive predators. Just wait until I...I said and got up transformed into a machine made of pure rage, as though Lilia were my daughter, going off to find that despicable wretch. The voice of the girl didn't know what to do with its desolate sound, disconcerted by the violence of my determination, and fell silent as she followed my footsteps. Luis would still be sleeping because only the devil himself knew at what time he'd come back last night, if, indeed, he had come back, because the shameless... I took the steps two at a time, quickly. I got to his bedroom door with the blood throbbing furiously in my temples, I don't know whether due to the sudden effort or to my furious anger. And just then I feared touching my son's body with my ire intact. I pounded on the door to wear down my rage, but without giving away the hell. Once, twice, nothing. Luiiiis!, the house boomed. Still nothing. I was about to try breaking it down when I thought I heard a sound in the lock mechanism and I remembered. I turned the knob and simultaneously pushed against the door with all my weight, and I knew that my son, on the other side, was at that very moment trying to lock it. Through contact with the iron handle, my hand became aware of that decision in his, but also of the clumsiness and the bad timing. The door opened suddenly and I landed a light blow, my onslaught paralyzing him. Over his shoulder I saw a naked woman flying to take refuge in the bathroom. I closed the door behind me and gave Luis a push that landed him in the middle of the room. Only then did I see that he was also naked. Get dressed!, I said, the words hurting my throat. What's got into you, old man, he said with a knife-like, grotesque cynicism that affected me deeply, not so much because of the cynicism in and of itself, but because it struck me as very similar to my own and without a bit of transparency to mask it. Get dressed, damn it! It was an effort for him to obey. I want to talk to a man, not a savage! In an irritating leisurely fashion, he turned his back to me to look for something to put on. I saw his long torso, his tight buttocks, his hairy legs, and, for a second, I could see myself, distant and identical, on an ancient day twenty-five years ago. I also saw the bottles, the ashtray overflowing on the nightstand. The posters of Charles Bronson, Ornella Muti, Bo Derek, and Che. I saw the woman's clothes falling from a chair to the dirty floor, just like his, and inhaled the stink of alcohol and the odor of two in the closed air. He finally found a pitiful robe. With his fingers busy making a knot in the belt, he came a few steps closer. What did you want to talk about, your affairs or mine? Shameless shithead, you've got a pregnant girl waiting for you in the living room downstairs and here you are with another woman. I heard, almost simultaneously, my own anger and a woman's sob. From the girl in the bathroom, no doubt, who had the good sense to stay hidden. What girl?, he frowned.

Lilia something. Lilia who? Don't make me any angrier, Luis! Aaaah!, now playful, Lilia. What are you going to do, Luis? Me, nothing. And you? I punched him straight in the mouth and he stumbled to the bed and fell on it. Still lying down, he touched his split lip as though he were helping himself bear the pain with his fingers, and he laughed. Raising himself up on one arm, the blood poisoned his words. And you, what did you do when you got my mother pregnant?, and he spit blood without moving anything other than his lips in order not to miss my answer. I'd like to kill you!, I said, without breathing more than my own air. And I, you!, he said with the weight of his chest thrown back, resting on both arms in order to aim his hatred. So why don't you get out of here, you little old shit! The blind conflagration of rage that undid me when I hit him overcame me now. I saw that my hands weren't far behind in wanting the disgrace, in longing to keep hitting and hitting. I was fighting for a girl, for her enchanting present beauty, for her inexorable tenderness, who had fallen like a bolt of lightening on this house and not the house nor anybody, except me, was supporting her in the flesh, as though born for that reason. My rancor was no longer based on the wish to protect a daughter as I believed, but disgracefully and hopelessly on the defense of the woman one loves in the eternity of a moment with the mortal dementedness of all the illogic in the world, whose prodigious beauty had been offended by the only face in the world that I could not destroy and that was, instead, attacking me, and I wanted only to take refuge in the heart, in the runaway heart with which I had woke up today. I though vainly of my years and I didn't want anybody

to take away a single one because with fewer I would-
n't love that girl, just as I hadn't loved before. Wretch,
I should make you marry her even if that means I have
to kill you! And I, with whom should I make you do
the same, eh? It was awful. Luis smiled in triumph,
but inside he must have been crying for that past that
seemed to be all that I had given him of my blood, and
that was breaking through my arduous troglodyte fortifications. I gave the door a shove and left so that my
son wouldn't see me die of rancor, or my own perver-
sity, that was his as well, force me to crush him forever
and change him into the man that I had to invent so
that Lilia wouldn't suffer any more. I felt his laughter
and my tears. Then I saw through them, at the far end
of the hall, Lilia who was disappearing madly down
the stairs, whimpering loudly, and I knew that she had
been listening at the door from the beginning. I ran
after her, in desperation, but I stopped when I got to the
staircase, thinking suddenly about the lock on the door
to the street, and I began to go down slowly, treading
on each of the steps.

IVÁN EGüEZ
(Quito, 1944)

Prior to achieving popularity with his short novel *La Linares*, Iván Eguez was known as a poet. His poetry collections include *Calibre Catapulta* (1969), *La arena pública—Loquera es-lo-que-era* (1972), *Buscavida rifamuerte* (1975), *Poemar* (1988), *El olvidador* (1992), and *Libre amor* (1999).

In 1975, he won the Aurelio Espinosa Pólit National Literary Prize for *La Linares* (1976). Subsequently, he has published four novels: *Pájara la memoria* (1985), *El poder del gran señor* (1985), *Lorena & Bobby* (1999), and *Sonata para sordos* (2000).

Egüez has published six story collections: *El triple salto* (1981), *Anima pávora* (1989), *Historias leves* (1994), *Cuentos inocentes* (1996), *Cuentos fantásticos* (1996), and *Cuentos gitanos* (1997). A number of his stories have been translated into English, French, German, and Russian, and included in Ecuadorian and Latin American anthologies.

Eguez's early narrative is distinctly baroque and sensual in character, reflecting the influence of Carpentier and Lezama. Over time, however, his prose has evolved toward the humorous and the dramatic. He brings to Ecuadorian narrative the picaresque, so characteristic of Spanish literature, and his more recent stories, after questioning the power society has over individuals, have taken on elements of the fantastic.

THOSE WHO ONCE LOOKED AT THEMSELVES IN WATER NO LONGER RECOGNIZE THEM-SELVES IN THE MIRROR*

How little the audience understood! How little everyone understood, when it came to destiny. To be a clown was to be destiny's serf. Living in the circus arena was a pantomime consisting of falls, slaps, kicks, an endless landing and dodging of kicks. And it was through this shameful rigmarole that you won the audience's applause! The dear clown! His privilege consisted in recreating the mistakes, craziness, stupidity, all the misunderstandings that plague mankind. To be incompetence itself: something that even the least of chumps could imitate. Fail to understand when everything is as clear as water; don't catch on in the least even when the trick has been repeated a thousand times; grope around in the dark, like a blind man, when all the signs are pointing in the right direction; insist upon opening the wrong door even though it has an enormous sign that says Danger!; knock one's head against a mirror instead of going around it; put an eye against the barrel of a loaded gun! People never get tired of this nonsense, since for thousands of years human beings have taken the wrong path and for thousands of years all of their searches and inquiries have only led them to dead ends.

The Smile at the Foot of the Ladder

HENRY MILLER

---

*From the collection *El triple salto*, 1981.

The applause was still resounding under the big top when Pitillín made his decision. In a dressing room beyond, the beautiful Gladiolito removed the saffron makeup she used on her cheekbones to offset her plump cheeks and she took off her spangled stockings as carefully as someone rolling a tobacco leaf, all under the beaming gaze of Vani the Magician, who´d become her lover like a bolt from the blue.

That afternoon, after the show, the easygoing Palaccino had gone to Pitillín to tell him officially that his woman was in love with somebody else. Those were the circus rules: Lovers had to share from the beginning their idyll with the oldest of the managers; he kept the problem secret, followed it without blinking the way he followed the trapeze artists, examined it like a magician's hat, weighed it like the tightrope walker's balance bar, and, if it was necessary, if it was something with merit and not a simple infatuation, he consulted with the entire troupe to find out what each one thought about the secret he revealed to them. Then, if there was no opposition, he approached the aggrieved to let him know what everybody else already knew.

Thus did he proceed with the clown: He took him to the dark, desolate track, he guided him, as though he were leading a blind man, to the railing of the orchestra which Pitillín, clowning, conducted; he turned on the center floodlight, he stood under the beam in his string tie and sequined jacket, he put the harp to his shoulder, he bowed and disappeared with a leap into the gloom. Then he lit the ring around the track, took the plumed horn and began to intone *I Pagliacci* by Leoncavallo, walking slowly around the sawdust track as though giving him time to understand and decide.

According to the rules, Pitillín had two alternatives: accept the opera and the holy peace, in which case all of his flying comrades offered a formal evening party in honor of the suicide victim; or not accept it, in which case the lovers had to leave the circus, a punishment equivalent to a death sentence.

After the ritual announcement, Pitillín decided to write that fateful letter forevermore. That's what he told Chaparrón, the disciple of his clowning, when the latter—worried about the euphoric melancholy his colleague had just displayed on remaining alone in the ring, improvising a recital of laughter and laments for nobody in the gloom—came into the dressing room to begin a dialogue characteristic of clowns.

"And what has befallen my lord, the Great Pitillín?"

"One doesn't say befallen, Chaparón, one says fuckafflicted."

"Very well, then, what has fuckafflicted my lord?"

"The fact that his neighbor the Magician is in love with a widow."

"And what's wrong with the Magician being in love with a widow?"

"What's wrong is that her husband isn't dead yet."

"And what does my lord have to do with all of this?"

"The widow is the wife of your lord and your lord should be dead."

"In other words, the Magician made his wife disappear?"

"He fucked her a few times and took her to his enchanted castle, but lord Pitillín, like the good actor that he is, is not going to follow the script or abide by

the rules. He is going to provide reasons for his decision in a letter."

"My word!" said Chaparrón, "and with the post so
unreliable."

"I will deliver it to you. Call them to the ring and
read it to all," said Pitillín as he took off his mask in
order to write.

And thus was it done. Called to the ring, all took
their places: Mudesquina, the tamer of wild beasts, in
the trunk of her elephant; Fidelius behind his mask;
Química on her combustions; Prince Igor in the
Impresario's seat; Abadón, the fat man, in the lion's
food tub; Chordelita on the tight-rope; Bubulina on the
edge of Frankenstein's coffin; Super Mélida on the
trapeze; the rest in a circle on the saw dust.

I met Gladiolito on the afternoon of a torrential
downpour, when the big top was poor and leaking
from all sides. In addition to being a clown, I was a juggler back then, and a tightrope walker and an acrobat.
While juggling one day, I asked for three lady volunteers to assist with the porcelain plate number while I
ran from pole to pole keeping them spinning, making
sure the dinnerware didn't fall and break. Suddenly, I
noticed how one of the volunteers—barely more than a
girl—took the plates from the table and spun them on
her index finger with incredible skill and grace, as
though they were screwed on. Then she picked up the
clubs, asked Palaccino for music, and began to perform
a notable series of juggling feats that won the audience's enthusiastic applause. She started coming to the
big top every day at rehearsal time, at show time, and
at my lunchtime. After a month of wooing her and
feeding her like a little bird from my hand, when our

season in her city came to an end, I had to steal her forever, if not for me, at least for the circus, because I knew
that whoever has tasted the ring and the applause,
whoever has seen the amazement and the happiness in
the children, and above all, whoever has seen the child
in the face of an adult, can never again leave the sawdust no matter how much it sometimes smells like a
tomb, an empty plate, a damp straw mattress. I knew
the price the Impresario charged to let her in: an hour
of feeling her up in his office getting her vital statistics
and then a whole night in his slaver's dressing room. I
took her the day after he deflowered her. And so the
years began to pass. And so began our wanderings
through everything from the unhappiest little towns to
the grandest capitals, like the one where Vani, the
Magician, joined our company. He was already famous
by then with the public, but especially with the members of the troupe, since his real magic consisted in
charming those who knew him. The closer somebody
was to him, the greater the charms she discovered.
Sometimes it was an abyss and sometimes heaven, but
always unpredictable, as Gladiolito put it so well. I
noted how fascinated she was with him, because with
every passing day she spent less time with me and
when she was at my side she talked more and more
about him, about his marvels. Until one day she
stopped mentioning his name. Then I knew that something had happened, I knew that I, but above all our
love, was, if not lost, at least gnawed, like the claws of
an ancient lion, holey like a penniless big top. When I
tried to get her back, to keep her, it was already too late.
She was not only the one who assisted him during his
magic numbers, who handed him the implements he

used for his tricks, who retrieved the endless handkerchiefs, umbrellas, and rabbits that came out of his velvet hat, who levitated like a cloud, like a saint in cho-
rus-girl stockings, she was, besides, the first to applaud
and thank him, because at that point Vani created for
her, renewed himself for her, and from a quiet magician
he had turned into a happy genie let out of the bottle.
Clearly, we were no longer the same. We who had once
looked at ourselves in water no longer recognized ourselves in the mirror.

I don't know what I felt then. Maybe a numbness,
an immobile agony, a paralyzing and pitiful mea culpa
that led me to torment myself, to accuse myself of having been careless during rehearsals, to recriminate
myself for having bored her with the same acrobatics
and pantomimes, for having made her spin around my
life with the monotony of a saucer spinning on a pole
day after day and show after show. And why not say
it, for having treated her like a queen, but in my own
way, forgetting that life always has new tricks up its
sleeve. I began to love her then from my anguish, from
the thorn in my heart, like Othello behind the curtain.
Her every word, every gesture, every silence were
weighed, picked apart, and filtered through the sieve of
my doubt, that coward's doubt that doesn't look for
proof but for the evidence to vanish, that doubt that
eats away but doesn't condemn, that has one like
Chordelita always on a tight-rope. I think I had fallen
into apathy then, walked with a blindfold covering my
eyes so as not to see what everyone else saw. Until
now, when Palaccino came, the orchestra baton, to put
a horn under my nose, to tell me in silence what the
whole world, including my own heart, was shouting

from the rooftops. As he walked around the track, I have admitted that in love there are no guilty parties, only makers, and I have said that while it's true that love lights where least expected, it remains where it's kept warmest. And that bit about how it's a plant that grows with flattery is the truest of truths. The grimace that shows through my clown's laugh is because I know that she's in love with him, and also with his tricks; but who am I to deny my dear whore, dear weakling, or dear saint her happiness with him? I'm not the Knife Thrower to kill her, I'm not the Lion Tamer to domesticate her. I'm the clown, the fifth wheel; so I leave this big top forever to wander the world tapping my blind man's stick until the end of time, with this miniscule drama the size of all of mankind.

FRANCISCO PROAÑO ARANDY
(Cuenca, 1944)

Though born in Cuenca, Francisco Proaño has lived in Quito for most of his life. As a diplomat, he has experienced, first-hand, decisive moments in the countries to which he has been assigned: the war of insurgents in Colombia's Putumayo, the disintegration of the Balkans in Yugoslavia, the dissident takeover and the brief hostage crisis that ended without bloodshed at the Ecuadorian embassy in Cuba.

Proaño the writer has published one poetry collection, *Poesías* (1961) and four short story collections: *Historias de disecadores* (1972), *Oposición a la magia* (1986), *La doblez* (1986), and *Cuentos* (a personal anthology, 1994). In addition, he has written two novels: *Antiguas caras en el espejo* (winner of the city of Quito's José Mejía Lequerica Prize, 1984) and *Del otro lado de las cosas* (1993).

His works have been translated into English, French, and German, and are found in nearly all anthologies of Ecuadorian short stories.

Above all, Proaño possesses a tremendous talent for creating sealed, hermetic, suffocating environments, with a prose characterized by long, open sentences. His characters offer passive resistance to the oppressive surroundings in which they are immersed and from which they dissect the action. They are living beings transformed into silhouettes reflected against a wall-screen, shadows peopled with memories. Exterior reality seems, in Proaño's works, a distant reference point which is, nevertheless, ominously present and transfigured: memories that re-cover their creatures in a maternal, fetal warmth.

THE SCATTERING OF THE WALLS*

This problem with the children is driving us crazy. For a time, those of us who are members of the neighborhood's Adult Committee, the only committee allowed, have enjoyed relative peace. Free of children, the life of the community has slipped by enveloped in a pleasant silence, namely, without shouting, without unexpected laughter or useless babbling, without the monotonous and terribly irritating to-ings and fro-ings of rubber balls, without surprising drawings on the walls upsetting our sensible daydreams. The gravity, the methodical confrontation with the day-to-day (which some, pejoratively, call routine), the composure, the silence, are, among others, the values that had lately reached, thanks to the eliminatory measures adopted previously, a significant splendor.

Recently, however, truly alarming matters have come to light. A few days ago, someone complained at the Committee's office that on the wall of his house there had mysteriously appeared a drawing evidently executed by a young hand. Could it be a joke, asked

*From the collection *Oposición a la magia*, 1986.

the complainant, nervous, and with reason. Because if it were not, it was clear that the matter had all the signs of high seriousness. The community prepared itself for the appearance of other disturbing events, which were not long in occurring. On the days following, and as though in response to a meticulously drawn plan, there appeared at different points in the area, new drawings, those sketches or half-finished designs with which we were already familiar: cats with string ties, scribbles similar to human shapes, smudges, signs cabalistic in the extreme, lines, circles, letters, even. Those who had an opportunity to see the drawings were able to discover something threatening about them, which explains why the Committee is at this very moment not only paralyzed with indignation but, in addition, troubled by ominous concerns.

At the same time, other occurrences have contributed to bring to a climax our fears. It happens that at any given moment in the course of the day, we might hear, as though filtered through the ramparts, in hidden walls, something like a chorus of children, a distant chant, or maybe that murmur, now almost forgotten, of children's voices learning or reciting at intervals the alphabet. The certainty of hearing a song of that nature in our grave surroundings has us veritably overwhelmed. Unless these are mere acoustical hallucinations, if there is something concrete, real, here, it would have to be a clandestine school, an underground children's circle, and that, for its part, would reflect organization, a system, something that exists among us and against us, right under our noses, which the security mechanisms adopted have been unable to detect. The Committee has thus seen its activities multiplied.

Members have organized volunteer patrols to stand guard both during the day and at night. Special inspectors have examined houses, basements, attics, even those sorts of room that at times, in our city, emerge stuck to walls or located inopportunely on roofs, but always dispensable, false, as though they were tumors or excrescences appearing unexpectedly on the buildings. But up to now it has been impossible to discover anything concrete.

From time to time, one of the volunteer teams will have—they tell us that they have had—a relative victory. Relative, because we're not dealing with anything more than the discovery of some few material clues: a forgotten notebook, a splayed toy, a pencil with an eraser worn and chewed, marbles and stickers. When these clues accumulate suspiciously in a specific district, *rezzias* are organized, the sirens of patrol cars are heard at night, the boots of volunteers come and go in the darkness, approaching at a run, receding into the distance. But, as far as we know, there hasn't been a single arrest to date.

The neighbors, who support the Committee with their votes or their economic contributions, sometime suffer actual spasms of terror. It happens, it can happen, for instance, that you are at home, peacefully reading, or working in your office, let's say, and, suddenly, you hear, you seem to hear, children playing in the street. Just like that, something so supernatural at this late date, after the eliminatory measures. The sound is unmistakable. You listen to their laughter, their skipping. There is—you have reason to believe—a rubber ball, maybe toys, but especially that laughter, those cries, those shouts, in the serenity of the afternoon. So you tremble, memories of other days come to mind, you approach the window in fear, pale, and there it is, all of a sudden, a window breaks and a ball comes into the room and begins to bounce among the furniture, from one wall to another, *boing, boing, boing,* in a nightmarish crescendo, noisy, maddening. Maybe you cry out, lose your glasses, or shake or stumble in agony among the furniture, or you have the strength to get to the street, to move toward the sound of a fleeing child's footsteps, but in the end you will not find anything but the usual sight of the street: desolate, long, just as it has been during these last years, ever since the eliminatory measures were adopted.

Or it might happen that you trip in the street, or on the stairs, over a toy forgotten by someone, and you stumble or fall and break a leg: From that moment on the circumstances will take on a different meaning, the investigators (infallible) will discover that there was something intentional in the forgetting, seemingly innocent, of a toy in the street; they will even talk about an attempt to eliminate you. Your terror will then be justified. Then there will be no rest for you.

The cumulative weight of abnormal events registered in these last few days is truly alarming. There is someone who has seen, rising over the rooftops in the distance, a kite. He claims, the informant, anonymous since we are now even afraid to sign a complaint, that he rubbed his eyes at first, that he imagined, maybe unconsciously seeking relief, that it was a UFO, those unidentified flying saucers, but his fear must have come to a boil, that is, become more real, precise, almost physical, on seeing that it was, unquestionably, a kite, and, of course, you know, the kite, the paper comet, as it's known, was tied to a string, and the string, well, there has to be a hand at the end of a string, correct?

They are even more occurrences. One is in the park and perceives, at the same time, suddenly, a strange rustle in the trees, the rustle of someone climbing, hidden or camouflaged by the leaves. It seems to one that one is hearing sounds forgotten a long time ago, those that children make on climbing trees. One approaches, looks, observes, with a stone in hand, ready, but doesn't manage to see anything; nevertheless, the noise was, indeed, there. Or it might be that one continues with one's walk and comes upon, hands over one's mouth, a circle like those they draw with chalk on the ground, to play with marbles, or perhaps one of those alarming designs they draw on sidewalks with compartments and arcane signs that they use to jump on one foot, in repetitive rituals.

But if the days pass fraught with unending frights, the nights reach, at times, the very limits of terror or nightmares. As we sleep—this is just one example—a child's cry wakes us. How? Where? In the room next door, in the house next door. The neighbors wake up, they jump out of bed, ready to apply one of the measures prescribed; but no matter how much they search, high and low, nothing appears; and the crying continues right there, over our heads, tangential, absorbed, hair-raising, as though it were struggling to transmit to us, or, better yet, to decipher, a dark message, an overwhelming threat. We might even go back to sleep, but our sleep will always be troubled, frightened, filled with the impression that someone, a child, breathes, panting next to our ears, that laughter, clear and ominously childish, runs through the hard spaces of the night, its subtle saliva moistens, implacably, our temples, our gray temples.

And always, at any hour, the vibrating sound of footsteps through corridors lost, unknown. The bells of tricycles we didn't know existed. The running on the other side of doors, among laughter or jubilant cries; the quivering striking of the earth that tops somewhere produce, the irregular to-ings and fro-ings of rubber balls, nearby, very near. The members of the Committee believe that little by little our psychological reserves are being sapped. The tiredness, the insomnia, the terror, is hopelessly changing and undermining us.

We sense the cracks in our ramparts, cracks through which the threatening sounds attempt to filter, the cries forgotten long ago. We have—all of us—the impression that beneath our houses, within our walls, there exist or grow caverns or spaces or rooms, hidden, unknown, there, where they must sleep, live, where they must have their classrooms or clandestine circles, those hidden places for their games, of conspiracy, we would say, which at times we imagine, during sleepless nights filled with terror, sweating, ashen.

We experience an inevitable collapse, a gnawing away at things, strange loosenings in the walls. If we move a picture from its place or change the frame of a mirror, we find, behind, in the very wall, something like a tunnel, a hollowness at whose base we hear a scream or a desperate cry, our own whimper of surprise or anguish. We no longer have enough time to erase the drawings on the walls because others appear the minute we turn our backs, each time more perfect, pictorial in color, volume, fantastic meanings. Over our heads the flight of kites razes the sky. With each passing minute and with increasing frequency, the whistles around us grow, the cries of irrational happiness that they hurl, that invisible mob, close, ready to make an appearance. Our terror comes to a boil. We fancy that at any moment, through the cracks, at this very dreadful instant, we will see them, we will see them advance, advance over us, with there being nothing left for us to do, undermined as we are, inert, unpardonably old and disheartened.

VLADIMIRO RIVAS ITURRALDE
(Latacunga, 1944)

A grant awarded by the Latin American Writers´ Community took Vladimiro Rivas Iturralde to Mexico for the first time in 1973, and what was to be a temporary stay turned into permanent residence.

Rivas's short story collections include *El demiurgo* (Quito, 1967), *Historia del cuento desconocido* (México, 1974), *Los bienes* (México, 1981), and a personal anthology of previously unpublished stories, *Vivir del cuento* (Quito 1993).

In addition, he has published an essay collection, *Desciframientos y complicidades* (Mexico, 1991); a novel, *El legado del tigre* (Mexico-Quito, 1997); and a novella, *La caída y la noche* (México, 2000).

The writer is currently a profesor-researcher in the School of Literature at the Universidad Autónoma Metropolitana, Azcapotzalco.

Several of his stories have been translated into English, French, and German, and included in a number of anthologies.

Critic Cecilia Ansaldo writes that "his pieces, lacking experimentation, breaks, and digressions, are clean structures in which the originality of the anecdote and control of language predominate. Themes and characters emerge from all corners of world culture, and the "Ecuadorian" in his work does not have the flavor of the regional.

According to Javier Martínez Palacio, writing in *Insula*, a publication out of Madrid, "The quality of his prose rises from his exploration of man as an elemental being and in the way he whispers into the reader's ear, with the rhythm, the nakedness, and the 'silence' of a movie camera."

THE INVISIBLE FOOTSTEPS*

That night I got home a little late. With the first crescendos of Berlioz's *Fantastique,* I also heard the first complaints, the first little knocks on the left wall. I foresaw that with the *fortissimos*—and the symphony abounds in *fortissimos*—the knocks on all four walls would become intolerable. Soon after, in effect, there came to me from his knuckles the censure sinking itself into the walls of my room. I forced myself not to listen to the witches' night and to go to sleep. Since Dominique wasn't there the following night—she'd warned me about a possible additional flight to Istanbul—I had to lock myself again in my room and listen to the last movement. It was ten-thirty, and the complaints of the night before were not long in coming, and they fed my wish to strike them all down with a *fortissimo* by Berlioz at full volume that would break with everything once and for all and bring from far away the *concierge* to witness a colossal incident, unique, inimitable, a scandal that would remain etched forever in the memory of that house that seemed to

*From the collection *Vivir del cuento,* 1993.

have no other. But I chose to play instead a different game, precisely the opposite, one which wouldn't in any way distance me from my antisocial conduct but, rather, confirm it. Creating an uproar in that house, I realized, was an operation similar to that of neutralizing myself, of spying on the others with my ears.

It took me some time to get to sleep. In the midst of that shrouded silence, imagines of Saint Michel and Saint Germain trooped through my mind, capricious, arbitrary: the pride, the arrogance, the indifference; the street poets, barely out of their teens; the vaguely Andalucian face leaning toward the lips of a blond; the watchmaker, absorbed, unaware of the movement on the street; the groups of students, Trotskyites, handing out brochures and flyers at the entrance to the Metro; the beautiful Hindu woman who could bring to the faces of those who looked at her something like the glow of the memory of first love or, in any case, something well beyond indifference or lust; the old woman at the foot of the Tour Saint Jacques feeding the little birds from the corners of her mouth, with a Franciscan beauty at dusk, attracting even the attention of those pedestrians accustomed to being surprised at nothing; the little man masturbating across from the magazine stand on the rue Séguier; the *clochard* refusing to accept from a *clocharde* the invitation to rest under the bridge over the Sully; the small group of boys playing *De terciopelo negro* on flute and guitar under the bridge over the Tournelle… It was then, as I was trying to reconstruct that song in my semi-waking state, that I heard footsteps coming from above. First I jumped out of bed and for a moment imagined that the whole ceiling was going to come crashing down on me with whoever was upstairs on top of it; in the end, that crash would have been a substitute for a *fortissimo* by Berlioz, for the frustrated uproar, a breaking of that jealously constructed order absorbed in its own contemplation. But the ceiling didn't collapse and the man continued walking to a point I was unable to identify. I assumed it was a man, given the heaviness of the footsteps. Lying on my back, with the dim lights from the street playing on the walls and the ceiling, I amused myself by following the path of those steps and observing at what point I lost the trail, when and where I picked it up, when and where I lost it again, by imagining the end-point of that route, and that sort of thing, a little like the game of the blind chicken or the *piñata* pushed by the wind or a cord or by the same stick that pursued it. The game forced me to recognize, in the first place, my own position in my room on the *cinquieme* as a point of reference. My bed was next to the window, the one to the right in the room, and the bathroom across from me, at the far end. Curiously, it seemed that the room on the *sixieme* was much larger than mine, or maybe that the man was moving much too slowly or, maybe at the same time, that his room was not of the same architectonic design, a truly rare thing in that old Napoleonic house that so respected, ostentation and all, measurements and symmetries. If this wasn't the case, then there was some problem with my perceptions, attributable to exhaustion and sleepiness. I concluded that perceiving a sound divorced from the body that caused it creates in us an erroneous concept of space: The space in question becomes larger than it is in reality; all space turns into sound. The matter was still on my mind when I woke up and heard the sounds again. First it was his alarm

clock. It was only on hearing his footsteps that I realized that I had always heard him, that I had always
been in a position to hear him, had it not been for the
breathing of the woman who at our side reminds us
that we also exist. But this time the only presence was
his, that of the man, above, on the *sixieme*, announced
by the alarm clock that I assumed was such, suddenly,
at six-thirty in the morning, a ritual presence.

Throughout that week, events conspired to leave me
alone early on the *cinquieme*. M. Lamont gave me thir-
ty additional pages of the programs I was translating.
At nine, in the light from the lamp, I heard him come
in, up the stairs. He had just arrived. He stopped for a
moment at the door. He wiped off his shoes on the
floor mat at the entrance, he went immediately to the
bathroom where he must have shook the rain from his
coat, he must have taken off his rubber boots and then
returned to his room. He must have forgot something,
because he went back to the bathroom. I heard the yellow stream hit the water and, immediately after, the liquid flushing in torrents down the pipe. He went to the
sofa and unfolded his newspaper. The man was clearly not the master of his own time in the course of the
day. Nor was he now, now as I listened, secret, distant,
intimate, in perfect symbiosis with the profound stillness of the house, to the nebulous purr of his television.
I stopped working for a moment and gave myself over
to a silence that carried me to the perception of something more. I was horrified to find myself in a state in
which all traces of life, namely, movement and sound,
were suddenly suspended. I had believed impossible
the existence of such moments, moments in which
nothing happens, in which everything seems to be sus-

pended and hanging by an invisible thread, of every-thing depending on nothing. Something must have been happening somewhere. I went to peer into the hall. Nothing, except the slight squeaking of the hinges on my door. Not a soul, not a movement; here and there strips of light at the edges of the stairs, and barely, bare-ly, the distant purr of the television on the *sixieme*. Suddenly, the precise word came to me, the one I need-ed for the phrase I was translating, and I returned to the lamp. I applauded with gratitude that word, which had rescued me from the hallway. I finished the first draft of the document, put on my coat, and slipped down the stairs. At the Blanche, I drank a glass of wine. I also ate a roll with Roquefort.

I don't know if it was that same night or another (custom offers the illusion of time's repeal) when I stumbled over the Miles David and Dave Brubeck records, nor if it was that same stumbling that made me look at them fearful of listening to them because of the censure that would come from above. I spent some time contemplating the photos I had taken of Dominique in Abignon. Photos in hand, I dreamed about her going with me to open air concerts, when I found myself surprised by the invisible footsteps. I emerged brutally from the daydream, hid the photos, and followed again the footsteps which forced me to rest from both my work and my nostalgia. I surprised myself literally reading the route of the footsteps. Now I could predict where they would go, what the man would be doing. His bed, I concluded, was not exactly over mine. I thought that my espionage would be more precise if, in addition, I reproduced, as far as possible, his room in my own. I took the covers and all the extra weight off my bed and dragged it to exactly where he had his. Now they were in the same place, namely, in the middle of the room. I could do something similar— though I don't think identical—with the rest of the furniture. I could even measure the light in his room, measure his time. Those footsteps had a precise rhythm: not the whimsical rhythm of memories or of images of the street, not that of any known music nor that of machines. They seemed only like breathing. Those footsteps were the rhythm and the man himself. But I should point out the provisional nature of that impression. There was in the character of those footsteps something much more concrete and nevertheless inapprehensible than what I was able to imagine. It began to seem to me to be logical that in those cells, where solitude was so rooted, and organized and compartmentalized and regimented (*Pas de musique dans la nuit, pas d tout, hein?*), one could know a man simply through his footsteps. In the course of that week of work next to my lamp, I learned of his weariness, his very discreet joys, his insomnia, his ailments (his indigestions, his long hemorrhoidal bowel movements), the rigidity of his schedule (a reflection of his bureaucratic obligations), the indispensable call of his alarm clock at six-thirty in the morning, his mental fatigue, his television tastes, his infinite lower middle class correctness, his loneliness. As for my neighbors, the old inhabitants of the house passed through my mind via a process of identification with the man upstairs. Their almost anonymous faces, seen in passing on the stairs, their movements, their sounds, had become almost abstract to me: They all became concrete, their small lives, in the footsteps of the man on the *sixieme*. They were those footsteps.

I believe it was the fifth day, the desire for coffee in the face of an empty sugar bowl, and it was almost ten-thirty when I decided to go up to the *sixieme* for sugar. I had worked feverishly that night and I don't remember having followed his footsteps. Two coincidences were being fused: my need for sugar for my coffee and the silence of his footsteps, of which I only became conscious on hearing my own on the creaking spiral staircase that led to the *sixieme*. I was about to return to my room in light of the suspicion that I would be badly received or somehow censured. Everything led me to think about that: my guilty need, the walls of the house, the silence, the hour, the absences. I gathered up my courage on the way and dared to knock at his door, so timidly that I couldn't have been heard. But, how could I have forgotten. His schedule. Behind the purr of the television I could hear the snoring of the man. Apart from whatever urgency (the sugar, for example), there appeared in me another need: to see his face, hear his voice, confirm that it was the same as mine, that it was the same as that of all those in that house, that it was the same as all those in the rue Mansart, that it was the same as all those in Paris. In my room again, I heard. The man woke up and in his footsteps I could make out, at last, enlightened by my typewriter and the brief incursion into the corridor, that which had been bothering me until then and dragging me along without my having fully realized it. In the first place, those footsteps were mercilessly indifferent, they ignored me thoroughly, which fact confirmed my status as a foreigner in that house; in the second place, there was in those footsteps a vague bureaucratic murmur; their rhythm was precisely that: the rhythm of the endless offices that now lived in him and peopled the house under the guise of a routine.

Though relieved in part and with the vague joy that follows from understanding what before was unknown, in the morning I spied as never before. First it was the alarm clock and, following that, the opening of the curtains, the gargling in the bathroom, the chaotic movements of morning calisthenics, the clearing of the throat, the cough, all of that at precise intervals in the silence of the house. I could tell him on the staircase that the night before I had gone up to ask for some sugar but he was already asleep. I could initiate a conversation. Paying attention to his movements made me careless of my own. I hadn't been aware of how late it was so I had to do everything quickly and clumsily. I didn't even shave. I was putting papers in my briefcase when I heard him come down the stairs. His footsteps were quick, urgent. I caught a glimpse of him from the back, descending the spiral of the staircase. I followed him, my footsteps echoing his. How I damned the *concierge* in the patio when at that very moment she approached me with a letter. It was from Dominique, from Athens. I wanted to ask the harpy about the man who had got away, but on seeing in her Cerberus, the cold, implacable guard and spy, and owner of the silence of the house, I couldn't find a single reasonable pretext that would justify a question that would make me feel guilty, an inquisitor like her.

Five days were enough to make the six-thirty awakening to his clock´s alarm very nearly a habit. On the sixth I woke before the hour. It was still very dark. It was the footsteps, now become a slow, painful dragging of slippers around his bed, that is, around my own. They came and went around me in a semi-circle. They opened at the sides of the bed and then they closed like pincers at the two extremes of the head-board. The circumference that that gloomy shuffle traced was almost perfect: The diameter began at my head and ended at the central lamp, where it stopped for a moment to contemplate me. I sat up immediately, turned on the lamp on the table, and forced myself to see the invisible footsteps. But the more I tried to see them, they less the moved. Their immobility, in fact, had made them invisible. I turned the lamp off and realized that they moved to the bathroom. I turned it on again and followed him. He turned on the bath-room light. I looked in the mirror at the swollen eyelids, the bags of exhaustion under the eyes. I drank a glass of water, gargled, and listened to the water flowing down the pipes. At that hour the silence was so deep that even the act of breathing echoed. He turned the light off and went back to bed, where the light from the bedside lamp still awaited him. He turned it off and must have fallen asleep immediately.

I woke up again after six-thirty. I distracted myself from what had happened hours earlier by concentrating on putting into words the dream I'd had about a double confinement: I was a snail in a spiral shell which a force superior to my own had enclosed in a matchbox. I pushed with my head to open it but enormous hands shut it again. I wanted to reread Dominique's promises but I was exhausted. I put her letter aside. Nothing came from upstairs. Only silence. The alarm clock hadn't gone off. And his footsteps were not heard. Nevertheless, I waited for them. To no end. The alarm clock hadn't sounded. I put on my slippers and wrapped myself in my bathrobe. I walked around the bed several times and it was probably that the clock was broke and the man was still sleeping, who knows, and they'll probably fine him or fire him or he'll receive from his boss a reprimand that will have him depressed throughout the entire day, humiliated and irremediably tied to a condition that will only lead him to despise himself. I must have stumbled into two neighbors who, *baguette a la main*, condescended to offer ambiguous smiles and restrained, oddly fearful greetings, after which, coldly puzzled, they returned to their rooms. I don't know how many more might have come out to watch me go up the stairs. I knocked hard, insistently, at the door on the *sixieme*—there was no number or letter or name whatsoever by way of identi- fication—and when I was able to internalize that sound, dry and peremptory, when I surprised myself knocking at the door as they had done previously to ask me to be quiet, I understood that now, now indeed, I had broken the order of the house, as when I had attempted to listen to the *Fantastique*, and that if I con- tinued doing so, the man would complain to the *concierge*, or might even go so far as to humiliate me with a joke, a harpy smile, a flood of questions. But it was too late: They had already called the *concierge*. I asked her to please wake up the man on the *sixieme*. She looked at me with pity, as one looks at a madman, and burst into a horrible guffaw. The neighbor on the left approached with a smile that was more like a gri- mace to tell me, taking me by the arm, that I would do well to go back to my room and wait there for a moment, because no one lived on the *sixieme*.

ABDÓN UBIDIA
(Quito, 1944)

A member of the tzántzico movement, Abdón Ubidia became one of its most prominent critics. He won fame as one of the finest story-tellers of his generation with *Bajo el mismo extraño cielo* (1979, National Prize for Literature). Subsequently, he published *Divertinventos. Libro de fantasias y utopías* (1989) and *El palacio de los espejos* (1996).

Ubidia's novel *Sueño de lobos* (1986) was acclaimed the best of the year. His novella *Ciudad del invierno* (1979) has come out in more than ten editions. In 1993, he published *Adiós Siglo XX*, a work for theater.

In addition, Ubidia has made important contributions to research into oral literature, writing studies to accompany two anthologies: *El cuento popular* (1977) and *La poesía popular ecuatoriana* (1982).

The writer's works are found in nearly all anthologies of the Ecuadorian short story and his stories have been translated into English, French, German, and Russian. His novel *Sueño de lobos* was published in English (*Wolves' Dream*, 1996, Latin American Literary Review Press, translated by Mary Ellen Fieweger).

Ubidia's narrative is governed by two predominant and comple-mentary ideas: the gamble and failure. His characters dream up grand projects, often outrageous, and they inevitably fail to bring these to fruition. But in the failure the true measure of the man appears. In *Sueño de lobos*, a great novel, a bank heist is conceived as an assault on heaven. The novel's conceits are, among other things, pretexts providing opportunities to describe Quito, a city of labyrinthine streets and hidden corners, intimately described in a fashion never before achieved. Only in Javier Vásconez do we find a comparable tragic pathos.

NIGHT TRAIN*

She heard a deep whistle followed by the clatter of a train approaching at high speed. Silent, trembling, with her eyes open in the dark, she imagined pounding rods and pistons, gusts of steam convulsively escaping from between rusted iron wheels and tracks mired in grease and mud, a wealth of steel upon steel. But that was absurd, the train station was at the other end of the city. It was impossible to hear anything that went on over there. It's true that insomnia sharpens the senses, electrifies them, extends their range, enables them to pick up signals, details that during the day remain hidden, drowned out by the riotous display of the rushing city. One can hear the periodic creaking of wood settling in wardrobes. Or the gnawing of small creatures digging tunnels and galleries in brick and lime walls. Or insects self-destructing against windows in the night. Or one's own breathing. Or, beyond, the murmur of a sleeping city—a distant din, the sum of restless mutterings, faraway cars fleeing, isolated howls, echoes of remote factories, solitary footsteps, sirens

---

*From the collection *Bajo el mismo extraño cielo*, 1979.

wailing, cries, probably, and songs, probably, coming from bars open until dawn. But the train station was at the other end of the city and it was impossible to hear what went on over there. Undoubtedly, she said to herself, it was only a dream. Undoubtedly, she was dreaming an attack of insomnia that was also a dream. She turned between the sheets. But the glass on the nightstand began to vibrate. Then the glass's vibration spread to the nightstand itself, and then to the floors and then the walls and finally it seemed that the entire house was being shaken by an earth tremor. She got up, took two steps, and was standing at the window. Just then a train, or whatever it was, passed by the house. There was no question. But she couldn't open the curtains; she was paralyzed by fear. When the vibrations stopped and the swift running of those innumerable wheels fell gradually silent, and the cold night air began to chill her bare arms and feet, she returned almost mechanically to bed. She kept her eyes fixed on the window, as though she could see through the curtains, as though she could go on seeing what she hadn't managed to see to begin with.

Much later, she fell into a broken, stupid sleep. Before six she heard the gobbling of the neighbor's turkey. An hour later and as always, she heard, or felt, a quiet bustling that slipped among pots and pans in the kitchen; it was her mother who had returned from church.

Now she was up. Tall, thin, enveloped in a gown as white as she was and resembling a habit, she went to sit at the dressing table. The old mirror with flowers etched around the edges returned a reflection that seemed to emerge from some watery depths, that face of hers which, in spite of moisturizing lotions and nutritive creams, was beginning to crumple around the mouth and eyes. And now, added to that, the traces of insomnia. Her normal paleness accentuated, her eyelids slightly swollen. It looked as though she'd been crying. But those eyes, still lovely, had forgotten about tears a long time ago. At least it was difficult to imagine tears in that oval face, rather stern, actually, rather disdainful and stoic at the same time.

"Why so early on a Saturday?" said the mother when she saw her appear in the kitchen doorway.

"Mama, you heard it!" she exclaimed. Before the mother could ask, she said in a rush, "The train!"

The mother's eyes widened in astonishment.

"It went past the house," the daughter said.

The mother couldn't think of a thing to say. She looked at her out of the corner of her eye: Those small eyes underscored by violet circles observed her closely. She was bathed in the morning light, hazy and gray, that came from above through the square panes of a narrow window. Immobile behind a small table covered with a white oilcloth, her body inclined forward slightly, holding a cup and saucer in her knotted, parchment-like hands, the mother looked the very image of Saint Ann. "You've had a nightmare," she wanted to say. "You mustn't worry about it," she wanted to add. She said nothing. It was better to say nothing. In these last years she had learned to fear her daughter. And now that she saw her, pale, tense, it was not worth doubting her word: Their day might be spoiled as a result. It had happened before. Yes, it was better to say nothing. Nothing would be gained by provoking her. Maybe she was having evil visions.

Maybe it was just nerves. "You'll soon forget about it," she said, putting the cup on the small table, as if the gentle descent of her arm accompanied by a fleeting frown were a comment. Her mind was blank. She could not think of a single thing to say.

The daughter observed the descent of the cup to the oilcloth-covered tabletop. She also observed the mother's narrow forehead. It was truly strange: With no more than an almost imperceptible movement of the eyebrows, amazement became pathos. Evidently, the mother had heard nothing unusual the night before. And if she had heard, she would have denied it. And forgotten about it. The elderly had their own forms of madness, their own stubbornness in which they hid, blindly, due to fear, due to tiredness, due to weariness, who knows why. And the mother was given to contrariness as far as she was concerned. And she would have denied it. But now she didn't know what train the daughter was talking about. "She thinks I'm hallucinating," she thought. "You think I'm going mad," she was going to say. But the words didn't leave her mouth. That would have begun an absurd argument. As on other occasions. That would have ended up by spoiling their day. As at other times. She said nothing.

"A train?" the mother said.

It was a question without emphasis, barely whispered, the intonation neutral, as though she were talking to herself. Because a change of conservation was in order, the daughter decided to avail herself of that air of contrariness and abandon, that familiar and worn-out gesture that was never anything more than a habit learned in the distant past, and to say to her, "Forget it, it was a nightmare," and to go on with any old comment that would dissipate the mother's concern.

"A train?" murmured the mother.

The silence of a mausoleum or a cave kept them suspended in a time without minutes or seconds. The daughter closed the top button of her bathrobe and shuffled over to the sink. The tap was dripping lazily into the shiny metal basin. She closed it tightly to stop the dripping. Now the silence was complete.

Salvation came from above, as though from heaven. On the upper floor, at the other end of the house, a bell rang, the father calling. "Dear Lord, he's awake," said the mother, and losing herself in a swirl of activity, she quickly prepared a glass filled with three parts hot and one part cold water from the tap, plus a teaspoonful of standing water kept in the refrigerator. "I'm bringing it right up," the mother said, her voice a thread only she could hear. A little later her footsteps sounded on the wooden spiral staircase.

The daughter watched her disappear through the balusters of the staircase. Then, apathetically, she called, "Pepín, where've you gone off to?"

She felt him press against her legs. He'd come out from under an easy chair. "Stupid cat, if you're not called, you don't come," she said to him, returning to the kitchen.

Pepín followed her with elastic contortions accompanied by short meows. She filled his bowl with milk and went to the door leading to the back patio. She opened it. Outside, the sun cast a frail light on everything. At the back of the patio, next to the posts from which wash lines hung, was Boby's empty doghouse. The poor thing died of old age, pure and simple. He must have been more than twenty. Towards the end, he did nothing but sleep. And not even Pepín's claws disturbed him. Slow, his back bound in a tangle of hair matted with filth because no one bothered to bathe him, his mouth always open, panting, eventually he had strength only to get up from time to time, sniff around the corners of the patio as though moved by an instinct he barely remembered, and return to collapse on the frayed rags in his doghouse. Finally, he died.

"Do you miss him?" she asked Pepín.

Pepín looked up at her with emerald green eyes, then closed them almost sweetly as he licked his paw and brushed it over his whiskers and ears. She talked to Pepín as though he were a person, just as she had once talked to Boby or, before him, to Tony, or as she had also talked to the canary and the macaw, to all the dogs, cats, and birds that appeared and died in her life and that were now no more than vague spaces in her memory, vague, docile shapes to which she always attributed rudimentary feelings of affection that they bestowed on her for almost nothing in return. One day, years before, she promised herself that she would stop talking to animals. "I must not speak to them as though they were persons," she told herself. On another occasion she vowed not to talk to herself out loud when she was alone. And at first she tried to resist the temptation to do both. But, little by little, the habits of an unmarried existence took over, and then she found herself talking to herself or to animals as though to do so were the most natural thing in the world. Now it hardly mattered. Pepín would be the last pet in that house. "No more animals," her father had said, months before, looking at Boby's empty doghouse. "No more silly suffering," her mother had insisted.

And, for once, she felt that they were right.

"Do you miss him?" she asked Pepín.

As Pepín again closed those crystalline eyes, she looked at the angle formed by the banister and the kitchen doorway, partially blinded from the light in the patio. Her mother was staying up there for a long time. There was no telling what she was saying to the father. "She shouldn't tell him about the train," she murmured to herself. She sat down at the edge of a chair.

With her elbow resting on the table, she placed a hand, visor-like, over her mouth. With the other hand, she played with a teaspoon laid for a breakfast that wasn't being prepared: a little coffee and two slices of toast with honey, to keep her weight down. Periodically, she tapped the cup, still upside-down on the saucer. She felt her mother approach from behind and look at her wordlessly. She didn't turn around, it wasn't necessary, and besides, she assumed that the look would hold the same old reproach: "Why didn't you get married?" she would be saying. She knew that all answers were useless. The mother had learned to shut herself up in her own way of thinking and nothing could get at her there. It made no sense to tell her that it was their fault, for their stupid insistence upon bloodlines that never existed, which time and again frightened off the man who had once sought her out with a shadowy and cautious persistence she never managed to explain to herself satisfactorily, and who, in some part of her memory, especially on sleepless nights, continued looking for her, circling her, clinging still to the fervor of old, and who, just maybe, she might have grown to love. It was useless to let herself be overcome now by pointless anger and to respond to that reproach with still another, equally pointless, because in any event, the mother said nothing; she folded herself up in a gloomy silence, though she would be wordlessly repeating the question she mulled over endlessly and never uttered, "Why didn't you get married? Why?", as she approached from behind and stood beside her, looking at but not seeing the immaculate porcelain cup still upside-down on the saucer, and asked whatever came to mind, about breakfast, for example, any false, hollow remark that would better serve to hide her thoughts.

"You haven't had breakfast yet?" said the mother.

An icy blaze flashed through the air.

"You haven't had breakfast yet?" said the mother.

"Yes! I've had breakfast!" her daughter nearly shouted as she got up abruptly and fled from the kitchen, propelled by the congested blood rising to her face, but it was not enough to make her cry, because, in the end, nothing was enough now to make her cry.

It was unreal, that rose-tinted gloom created by the drapes partially drawn. At the far end of the room and looking out of place, the tall mirror on the dressing table shone between two sets of half-open drawers. The same effect of light bursting into shadow was repeated on the tiny colonial painting. Jesus's white face looked like a cutout against the deep background tones. Below him, from the unmade bed, tangled sheets and quilts spilled over in a thick, soft cascade. There were clothes on the yellow damask hassock shot through with gold threads. The closet doors stood ajar and two of the dolls in her collection on the mahogany shelf had fallen over, one on top of the other, probably knocked down by an unnoticed swirl of her long bathrobe's lace hem. There was much to be done there. Without thinking, as though moved by a timeless impulse, she began to straighten up the room. She would first have to open the drapes and the window so that the light penetrated completely and the fresh air replaced the stale, erasing, once and for all, the last vestiges of the night. She would abandon herself to the old habit of reordering today all that had been disordered yesterday, because in that way time weighed less and, in addition, the past seemed to be erased, transformed into a new hope, a new beginning or starting point, as open drawers were shut and wardrobe doors shut as well, with all her clothes inside, and the unmade bed made and the two dolls on the mahogany shelf returned to their rightful places in that long congregation of candid effigies, tall, short, fat, thin, white, brown, pink, perfectly preserved from the years of her childhood. Beyond the doors of her bedroom, now impeccable, the living room, dining room, and hallway floors awaited her care, a Saturday and Sunday morning obligation self-imposed, whether or not a maid was employed, whether or not she was feeling well.

The father found her bent over the floor polisher that buzzed among the furniture still encased in protective linen covers in the corners of the living room.

"But, my dear, you're going to make yourself ill, we could hire someone to do that," he said.

"It doesn't pay," she replied, "they never do a good job. No one does a good job."

The father assumed his habitual pose, serious and solemn, as though preparing himself to continue the scolding. But it wasn't worth it to do so. That wasn't what he wanted to say to her. Then he considered asking her about the new maid who would begin work on Monday. But that wasn't what he wanted to say, either. Rather small, bent, graying hair, a very short and graying beard that looked as though it were pasted onto a face lined with wrinkles, the father couldn't find the appropriate tone for a change in conversation. He merely coughed two or three times. He was dressed to go out. He only needed to put his jacket on, and his homburg.

"It seems you didn't sleep well last night," he said at last. His voice sounded hollow.

"Did mama tell you that?" asked the daughter, as though anticipating what he was going to say.

The father frowned. He didn't know how to respond. Then he nodded as he took off his glasses and searched for a handkerchief to clean them.

The daughter watched him put his glasses back on.

"It was a nightmare," she lied easily as she turned on the floor polisher. Over the buzzing of the machine, she heard her father say, "About the train?"

The daughter switched the floor polisher off and turned toward him. "A nightmare," she insisted. "Something didn't set well. There's nothing strange about that, is there?"

The father pursed his lips, displeased. "My dear wife no longer understands things very well," he would be thinking. "I'll have to talk to her about that," he added to himself, getting ready to go off to look for the mother. The daughter turned on the floor polisher and the buzzing removed the old man's footprints and she rediscovered, with each of the machine's movements, forward and back, something like a hidden meaning in that task of polishing the waxed floor, a

kind of calling out, precise and reiterated, from someone who would never again return.

Later she saw him walking through the hallway. He
looked tense, caught up in something unpleasant that
wasn't quite indignation, or, rather, caught up in indignation gone awry. He would have preferred to spend
the entire day (as he did nearly every Saturday) with
friends, away from home (because of the unpleasant-
nesses that occurred punctually every Saturday) but
with his conscience at ease, feeling absolutely in control, justified.

"Are you going out, papa?" asked the daughter, a
question that was also an answer.

"I don't know," the father responded. But he did
know. Apparently, something was amiss there, within.
Maybe his complaints to the mother had been excessive
and now he felt guilty. The mother would be off in
some corner of the house now, her face contrite and
tearful. He, of course, didn't have to complicate matters like this. No one dictated his comings and goings.
No one stopped him from doing as he pleased. But it
was Saturday. And he was a man of habits and anxi-
eties, and his habits were precise and established,
though there were times when he found them intolerable. Retired ten years before, he continued to observe
office hours during the week. "I'm going out to attend
to some business," he would say early in the morning.
And that "business" amounted to no more than paying
monthly light, telephone, or water bills. An occasional
formal call. A funeral, perhaps. The rest of the time he
spent on benches in city parks and plazas, waiting for
midday in order to return home, just as he had
returned home from work years before. However, he

felt obliged to spend Saturdays and Sundays with his family. Except that sometimes his sense of duty and his secret desires were not in accord. At least not on Saturday. Then he would be overcome by a desperate feeling because he was unable, through his own fault, to do that which he wanted to do. All of that while his friends had already begun to gather in some dim corner to which they had been faithful since the days of their youth, and which she and her mother could barely imagine, enveloped in a smoky haze produced by hand-rolled cigarettes and the smells of cane liquor, fried pork, cow-foot soup, and all the rest. Thus, there were complications. Thus, it was necessary to invent some unpleasantness, something, anything that would serve as an excuse to join the weekly get-together, as always, throughout his entire life, especially now that those who gathered were fewer each time and more decrepit, now that the mind had begun to distort events that existed solely in the confusion of a distorted memory, given that no one could point to the spot where they had occurred because it had vanished or been erased by new asphalt and new, winding streets in that changing, unrecognizable city.

"Are you going out, papa?" she asked and the father replied that he didn't know, but she saw him hesitate under the living room arch, then leave and return with his jacket and his hat on and his dark raincoat folded over his arm.

"Take care, my little girl," he said, almost reverently, and she didn't have time to say to him, irritated, as on other occasions, "Your aging little girl," nor did she have time to say to him, "Be careful, papa, the floor," because the father was already out the door, quickly, each footstep leaving a small, dark print on the gleaming waxed floor and she had no choice but to follow them with her machine alternately purring and roaring, reestablishing the waxy shine, making it smooth and splendid again, like crystal.

The light was a silver stain on the floor and a chiaroscuro of vertical light and shadow on the drapes. A carved cedar table stood on the rug—a soft brown oval—in the center of the living room. It was crowned by a molded glass vase filled with fresh hydrangeas. In the living room's limpid air, isolated beams of light glinted off ashtrays, lamps, wall decorations, and little glass and porcelain figurines standing here and there, arranged one by one on glass shelves. She had changed her clothes now. She wore a silk blouse in muted tones, white slacks with wide cuffs, and, over the curlers in her hair, a scarf that matched her blouse. She looked fresh, almost rejuvenated after hot and cold showers. She smelled of talcum and soft perfume. And on her partially made-up face, in her eyes still lacking liner and mascara, on her mouth already covered with dark lipstick, a pleasant anxiety briefly fluttered as she stood, half-hidden by the living room arch, contemplating, detail by detail, the places over which her hands had passed and passed again, polishing, cleaning, arranging with uncompromising zeal. But the anxiety on that face was not just hers. It seemed to emanate from objects as well, from the empty spaces, from the play of light in the room. It felt like a new aura that enveloped things as though, in that instant and for that single moment, the objects were a little more than just themselves; as though they had grown a new and pleasant layer that was not made of light nor of air, but that existed and called out from rugs and lamps, from the opaque depths of the furniture upholstered in scarlet velvet, free now of the slightest trace of lint. There, everything seemed to be waiting. The living room itself seemed to be waiting for something or someone from within that newly acquired tidiness that beckoned clamorously.

But that daydream collapsed almost immediately. It didn't last as long as it once had. Like a bubble escaping from dark, watery depths and ascending violently toward the surface, a cruel mental outburst reminded her that the hours of waiting were over, that in that house no one—and certainly not those cold objects—waited for anything any longer, and, as a result of that spectacular mental fall, they returned to being themselves, to being as they truly and customarily were within the intimidating cleanliness of the room suddenly transformed into a mausoleum: dead. It wasn't an expression of horror or anguish that upset her face. Nor was it a cry of fright that brought her hand to her mouth. It was simply an unexpected shudder zigzagging through her body. Or, rather, a sudden sensation of cold. A second later, she practically ran through the house in search of her mother with an idea fixed in her mind.

"Mama!" she called as soon as she saw her, bent over a pile of clothes, exaggerating, as she always did, her household chores.

The mother turned to look at her, nonplussed. She seemed to have awakened, suddenly, from a long sleep. She looked at her, perplexed, and then looked away, and with no desire to find out what this was all about, she buried herself again in her task, as though returning to some suffering or painful animosity, and the daughter understood immediately: She was considered the guilty party, and with reason, for the complaints of the father.

She tried then to fit herself into the mother's own special time and to control the urgency that had taken her there. She had truly frightened her. On calling out, her voice had risen to a scream. That had not been her intention. She merely wanted to ask that the mother forget her quarrel with Aunt Antonia and call her, inviting her to visit. That was all. She would put up with her aunt, and the aunt's daughters and their children, because that was preferable to enduring a stupid Saturday afternoon watching the hours pass, one by one. Saturday afternoon had opened in her an enormous emptiness in time, and she had nothing to fill it, and it was essential that it be filled, even if that meant a visit with Aunt Antonia and her fidgety conversation about all that had happened (or was going to happen) to the family, including its most distant members, for whom she served as a kind of full-time honorary directress and guide, since she didn't mind going to wherever it was necessary to go in order to address any and all offenses caused by the many upstarts who had slipped into the family due to the thoughtlessness and lack of discrimination of that new, modern, inconsiderate generation whose members let themselves be dragged along, unawares, by the first friend, fiancée, pretender, and so on to cross their paths. An implacable, monumental conversationalist was Aunt Antonia, which did not prevent her daughters, nonetheless, from providing her with new, alarming data, nor did it stop their children, three tireless little demons, from dashing through the entire house and knocking into and upsetting everything; all of that was preferable to feeling yet again, in that empty house, in that empty living room, the icy sensation of silence and death, especially now that the brutal lightning bolt of lucidity had led her to fear, in those moments of solitude, what might lie behind that monstrous train that had begun to appear in her nights of insomnia or of nightmares.

"Mama," she called again. Her voice sounded firm, dispassionate.

The mother didn't respond, or perhaps that was her way of responding. The daughter, maintaining the same indifferent tone, said, "Are you going to call Aunt Antonia today?"

The mother felt obliged to answer.

"No," she said dryly. She remembered Aunt Antonia's affront the week before.

"But, mama, don't dwell on that, it's not worth it, everyone will only get more resentful," replied the daughter, barely controlling the indignation she was beginning to feel.

"I called her last Saturday and she kept us waiting all day," said the mother, now perfectly convinced that she was justified. "You can call her if you like," she added disdainfully.

The daughter didn't respond. It was pointless. Aunt Antonia' quarrel was with her mother. Therefore, she would have to call. But she wasn't going to. It was useless to insist.

The mother had moved her head to the side in a gesture of resignation and abandon. She preferred to risk losing all with Aunt Antonia. After having lost so many things, one more hardly mattered. She preferred to persist in her loneliness, to withdraw definitively, to raise protective barriers. It was clearly useless to insist. Besides, that first urgent need to fill the house with people had passed by now. And a visit from Aunt Antonio would be no more than what it had always been: a substitute, an imitation, a pretense that didn't suffice to fill, not even for a few hours, an emptiness for which, in the end, there was no remedy.

"That's all right, forget it," murmured the daughter.

The mother, expecting another response altogether, turned around, amazed. She had been prepared for an angry reaction and, instead, found herself with that unexpected meekness and, at the same time, saw on her daughter's face a kind of strange, absorbed serenity that contrasted with the near-anguish of a moment before. Something was happening within her that the mother just barely managed to discern. "She's had another vision," she said to herself. And she remembered the first call that had startled her when the daughter burst into the room. And that call began to resonate in her mind like a plea for help from someone drowning. And her daughter's pale face seemed to be that of a drowning person. Thus, the blind impulse to save her was stronger than her resentment or her rancor, and though she didn't understand very well what relationship there might exist between that sudden need for a visit from Aunt Antonia and the dark suffering eating away at her, giving in to a tactic she suspected would be worthless, she said almost without thinking, "I'll call her."

The daughter watched her turn slowly and move toward the door. That decision weighed heavily on her. She didn't want to make the call. Seeing her like that, hands folded over her stomach, footsteps slow and hesitant, she asked herself if at the age of sixty-eight, or rather, after sixty-eight years of living, people still had a right to vanity, or even to dignity.

"It would be better if you didn't," said the daughter.

The mother stopped for a moment, as though relieved. But then she continued walking to the phone.

"I've thought it over carefully, mama. Don't call her. Let this be a lesson to her. In the end she'll give in," she said, following her. She restrained her gently by the arm and the mother agreed, allowing herself to be stopped, freed from guilt now.

"Come, mama, it's already late, we should have lunch. Papa won't be coming," she added, guiding her to the staircase.

They went downstairs and the mother murmured, by way of consolation. "She'll call in the end. And if she doesn't come, her daughters will. You'll see." The daughter didn't hear her.

Now they were seated in the living room, facing one another. The mother dozed with a rosary in her lap. Her breathing was calm, even. Hot sunlight shone obliquely through the window, casting its rays on the velvet furniture, changing it from scarlet to crimson. In the hallway the light that came from the back of the house acquired a blue-gray tint as it mixed with the shadows of the high ceiling. In all of that silence, one periodically heard, like an echo, footsteps or voices, neighborhood children joking with one another, long-haired and casually dressed according to the latest styles. At one point the mother woke up and asked if anyone had come. At another, she found the courage to say, "If they do come, it would be better not to mention last night."

"Whatever for?" responded the daughter. "It was a nightmare."

A little later, the mother suggested that they go see what was on TV.

"I'll stay here," said the daughter. The mother left.

After a little while, the old woman came back and said, "Would you like a cup of coffee?"

"No," the daughter said.

The afternoon changed from an intense yellow to orange, then to blue and later to violet. It was time, then, to turn the lights on.

The father returned when it was already very late. The mother had waited for him in a perpetual state that got worse with each passing car, with each sound coming from the street. The daughter, in her room, heard him come in as he came in almost every Saturday: a little tipsy, humming the first bars of the same old *yaraví*. His severe, customary authority, that habitual solemn, preoccupied air, was affected by drink—and affected, according to the mother, by his friends' advice—changing to a deaf belligerence, a little lazy and malicious, that never went beyond reproaches, naturally, always aimed at the mother and never fully stated, and that the daughter had no interest in deciphering. Now, as always when the father arrived in that state, she heard them argue, say things, accuse one another, perhaps. All in half-words and at a volume that was never as low as they would have wished. At times, however, the father shouted. At times the mother was unable to suppress, between one sob and another, her protests. The daughter listened to them in her dark room, without knowing if it was anger or pity she felt. She wanted to go to them, to tell them to be quiet, not to waste like that the time left to them, and to tell the father to stop making demands of life now, as she had done, and to tell the mother to stop crying, as she had done, but the certainty of not being able to penetrate their world, of being unable to break that intricate game of obsessions, kept her in her room, immobile and with her fists clenched, listening in silence to that battle that was as decrepit as its protagonists.

At last the parents were quiet. And the night began to sound with a uniform buzz. And the noise of cars and pedestrians gradually diminished. And it was the time of insomnia. Of the perfect lucidity of insomnia. The time of abysses and of anguish. And then she saw herself as though she were someone else. And she suffered with and felt pity for that other person who was herself. She saw her situation clearly: the blocked tunnel, the dead end road, a life consecrated to burying that old couple, beings, like her, from another time, who were united now only by the memory of love. After them blackness would follow, the certain night, there wouldn't be time for anything anymore. Then she had an overwhelming urge to pray that pagan prayer that was hers alone, and not to a merciless Christ from on high. She closed her eyes in the dark and devoutly accepted that inner summons, that blessed absorption, that profound internalization that she poured over herself, that she poured over herself from within, allowing it to discover its own silence, its own darkness, the true and not the false silence and darkness outside. And thus she was able to think about that distant country about which she knew nothing except that it was distant and warm, perhaps, and about which she could only sometimes think.

She was pulled from that ecstasy by the train's first whistle. It was so far off that at first she thought she had merely imagined it. But the whistle sounded again. She got up quickly and began to dress. And she had no time for fear because something broke loose in her soul and it was like a scale suddenly off balance and pointing in an unforeseen direction, nor did she have time to go to the wardrobe to take anything along from there because the train was approaching now at a dizzying rate among puffs of vapor and the deafening roar of powerful machinery that pounded and rattled like the reckless rhythms of her own heart and her gasping breath, all of that as she ran through the house in order to catch the train that came for her, there was no doubt that it came for her, because now she heard it approaching and heard the movements of the pistons slow and the brakes sound, so she stopped running and began to walk, almost at a normal pace now, and she took time to arrange her blouse and to smooth her hair just as she reached the door and opened it.

JUAN ANDRADE HEYMANN
(Quito, 1945)

Something of a child prodigy, Juan Andrade Heymann burst on the literary scene at sixteen years of age with a surprising collection of stories, *Cuentos extraños* (1961) that broke with the realist tradition in Ecuadorian literature and linked the author to that precursor of the Latin American vanguard, Pablo Palacio (1906-1947). *Coros* (1965), the author's poetry collection, as surprising as the stories published earlier that same year in *El largato en la mano*, confirmed his gifts as a sarcastic humorist of irreverent, iconoclastic literature. His published works also include other, lesser story collections, as well as plays and articles.

The collection *Veinteséis años de vacaciones* (1988) brings together works written between 1985 and 1988. The novel *Las tertulias de San Li Tun* (1993) is a repetition of the formula found in *El largato en la mano*, and thus lacks originality.

Andrade involuted from the deliciously irresponsible texts in *Cuentos extraños*, *Coros*, and *El largato en la mano* to the deadend of socialist realism that characterizes *La erección de San Fernandito*, *Anécdotas de vuelta y media* (1973), *Cuentos del día siguiente*, and other works. He has yet to achieve in his more recent works the quality of his early stories and poems.

THE GATOR IN THE HAND*

It's exactly twenty-six days today since she abandoned
me. Though maybe not exactly twenty-six days. But
don't assume the fact that I may be wrong about a few
hours more or less is due to carelessness. My conscien-
tious nature would not allow me to offer a fact that
would alter crude reality. The thing is, I don't have a
clock. And if there's anyone who's not sorry about
that, I am that anyone. I hate clocks, and I especially
hate alarm clocks.

When I said that on that winter morning a month
ago I suffered a terrible disappointment at her leaving,
I refer to my muse. I hope to be able to express the
magnitude of the nightmare that the separation has
caused my impressionable personality. It was martyrdom, agony. At first my shattered nerves couldn't bear
the slightest stimulation. At any sound, no matter how
faint, I felt a violent shock such that, when Klaus
dropped a glass, I fainted. Fortunately, the incident
had no further repercussions, since it was an unbreakable glass. And I say "was" because now, at this date,

---

*From the collection *El lagarto en la mano,* 1965.

it no longer is: It ended up breaking, one afternoon, in particularly spectacular circumstances. Klaus (I'm talking about my friend who, strange though it seem, is not related, not even distantly, to Mao-Tse-Tung), Klaus and I had been drinking lemonade in one of those critical spiritual moments of artistic solidarity. As we exchanged laudatory phrases regarding our past creations, we managed to empty the nineteenth pitcher of lemonade. I, by way of expressing my gratitude for his sensitive critique of my poem "Othello," delivered a panegyric to his best painting, an exquisite still life titled "My Mother-in-Law Eating Peanuts," when I suddenly noticed something inexplicable in his behavior. It was like a presage of the tremendous drunkenness that would seize him in the minutes following. In order to disguise my concern, I continued to assert that the Othello of my composition was not treated very well. (I note here that the Othello in question has nothing to do with that other; we are dealing in this case with the *concierge's* little Pekinese.) Klaus, who had lost all interest in what I was saying, went to the window and, sitting on the sill, began to sing an old ballad. It was a fact: His brain was imprisoned in citric acid. I'll never forget how overwhelmed I was with each one of his precarious swayings. His eyes danced with astonishing rapidity. His long arms rocked giddily. His head moved in a closed circuit. His entire being shook with atrocious spasms. Poor Klaus, I always suggested that he not drink more than seven liters of lemonade. Finally, the famous unbreakable glass he had in his hand slipped from his grasp, and he, most imprudently, tried to catch it. I approached to observe. The two objects fell with the speed of a bolt of lightening. It was the first opportunity I'd ever had to verify gravity's force of attraction on a respectable scale. Moved, I decided that from then on the Earth would enjoy my deepest respect. With the great anxiety so characteristic of me in situations of this sort, I sat down on the sofa, stretched my legs over two cushions, removed a hair from my trousers, loosened my tie, and sneezed two-and-a-half times. Counting on my fingers, I did the math: I lived on the tenth floor. I thought, thus, of the enormous difficulty I would have gathering up the fragments and splinters of my friend. There was nothing for it but to get a vacuum cleaner. Nevertheless, in light of the capricious events I have just related, I nodded off. Through half-closed eyelids, as though with affected carelessness, I was able to see the apartment door opening. I was stupefied, immobilized, dumbfounded. There appeared Klaus, Olympian and calm, thin and emaciated. Yes. It was he, the true friend who will go to whatever lengths necessary to maintain intact the ties of fellowship. My comrade, in spite of having fallen from a formidable height, had no misgivings about returning as though nothing had happened. I hurled myself forward to receive him, I grabbed with ardor his long nose and twisted it several times, to convince myself that he wasn't a ghost.

"Hard head!" I shouted with genuine spontaneity.

"Hello."

"It that all you can say?"

"What else?"

"You're all right? You're not damaged?"

"My legs hurt a bit…"

"That's all?"

"That's all. Since the elevator's not working, I had

to walk up the stairs. You know how exhausting that is, with my arthritis."

"Klaus, please react!"

"Who? Me?"

"But what's wrong with you? You disappoint me. Talk, tell me about it, the details."

"Do you think that something extraordinary happens when one comes up the stairs? Well, it doesn't. It's just an interminable series of steps."

I was overcome by a painful uneasiness.

"Your apathy causes me a great deal of anguish," I said. "You know very well what I'm talking about. Tell me, why are you alive?"

"Because I'm not dead…"

"Damn you! But why aren't you dead?"

"Why? The truth? It's not my fault."

"So it's a mystery? I don't understand: ten floors, ten…"

"Ahhh! You want me to explain the part about the fall?"

"Evidently."

"Why didn't you say so?"

"Fine, fine… Don't try my patience…"

"It was really very simple: The fall began normally, but after some fractions of a second, I felt a ringing in my ears…and then, bang!"

"Bang! And then?"

"Well, what a surprise! Guess where I found myself."

"On the ground."

"No. In the arms of an old woman. She smiled at me sweetly and said: 'Don't let this happen again, young man…' Then she set me down gently on the sidewalk, gave me a card, and continued on her way."

"That's very rare, these day, people behaving so courteously."

"Very true."

"And what did the card say?"

"I haven't looked at it yet."

Klaus pulled out of his pocket a small card that said:
                    AGENT ZP-19753
                    SALVATION ARMY

"I was lucky," he exclaimed.

"It's extraordinary," I responded. "It's an extraordinary adventure and truly inexpensive."

"That it is, in fact…"

Before saying another word, I took precautions. I went to the window and closed it.

"Yes, extraordinarily inexpensive, dear Klaus: You owe me only fifteen cents."

"But, why?"

"That's what I paid for my unbreakable glass."

JAVIER VÁSCONEZ
(Quito, 1946)

Javier Vásconez studied literature and philosophy at the University of Navarra and, subsequently, in Paris. He has dedicated his life to literature as writer, editor, and bookseller.

The author's published story collections include *Ciudad lejana* (1982), *El hombre de la Mirada oblícua* (winner of the Joaquín Gallegos Lara Prize awarded by the city of Quito, 1989), *Café concert* (1995), *El secreto* (1996), and *Un extraño en el Puerto* (1998). In 1983, the short story entitled "Angelote, amor mío" was awarded an honorable mention in the short story contest sponsored by *Revista Plural*, a Mexican cultural magazine.

Vásconez has written two novels, *El viajero de Praga* (México, 1996) and *La sombra del apostador* (1999).

His stories have been translated into English, French, and German, and have been included in virtually all contemporary Ecuadorian short story anthologies.

Vásconez is an implacable narrator who makes no aesthetic or ethical concessions in his works. His stories and novels, profound, charged with obsessions, are not limited to the exploration of decadence of a social class. His characters inhabit the city of Quito as they would a jail cell, and carry within a heavy load of guilt. Thus, whether they are in Quito, Barcelona, or Prague, they cannot escape from themselves. Like Onetti's characters, those created by Vásconez know that they have been found guilty and are able to free themselves only in dreams or in subversive acts, though the understanding they achieve as a result may not be the liberation sought. The author's most recent works transform the writer into a character, turning him and the world in which he lives into a fiction, with channels of communication opened between characters, thus converting fiction itself into the only world possible, and the only world in which it is possible to live. It may be that what we have in Vásconez's fiction is the search for the absolute narrative.

A STRANGER IN THE PORT*

for Iván Oñáte

1

At that hour, when the sky turns orange, one tells one-self so many stories, so many ports and ships setting sail, silent in the dawn, that the images begin to spin, overwhelming and confusing, like a movie in a quiet cinema, and then the ideas settle down little by little until they form a wall of silent, solitary confinement with the city. Now, when I've poured myself the first whiskey of the evening, after having given myself over to the flow of that story that begins with the ship's foghorn sounding in the mist of the port, though in that city there never was a port. Nevertheless, the boat had already come alongside the docks, sounding its foghorn again. Now I can confirm that the café was deserted, because there was nobody to follow from the gloom the movements of the ships at dawn.

I was anxiously awaiting the arrival of someone at that hour, maybe the sudden return of the protagonist who would appear sooner or later, that much I knew,

*From the collection *Un extraño en el puerto*, 1998.

walking in the rain, and I thought that maybe instead of a man, it would be a woman, with a wasted face, shiny, as though she had just been crying, but there wasn't a single visitor that made this story possible, nor a woman waving a handkerchief from the docks.

From the study I could see the arrival of a ship flying the flag of Italy, coming in very slowly in the Andean night. Each time I poured another whisky, something I did often, I imagined the breakwater and the lighthouse that completed, together with the seagulls, the detailed sketch of the port. It was then that I saw a man walking quickly toward the tavern and, after glancing furtively to either side as though he feared someone might be watching, checking his coat pockets and then taking an envelope from one of them.

Meanwhile, the boat from New York had dropped anchor, without a sound, as silent as an elephant about to fall asleep. A current of wet, salty air evoked within distant resonances. On seeing the port facilities, as impersonal as those of Hamburg or Shanghai, I realized that I was looking at a familiar landscape.

From the very beginning, I knew that the man's presence was no coincidence, though it took me a minute to understand that he wasn't there so that the customs officials would see him go into the immigration offices, nor so that I would calmly tell his story. Now he had left the dock and was at the immigration office, as alone as the first time he came to the city. I doubted his existence in the days that followed, and that he might have a life of his own, but he had returned to remind me that that was not the case.

I had gone too far, because the man was vulnerable in that lonely port, and he had the enigmatic air of the recently arrived. I could follow him anywhere and observe him from a bar. No doubt I was playing at being a controlling god, somewhat base, even: I knew so much about that man that sometimes I surprised and embarrassed myself, but there was nothing I could do now because the die had already been cast.

I remained in bed, with a cigarette burning in the ashtray and a book by Patrick Modiano open on the pillow. At the foot of the night table, a shaft of light from the lamp fell on the books piled carelessly on the carpet. There was no sound from the street. All I wanted to do was to finish this story, which could have happened in any port and perhaps was about to begin: A traveler who has just come off a boat remains for a moment on the docks, the breeze blows his hair as, his step firm, he heads for the immigration offices, but no one is there to meet him in spite of the fact that he has been dragging his misfortune from Prague.

As night falls the spell begins, the uninterrupted line of rain, and then one starts to tell oneself stories in order to be able to sleep and so that ordinary life in the port city will begin to make sense: The deafening sound of the cranes hoisted against the sky, the ship surrounded by grease stains, and the glow of streetlights diminished by the fog were taking on the consistency of a nightmare. And so I continued drinking and attributing to solitude this emptiness contracted in childhood. It was enough to be able to imagine and share with someone that accordion music played in the port tavern. I no longer cared what would come later because I was certain that I knew the story of the girl abandoned by her father, so I turned the course of my thoughts her way.

"She's a little touched in the head," Señora Maruja said when one morning I went down to buy bread and Maria had just left with a newspaper under her arm.

Maria was fat and freckled, and as vulnerable as her eyes softened by the morning light. Though they had lost their initial glow, there must have been a time when they were innocent.

"She seems fine," I said, "Is she an orphan?"

"No, she has grandparents. I imagine she's a burden for them. First she went off with an Englishman who wandered the Amazon with a cat. Then with a singer they call the Sicilian."

After that, every time I ran into her at Señora Maruja's, and when I saw her wandering around the neighborhood, I invented a past for her because, like most people, she probably had a double life.

One afternoon I looked out the window. She was standing in front of a bookstore, and I saw that she directed a pensive, unforced smile my way, as though she had always known me. She had raised her chin over a car parked at the curb so that I could see her stooping to look at herself in the rearview mirror. She neatly applied lipstick, reaffirming an alliance between the two of us that didn't exist.

At night I began to follow her in my imagination: I absurdly proposed to force the course of events. It would have been impossible to enter into her mind without ending up impregnated by her. There was something vaguely anomalous about her eyes; she conceded only a second to any individual, as though she were guilty of something, or feared being accused. Nostalgia and fear colluded in her, because she lived changed by the indelible memory of her father. While her eyes possessed a clear capacity for tenderness, there was in them a sustained fear, implicit, as though they were threatened by the possibility of a future attack. I searched my books in vain for an illustration with a replica of that face that secreted a sadness as inflamed as it was profound. It was a defensive act on my part, almost gratuitous, since in reality I had no desire to learn Maria's history, though the ghost of her illness hovered in my mind. "When her father announced that he was going to New York, she suffered the first attack," Señora Maruja had told me.

That night I went to eat alone at the Paris. I got home late. Then I was awake until dawn, gazing at the shadow of the tree on the wall of my study and listening to the sounds from the street. Shivering, with my coat buttoned to the collar, I walked to that restaurant open until dawn, where they serve a tasty chicken soup. The place was a disaster and there was little difference between the dirt and the cold inside and the night of misty rain outside. Behind the counter, a man with exhausted eyes gave orders to the waiters. The music was blasted violently into the street where it was extinguished among the glow of the passing cars.

From time to time I interrupted my task, imprisoned in the labyrinth of a story I was writing. I had a bottle of Cutty Sark at hand, with the frigate sailing over the illusory breaking crystal waves: Maybe it was the same story from which I could no longer emerge without the help of the wind pounding tirelessly against my window. Outside, the moon poured its entrails over the interminable night. However, I thought that I ought to slip gently and skillfully into the story.

Time and again I returned to the memory of Maria,

who wasn't surprised on seeing me eating at that restaurant where I went alone to take refuge from insomnia.

Finally, I had before me the steaming chicken soup and was beginning to feel happy, when I saw her playing gaily with her purse in the light from the narrow counter. That place harbored men of the night and Maria had borne with indifference their muttered comments. Neither the enthusiastic expressions nor the foul language directed her way seemed to affect her poise. She laughed when the owner pushed a saucer with change her way. Suddenly she fell silent, as though she were looking into a mirror, clapping her hands in a gesture of innocence. She was wearing a long dress with a full skirt, the lace neckline emphasized even more the bead necklace that gave her the air of an orphan, while her chubby hands pressed the purse against her chest. She stopped two paces from my table. I noted that she was a little stiff, as though she knew that she would not be welcome, and then she leaned toward me to say, "You're Javier Vásconez, the writer. And you usually buy the newspaper at Señora Maruja's."

"So what's the point?"

Maria didn't miss a beat. She had taken a seat, placing her purse between us. She must have felt my uneasiness, because she smiled sweetly as she watched me play with a fork.

Then she dumped the contents of her purse on the table, looking for a tissue to blow her nose.

"I've read some of your books. *El secreto* had me shaking with fear," she said, laughing.

"The critics have a different view."

"Where do your ideas come from?" she asked, her hands resting on the table. "I just write post cards that my dad doesn't answer."

"You write letters?"

"Of course, and then I forget to mail them," she added.

"Writing is just like making a chain," I said. "We invent stories, we write the lives of others because nobody is satisfied with the one he got by chance."

"It must be nice," Maria said, impressed by my words. "It's like living several lives at the same time. There must be a reason for having a sickness. And having a mother dead in an accident and a father living in New York."

"What sickness?" I interrupted softly, filling the glass with beer.

"Don't play games with me," she said shaking her shoulders insolently. "Señora Maruja has told you everything. Including the part about the insane asylum."

She leaned back in the chair, reaching for her purse.

"Yes, she's very talkative," I said.

It's true that a few days before I had relived the scene from the study, I had even thought about including a lie to soften with a magnanimous gesture the episode in the bank, but I refused to do it. I wanted to put a name on the imbecility that made the matter possible. Maria would never forget the deafening growls of the dog, because it continued to bark and to paw victoriously in her head until she woke up in the insane asylum. It's easy to imagine an epileptic fit, anyone who witnesses one can imagine the devastating violence.

"The guy at the bank acted like I had the plague," Maria said, her slow, chubby hands shaking, clasped in anguish on the table. "The idiot went and called the insane asylum."

"There was no reason for that," I agreed.

"Imagine, having a dog at the door."

Going into that hospital must have been like walking around an unknown city, friendless. Maria made an effort not to vomit, disoriented, convinced that she would never get out. And so, when finally they went to get her two weeks later, the city had a powerful odor of earth and seemed to her more familiar and legitimate than ever, although in fact it imitated the sounds, the fleeting shadows of the insane asylum.

"And the Sicilian…"

Maria remained deep in thought, with her hand resting against her chin, making me feel old, as though we had nothing in common. She could leave, or disappear as gently as she had gone into Señora Maruja's, weighed down by the night, leaving me with a memory as ephemeral as the flame of a match. I gazed at the glass, empty now, and wanted to say her name in the cold gloom of the restaurant, but she leaned forward until I felt her breathing next to me.

"You will never understand. The Sicilian was different, he gave me rides on his motorcycle and taught me to sing. For the first time, I was in hotels with ceiling fans and cockroaches crawling on the windowsills. I even ran naked on the sand. And riding on the motorcycle was like being transported, who knows where."

"You like motorcycles?"

"Riding on one is like flying. Imagine, he had a Harley Davidson."

"She pulled out a crushed tissue with lipstick stains on the edges, and she emphasized the shine of her face like an oriental mask. Very calm and happy, she began to blow her nose.

There was nothing I could do for her then, because I didn't even know the man. Maybe she had talked in order to hide what she really wanted to say. Now she was crushed and spiritless, and I realized that she would continue wilting until dawn in a love that was a lie.

"Do you want something to eat?" I asked.

"Soup is for old people," she affirmed. "My grandparents eat a bowl of soup before they go to bed. How awful!"

"We writers are born old," I replied.

"No," Maria said, heatedly. "You're younger than my dad. Though I haven't seen him for a long time."

I had begun to want what her eyes hid when I noticed an expression of sadness there. Suddenly she began to laugh, a loud laugh, without tears, in spite of the fact that the laughter no longer belonged to her, because it had become as indecent and real as the tissue in which she had left her joy.

Now her hair was mussed, and her eyes were shining because she'd guessed what I was thinking. It was very clear to me. I saw her lean forward to whisper something to me, certain of what I was going to say as, shyly, took my hand.

"Yes, kiss me," she said. "Because that's what you want."

She was so close that I couldn't breathe. I kissed her, knowing that when I stopped kissing her she would no longer be with me. Then we stayed there, neither one of us moving, without knowing whether to accept or even to recognize what had happened.

The study was now thick with cigarette smoke. The ashtray on the green cushion was filled with butts. The silence was charged with living, moving shadows. I kept imagining the cargo ship leaving. In the middle of the night, with the light from the bedside table shining in my face, I felt a vague uneasiness whose origins I couldn't identify. I'd begun to get drunk slowly and no longer cared. My hand had slid over to the table, I picked up the glass and the bottle without knowing where I was nor how to continue with Maria's story, because she had once again denied me the possibility of completing her life. Outside, the rain and the street light were reflected against a tree, while a distant murmur began to put me to sleep. Nothing could compare with the vertigo whisky produces, not even the distant sound of foghorns or the mist coming into the port from the sea.

I saw how the man moved slowly, back and forth, standing, finally, deep in thought at the counter, holding his gabardine, valise, and documents in his right hand. Invisible, with a grease stain on his tie, he didn't seem to be going anywhere. He simply blinked, putting his hand in the pocket of his coat while the policeman took his passport and stuck his index finger between two pages. He glanced up at the passenger and asked:

"Are you in transit?"

"Not exactly..."

Then he fell silent. One look at the policeman was enough to put him on the defensive. Suddenly, his self-confidence was gone. It must have taken him a moment to notice the surly, even malicious, note in the policeman's question. That policeman, who was at one and the same time all the policemen he had encountered in his travels, made him feel bad and, perhaps, guilty.

"The resident's permit is in order," he dared to comment.

"Take it easy, doctor," the policeman remarked coldly, the arrogant tone of voice more pronounced, while a dismissive movement of the hand contributed to absolving him of a suspicious past.

"They should give you a new passport. There's aren't any empty pages in this one."

"Yes, you're right," the doctor replied with disinterest.

And so, I went from one end of the story to the other, without understanding what the physician was doing in the port. Now he seemed to be an exile from himself, he hesitated for a moment and then headed for the door, alone, following the desire to continue, as though he were returning to the same starting point from which he had never moved, because he would keep going around, tenacious, until completing the circle. It was like watching a man through binoculars, and when at last the tension had passed, I was annoyed by a nagging suspicion that I had left something out. Maybe the slightly suspicious way he held his bag while the policeman questioned him.

The mist had lifted from the sea and floated in spirals over the port's streetlights. The man went out to the street, finally, got in a taxi, and headed for the Floresta, where Elmer was probably waiting, the prim cat, unscrupulous and taciturn, who was shedding his fur.

2

"What can I do?" Señora Maruja asked one afternoon, her tone forced, when I went to the store to stock up on cigarettes and whisky. "She comes every morning, she eats a bag of figs. And she doesn't stop talking. She treats me as though I were her mother. And she come in with suffering as old as her grandmother's wrinkles."

At the corner, no more than two paces from the store, a leafy Andean cherry tree was blowing in the wind. The warm odors from the garden grew more intense. A web of shadows spun around the wall surrounding the house. The weather was going to change and that night the moon would lazily bare itself again very close to my window.

"Forget about her. She's not a child anymore," I said, putting the bottle into a bag, though I might have been lying.

"She always talks to me about her father," Señora Maruja added, as she worked with a scissors, cutting strips of newspaper she would later use as napkins. "It seems he promised to write, but the letter never arrived. And the poor thing goes around sighing. Besides, there's that Sicilian who rented the back room, in her grandparents house."

"And when did he leave?"

"He took off four years ago," she said, lowering her eyes. She stared at the scissors and the pile of papers on the *Vistazo* magazine. "Nobody loved Maria as much as that man, but he had to leave anyway. He didn't have a job. The grandparents depend on the rent from that room and on their savings to get by.

"What did he do before he left?"

"He repaired TVs. Someone said that he sells shirts now, in New York."

"The attacks came after that?"

I imagined her walking in the Alameda Park with her father, a man who almost certainly couldn't appreciate the devotion in his daughter's look as she leaned against the trunk of a cypress tree, licking an ice cream cone. There probably wasn't anyone else in the park at that hour, and maybe Maria had leaned against the tree with her head turned up toward the man who looked at her, indifferent, smoking.

"It's hard to say when it all began," Señora Maruja concluded. "I don't know if it was before or after. And now she just goes around sighing for a guy who's not worth it."

"And what did he have to do with it?"

"Imagine how it shocked her grandparents when he took her to a beach in Manabí."

"It's obvious that you worry too much about her. The sea does everybody a world of good," I replied, beginning to lose interest in the story.

"The terrible thing was when she got back," she said, straightening up in her chair.

"That guy, is he from Sicily?"

"No, he's from Ibarra."

To get away from Señora Maruja, the park where father and daughter had taken a walk, the man who made the sea possible for her, all I had to do was cross the street."

Maybe there was something Señora Maruja wasn't telling me. She was as cautious as someone who was about to change her mind. That's why she didn't mention what I already knew: the history of that man, given that as far as she was concerned the Sicilian was an imposter.

It's may be that everything began in a bed in a hotel room. The lovers must have been holding hands under the wrinkled sheets that smelled like someone else had already slept on them. The boots cracked at the toe and tossed next to the chair, the poncho from Argentina and the guitar leaning against the wall. In the middle of the night, awake and beside herself with fear, Maria probably concentrated on watching the face of the man who snored at her side, a man wasted by alcohol, sleeping under the sad, accusing sound of the rain, as though she were not herself but what love must be.

Thinking back on those hotels, her suspicions must have been confirmed, I thought, lowering my gaze to the ashtray, where I touched the ash with my fingers and even brought it, perversely, to my nose, suspecting that Señora Maruja was right. At the time, I had deliberately, meticulously set the scene in all those filthy rooms where she woke up at dawn, overwhelmed by fear. Involuntarily, she had touched the sheets, while she felt under her fingertips the almost invisible trail left by a cockroach, but when she sought protection in the arms of the man whose hoarse, melodic voice she admired, she found herself face to face with a stranger who could offer her only the pretense of love.

"The guy was a bum," Señora Maruja told me two days later, as she stacked cans of tuna on the shelves. She was only seventeen and already she'd complicated her life.

"Maybe she liked going to those hotels with him," I said.

"That came to an end, but the fits returned. And

now all she does is wait for a letter and the next fit. The sickness has become so cruel that it's turned her into a sleepwalker."

"Maybe it was the love she felt for the man," I objected, taking a cigarette out of the pack.

On the days following, while I alternated working in the bookstore and in the solitude of my study, I tried to guess the cause of her illness. I decided to ignore the belief in genetic causes and superstitions about the moon. Little by little I modified my inquiries, until reaching not so much the causes but the terror that the ailment produces in its victims: I was certain that I'd entered a dangerous tunnel, where time didn't exist, as though the bridge spanning the banks of a river had collapsed, leaving travelers incommunicado.

I remembered the first time I saw her, sitting at the counter in the store. Her face was turned toward the morning light, her lips tight with fear, and a nervous hand grasped the beads of her cheap necklace. In Maria's wasted eyes shown an intelligence, an ability to see through things. At times as she watched us out of the corner of her eye, and her features seemed to vanish in a confused expression. The absence was as brief and fragmented as a flash of lightening. It lasted no more than a few seconds, but during that time Maria was no longer with us.

That was part of the horror, the inability to land at the port so longed for and perhaps forever out of reach, after having traveled without memory through an unknown land. It was as though she remained exposed to the shame of walking naked through those lands so that when she returned she remembered nothing, except for the fact of having lost in the crossing several hours of her life. When she was in the most violent stage of a fit, the crisis doubtlessly occupied the privileged status of ceremony. She must have hated those spasms. They're coming now, she would say to herself, without daring to scream from the threshold of fear.

That's what I must have supposed the morning I found her talking to Señora Maruja, because the fear was like a long corridor that disappeared in the darkness of her throat.

Where was she going to end up when she collapsed in the throes of an attack? What strange ports and lands did her delirious mind touch during those moments? I imagined her defenseless, surrendering to the inevitable: the fat body stiff while she tore at her blouse. The fit began with a loss of consciousness, and she collapsed, biting her tongue until it bled. It was as though the blood were the only towline she had, the lifesaver in the face of an inevitable shipwreck, because accepting the forgetting meant cutting herself off from life. Her face must have been white and suffering, her eyes fixed on her grandmother, given that every illness needs an interlocutor to exist.

Maria wasn't completely alone during the attacks because the illness kept her company. On slipping into the home stretch, after having fallen into the vertigo of the convulsions, a radical change came over her. Finally, she found herself face to face with something she knew and maybe loved too much: the moon's embrace. I imagined her, then, fulfilling the blood ritual, naked, with her breasts facing the night, exposing herself without shame to danger, as though she wanted to be possessed by an unknown hand. I imagined that she must have had a servile relationship with the sickness, though no doubt more legitimate than with love, because during those journeys she maintained a long and lasting tie with death.

3

Maybe I was falling in love with her, given that I spent the afternoon changing her features. It was as though the excitement shining in her eyes had erased the nearness of the rain, knowing that the afternoon was lost, since Maria wouldn't be coming back. She had no reason to give me what my fantasy wanted, a childish illusion, since everything had been buried the moment my lips kissed hers.

I raised the collar of my coat and headed for home. Because of the rain, I had to take refuge at Señora Maruja's. I greeted her as I picked up a package of cookies, but as I made my way to the cooler to get a beer, I heard her measured comment at my back:

"The weather is nasty. It's going to rain all night. Look at the street," she said, indicating the mud at the curbs, but without taking her hand out from under the shawl.

"Yes, we're going to have rain for a long time."

"And more leaks in the roof," she commented.

"Tell me about the Sicilian, Señora Maruja," I said, looking her in the eye.

"Ah, so you're getting interested," she replied. And with a gesture of indignation she said, "I don't like to make assumptions, but that guy isn't going to be back. Better for Maria, because if the affair had gone on much longer…"

"What do you mean?"

"She's not going to recover from what he did to her."

"Don't forget that she was already sick before he came along, Señora Maruja."

"He had the motorcycle and the guitar, her reasons to go on living."

"Yes, he had the answers," I concluded.

The dim lights of the port were softening until they formed an imaginary line in my mind. All that remained was the confused, arbitrary illusion of what might have been a fantasy. The night had heightened the mystery and served only to make me fill my head with whisky, after having surrendered to the solitary whim of simulating Dr. Kronz's return to the Andean city, carrying a bag and maybe a letter for Maria. Little by little, the screams of the seagulls, the smell of the sea, and the proximity of the ships faded, giving way easily to the first light of day. I wanted to continue surrounded by the nighttime lights of the port, contemplating the skeletons of the boats, imagining them in all their splendor, because I refused to believe that they would be lost in the morning and for all time.

I got up and removed the whiskey bottle from the night table. Then I made coffee and went to the window. On opening it, I confirmed that the wind had anticipated the dazzling morning light. To my right, the light was gaining ground and forming eddies that contrasted with the violet and gray backdrop of the sky. An almost impalpable stratum, as thin as a covering of frost, had spread and was lighting up the city. Now it was tinted with the same violet and orange tone with which old love letters are written.

I stayed at the window, smoking a cigarette, very still. It was years since I had had the sensation of being displaced, but when at last the city emerged from the shadows to remain suspended under an orange arch, I experienced a momentary peace: I understood that I was on the threshold of happiness, because that soothing light had been prepared for me.

Then I saw her crossing the street, in no hurry, her hair uncombed as though she'd just gotten up. From the sidewalk she looked anxiously at the open window and signaled for me to come down. I left by the kitchen door that leads to the garden with the fig tree. Señora Maruja came in, her lips tight, nervous, shaking her head. The fig tree's perfume was mixed with the wind. For a moment it seemed as unmistakable and contagious as the memory of Maria, when she woke me up in the middle of the night with the dazzling vision of her eyes and I felt for her a compassion that grew in the gloom of my study.

Señora Maruja didn't give me time to say hello. Instead, she greeted me with a weak, sad smile as she pointed to the corridor.

"Please, the telephone," she said quickly. "Maria had another fit. Her grandparents' telephone is out of order. You have to call a doctor."

As I went to the phone, she sat on the stairs and began to play with her hair, fashioning a braid that half-covered her shoulders. I recognized Dr. Kronz's voice on the phone, assuring me that he would be over in ten minutes.

Then I went to the bathroom. I left the bedroom door open in order to hear the sounds from the street: I quickly brushed my teeth while running a comb through my hair. I thought that the doctor had exaggerated, but when I looked out the window I saw his old Mercury parked at the curb across the street.

Very slowly, carrying the same bag with the metal handles that I'd seen the night before in the port, he looked up from the street to find the number of the house. He wore the same blue pinstriped suit, the same shirt with the cuffs extending beyond the sleeves of his jacket. Then he followed the stone path until he came to the old woman who was waiting for him next to the geraniums at the door.

I noted the pain in the faces of the old couple when we entered Maria's house; they appeared to be living a nightmare. The grandmother, barefoot and sobbing, grasped the doctor's hand, and he discretely accepted her affliction. Dressed in a wool robe frayed at the edges, the old man attempted to maintain his dignity, furiously cleaning the ashes in the fireplace. Señora Maruja asked his if he would like anything. The old man got up from the fireplace and went to the bathroom. The air reeked of cologne. The first thing I saw was a ray of light imprisoned between the bulky round ochre figure in the bathtub and the rod that held the curtain stained with humidity around the edges. The doctor walked without a sound to the sink and placed his bag on the wooden bench. Behind me, I heard the convulsive sob of the old woman.

"How could I sleep if Maria was late getting back last night," the grandmother said with a sigh. "I asked her if she wanted anything. She was very pale, I know that look."

She stood there in the doorway while Señora Maruja held her head against her breast. The doctor leaned over the bathtub. Then he rolled up the cuffs of his shirt and put his hands in the water. The tub was filled with blood. Then I saw the doctor's hands struggle with Maria's inert body. She had fallen, stricken by an attack as violent and sweet as blood and love, because she had been unable to resist that connection with which she was clearly condemned to live, because the intensity of that love begun so many years ago was absolute and forever.

The doctor turned suddenly and asked me to help, while he carefully held Maria's head. I didn't want to make an excuse to avoid the horror of seeing the naked body that rested in the water. Her hair was wet and her cheeks coated with a stiff layer of blood, though she breathed without difficulty. I heard a cavernous sound in her throat. Her large breasts floated like moons, very round and drifting, making waves on the surface of the water in the tub. The doctor breathed heavily as he held her under the arms. Finally, we carried her down the hallway and put her on a rug in the living room. A bright, reddish stain spread along the floorboards.

Now Maria's face was serene. Her eyes fixed on some distant point and that gave her features a mysterious truth. She seemed to have voluntarily chosen that sleeping state to avoid the futile waiting for something that would never come.

Bent over the sink, his neck red from the effort, the doctor's face was clearly reflected in the mirror. After washing his hands, he straightened the cuffs of his shirt and turned to look for something in his bag.

"And so... What are we going to do?" the old woman asked him.

"Nothing. There's nothing to be done," the doctor replied dryly, ripping open the package with the syringe and examining the contents of the ampoule.

"We have to wait until she comes to. I'm going to give her a sedative to relieve the muscle pain."

To my left, Señora Maruja murmured, "Where does she go when she's not with us?"

The doctor bent over to give her the shot and the expression on his face softened around the cheeks.

"Believe me, this is killing us," the grandfather said, his voice almost inaudible. "They said it could be controlled, but with the way she lives. She gets to bed late. She drinks…"

"She should take care of herself. Alcohol isn't good for her," the doctor responded, closing his bag.

Suddenly the voices became unreal. There was a moment during which I confused the gray pigeons in the neighborhood with the seagulls in the port. Then there grew in me the inevitable need to invent, when I saw the doctor walking again along the docks, carrying the bag in which he most certainly had a letter for Maria.

Amazed and delighted by the turn events had taken, with the certainty that at last I had acted freely, beyond my imagination, I knew that at that moment the doctor could just as well be in a hospital as landing in some distant port where a ship would probably be about to weigh anchor.

Señora Maruja left the house, promising to return at midday with a bag of rolls. Maria had moved her arm under the blanket, though her look was still lost as though she didn't want to recognize anyone. The grandfather had been studying me as he stroked Maria's face.

"Excuse me, I haven't had the pleasure."

"I'm a neighbor," I told him.

After they paid his fee, the doctor took his leave, satisfied and thankful. Nodding his head slightly, he put the check in a pocket of his jacket. That was when I approached and asked him if he had brought the letter for Maria.

"I don't understand. What are you talking about?" he asked me, perplexed.

Then I went home, taking care not to go by way of Señora Maruja's. I walked calmly, without looking at the cars that passed by on the street. There was only the city with its houses and its grimy neighborhood pigeons. I stopped at the door and lit a cigarette. Though the doctor hadn't brought the letter, I listened to the foghorn howling in the distance, persuasive, like a boat that at that very moment would be docking in the port. The waves kept rolling in, tirelessly, and most certainly dragging paper and bits of wood to the edges of the seawall, because there, where the high plateau and the Andean city began, I heard the foghorn again.

JORGE DÁVILA VÁZQUEZ
(Cuenca, 1947)

This prolific short story writer has also created plays, poetry, and novels.

The author's story collections include *El círculo vicioso* (1977), *Los tiempos del olvido* (1977), *Narraciones* (with Eliécer *Cárdenas*, 1979), *Relatos imperfectos* (1980), *Este mundo es el camino* (1981, winner of the Aurelio Espinosa Pólit Award for 1980), *Cuentos de cualquier día* (1983), *Las criaturas de la noche* (1985), *El dominio escondido* (1992), and *Cuentos breves y fantásticos* (1994).

He has published two novels and three novellas: *María Joaquina en la vida y en la muerte* (winner of the Aurelio Espinosa Pólit Literary Award, 1976), *De rumores y de sombras* (three novellas, 1991), and *La vida secreta* (1999).

Dávila´s three poetry collections include *Nueva canción de Eurídice y Orfeo* (1975), *Acerca de los Angeles* (prose poem, 1995), and *Memoria de la poesía y otros textos* (1999).

The author´s essays are entitled, *Ecuador, hombre y cultura* (1990) and César Dávila Andrade, *combate poético y suicidio* (1998).

Finally, he is the author of three plays, *El caudillo anochece* (1968), *Con gusto a muerte* (1981), and *Espejo roto* (1990).

His stories have been translated into English, French, and German, and included in many anthologies.

Jorge Dávila Vásquez is an indefatigable writer, whose world is one of small lives lived in the provinces, characterized by hidden passions, hypocrisies, and religious faith. His best writing is found in stories of the intimate, delicate, humorous, and, occasionally, sordid facets of life. Recently, he has begun to experiment with fantastic tales and prose poems.

THE SILENT FLIRTATION*

for Diego Araujo Sánchez

It all began when cousin Lety arrived.

That cousin whom the entire family had turned into a fount of silence.

If someone said, for example, Cousin Alberto's daughters are Lucia, Rosita, and that other one, it was clear who "that other one" was, because even her name had dissolved in waters of pretense, tersely.

At first, neither Rafaela nor Elida was able to understand the why of that sudden silence, of that uncertain omission, of those hypocritical coughs that surrounded like a screen a nearly invisible relative; nor did they understand the reasons for a forgetting that even mutilated photographs, leaving dreadful, inexplicable holes, made dates imprecise and sowed contradictions in conversations on the topic.

Lety had become visible the time the grandmother, half dotty on occasion, said something like, the poor

*From the collection *El mundo es un camino*, 1981.

girl, Lord knows why, suddenly, maybe art, perhaps those who dedicate themselves to acrobatics and the mountebank's trade, well, that one, no, or at least I don't think they could be very honest, but that, in the end, those were things you found even in the best families.

So Cousin Levy wasn't very honest! It was a revelation that came to their lives during a fidgety time, filled with mistrust and surprises, that had them divining mysteries at every turn and in all that before had been innocent, unimportant, routine; that had them running to the window the moment they heard the sound of an auto stopping or passing by in the street, the moment they sensed the footstep of someone expected, who never arrived except in their imaginations, the moment the doorbell sounded, as though the woman who brought the milk every day or the man who delivered the vegetables announced an unreal and magical presence. A time of sighs for no reason, of languid looks and photos of movie stars prolifically clipped and devoutly saved between the pages of history notebooks or an algebra text by Baldor.

And, soon after the revelation, suddenly, bang, like a bolt of lightening in a field of wheat, the telegram "tomorrow, that one, Lety." She, the cousin in person, and not alone, no.

She introduced him as "a friend." He took a room at the Hotel Margarita. He was blond, tall, with a boyish face and lips reminiscent of hidden photos, a moustache that evoked unmotivated sighs and a bearing that brought to mind excited little dashes to the balcony.

Elida and Rafaela decided very soon that Cousin Lety, in spite of being enchanting, of using expensive cosmetics and fine perfumes, in spite of those eyes so thoroughly trained that they could turn into fans of rubendariesque poems and also open ever so wide and remain fixed like those of a gentle calf; in spite of her dresses of sumptuous fabrics, her gestures like those of an actress on stage, and her way of talking reminiscent of the lovers in the radio soap operas they were so familiar with, in spite of everything, she was old.

Old, yes sir, ahhh, and he, so handsome, my God, his face so innocent, that you wanted to take care of him, to cuddle him, so attractive, so…

"He's refined, your little friend," the grandmother said, with a tone halfway between sly and satisfied. "Gentle, he has good manners."

And the two adolescent cousins looked at one another with a smile in those eyes of sun-drenched water.

The first visits of the lovely Don Diego—that's what they called him, taking advantage of his limited knowledge of literature in their games of near-love—were of the utmost courtesy and distance. But little by little the atmosphere filled with blazing birds, bluebottles, and dragonflies that swam on the surface of warm, silent ponds smelling of hollyhock and orange blossoms.

Of course, only four persons in that house breathed that air of birds, insects, and orange blossom whispers: Diego, Leticia, and those who were perhaps responsible for generating them, Elida and Rafaela, who said no more than a word here and there, barely smiled, brushed against the back of Diego's hand on passing, like that, as though by accident, or let their hair down in the presence of the guest, with an ingenuous, innocent, and malicious gesture; or licked their fresh lips, perversely; all in the midst of a pleasure and a gloating that they were unable to explain to themselves, nor did they wish to, laughing, whispering, sweet, honeycombed, in the dense perfume of the morning honey.

Diego, who did little more than smile, half ignorant of the game that enveloped him and half flattered, secretly flattered.

And Leticia, who was beside herself, who was unable to hide the bitterness, the anguish, that so much youth produced in her, such an extravagance of life, and who began to remind the girls of those formidable women in books, who kill for love or out of jealousy, those women who in old paintings appeared with eyes very like hers in one of the photos she'd taken out of her album of artistic memories to show them.

The other members of the family continued to live in another world in which not a single bird of illusion seemed to flutter, not a single butterfly left a bit of fine dust frivolous and silvery on eyelashes; a world, in short, in which the only dragonfly capable of adding a brief touch of sonority, the only bluebottle that flew about with a black and sparkling buzz was the grandmother in whispers with one of the uncles or aunts, about the extreme youth of Lety's little friend, about the way she gazed at him, almost with veneration, the same way she had looked at the saints when she was a child, and he, as indifferent as those very same saints, no?, about the finery of the girl, what are you talking about mamita, girl, girl, how can she be a girl if I'm forty years old and she, she's so elegant, no?, such expensive clothes, no?, and the smell, that woman does indeed smell like they say in *Don Quijote*, of amber and civet, though we wouldn't know the one from the other. Ay, mamita, you're not taking your medicine, there you go again, talking nonsense. There's nothing to be done about old age.

But apart from that insect muttering, everyone apparently immune from the feverish wind that trembled among the walls of the house and shook the four from within, putting the colors of rouge on the cheeks of the girls, turning Leticia mortally pale, flogging the little blond moustache of the pretty Don Diego, his pastel frock coats, his fashionable trousers, his silk handkerchiefs.

The feverish crisis reached its climax the morning following a night of nightmares in which Leticia dreamed that she had drowned in a swamp covered with flowers. She wanted to feel disgust for that exhuberance floating on rotting waters but felt only something vague, like an unspeakable fear. It was a night she spent flailing about, trying to come up to the surface, to consciousness, going back to sleep and falling into the quaking bog, sinking and abruptly coming out into darkness, into half-sleep, into insomnia, until four in the morning.

At nine, the hour when the pretty Don Diego arrived, the girls noticed that the cousin was sleeping profoundly. There was a game in their complicit looks, silent, gay.

Rafaela stood at the door, while Elida descended and, after carefully inspecting the lay of the land and ascertaining the total absence of the uncles and aunts, the grandmother's spell, the servants at the market, took up her post in the garden.

"She's asleep," she said, opening the door just as he was about to ring.

"I'll come back…," he said, hesitating.

"Wouldn't you like to wait for her… wouldn't you like to come in?" Somewhere in that vacillating voice, he believed he perceived a secret invitation.

"Very well," he agreed.

Near the living room, Diego felt the febrile brush of the hand, the agitated breathing, now in the door, the bosom, the body, the face.

"I…," he murmured.

Elida smiled, excited, with her eyes half-closed, pressing, longingly, against him.

"Be careful," warned Diego, but her warm mouth was already against his, her lips on his lips, searching for them, playing with his blond moustache. His hands trembled on the girl's body, and she slipped away instantly, to stand guard on the second floor, at Leticia's bedroom.

"She's sleeping," said Rafaela, holding out her hand. In that instant, Diego was fully aware of the rarified air. Then, the same feverishness, the trembling, the fleeting fear, the mouth, the body, the hands that searched for what they knew not in that young, sweet fleeing, as brief as that of Elida. Elida, who murmured at Leticia's ear in the artificial darkness of the bedroom.

"Lety, Diego is here. What shall we tell him?"

"Ah!" She was frightened, as though coming out of a brief death, opening those enormous eyes and sitting up. "Tell him to wait for me, I'll be right down." And she stretched, yawning.

Elida left the bedroom. She whistled. She had a canary in her breast, and on her mouth the taste of lotion, so strong that on noticing it on Diego her grand-mother had said, "But Lety's friend is more perfumed than a woman."

Her trill broke a caress barely begun in the living room, and for the rest of the time it dissolved into little smiles, word games, double meanings, until Leticia came down the stairs as though she were a heroine in one of those old romantic movies—that sometimes their mother allowed them to see after making sure that they weren't for "adults, with advisories"—with her hair loose, her bathrobe with the lace at the chest half open and a still lovely leg revealed with each step.

"My love," said Lety, kissing the pretty Don Diego next to his mouth, on one end of his little blond moustache. "We're leaving tomorrow, so if you want to buy some of those things made by our people, whatever, embroideries, weavings for your mother, or a bit of filigreed jewelry, those things you call 'marvels,' you'll have to do it today."

The girls looked at one another in silence and left the room without a sound, feeling on their fresh, palpitating, indecisive bodies Diego's gaze; slight disturbances still shook him, they noticed, as well as the concern in Lety's eyes, something close to fear.

They watched them leave the next day.

The entire family went to the station to say goodbye.

The girls played, both of them, with a finger to the lips, as though inviting him to keep silent, or blowing furtive little kisses. Diego smiled, a little bit sad. Leticia, relieved with the present, but uncertain, mistrustful, with something bitter fluttering around the future, chattered, promised to write, adjusted a dreadful hat that everyone noticed; kisses for the grandmother; caresses that had something clawing about them for the girls; hugs for the uncles and aunts.

He, on holding out his hands, pressed, sweetly, complicitly.

The eyes of the two shone when the bus left, raising a luminous cloud of dust.

The family walked home, carrying on a conversation about this and that, apparently inane, but filled with relief. A relief summed up by the grandmother's words, at which, though she had expressed their thoughts, they told her to hush.

"Well, at last they're gone! The visit dragged on much too long!"

"A lovely day," Elida sighed.

"It is," Rafaela agreed, her eyes and her thoughts flying after the worm of dust that was disappearing now around a distant curve. "It is."

And they smiled at one another, in silence. A silence charged with tiny secrets.

SONIA MANZANO
(Guayaquil, 1947)

Known initially for her poetry, Sonia Manzano won the national bi-annual novel contest in 1993 for *Y no abras las ventanas (zarzuela ligera sin divisiones aparentes)*. A collection of stories, *Flujo escarlata* was published in 1999. Manzano has won numerous prizes for her narrative creations. "George" is one of the finest stories ever penned by an Ecuadorian writer.

GEORGE*

My friends are strange, but I'm much stranger than my friends. This fact is confirmed by the generalized murmur my dress—thoroughly masculine—provokes when I enter, arm-in-arm with my second husband, the social gatherings that the painter has organized on several occasions, the one missing half an ear and to whose sensually cadavarine paintings (so inclined to exploding in a rotten range of yellow tones that open on mere contact with eyes skilled at the art of seeing enormous sunflowers die) I´m so powerfully drawn.

My second husband does not constitute an obstacle to my aesthetic appetites: I can get rid of him as easily as if he were an umbrella; he can do likewise with me: He ignores me when his sense of elegant pimping thus ordains. The day it occurs to him to make some sort of complaint he will become one of those obsolete memories on which I trample with my disdain each time I'm obliged to bring them to mind.

Beginning here two gatherings ago, my extravagant fellow gatherers have mentioned to me that the pianist N, self-exiled from some misty country, does not cease

*From *Antología de narradoras ecuatorianas*, 1977.

to inquire of anyone and everyone the maximum and minimum details of my congested existence. According to them (the very strangest of my friends), he is impressed by the libertine way I move about in center field in a game utterly lacking in rules. What's more, not content with the results of his investigative labors, he has begun to fire whimsical assumptions at my person (assumptions such as that of affirming that the silk scarf I wear around my neck serves to hide the unmistakable marks of those distressing wounds that on occasion I bear with at least three of my four apocalyptic horsemen).

The pianist has the eyes of a sorcerer and the complexion of English straw. He coughs persistently, as though there were a portion of clots obstructing his trachea, and he smells of camphor-scented alcohol (it may be that before getting dressed he rubs his body with moistened cotton balls to neutralize thus the aroma of living death that wafts from the collar of his shirt).

With the private lessons he gives to sickly young men, he is able to round out a tight budget, managing, besides, to establish contact with monetarily powerful mothers who are able to see in him a half-hemophilic Rasputin with whom they can share tedious afternoons in which the only tempting activity is to listen to the gurgling of blood in arteries not their own.

I dressed in reserved black to go to the farewell gathering that we organized, practically from one minute to the next, for the painter with half an ear, who two days hence was to go to Brazil for one of those shows of trees from the branches of which the shoes of professional suicide victims hang. I lacked only a whippet, so I told my husband to come along. I also lacked a coachman's whip to put the finishing touches to my equine image. Lacking the whip, I took along repressed lashes on the tip of my tongue, ready to be unleashed on the first naked back that appeared in my path.

I penetrated the salon with my usual haughtiness and went directly to the piano. My husband joined the group of hermetic poets who had positioned themselves, deliberately, at the entrance so that everyone who came to the party would be forced to stop and listen to the systematic discrediting to which they were subjecting decorativist literature (destined, according to the hermetics, to fall under the very weight of its ornamental excesses).

I rested my elbows on the top of the piano and allowed a lace handkerchief to fall from the dovecot of my plunging neckline. Then you began to sing, in a husky baritone, a song that you said you had composed a few days earlier, and to which you had given the suggestive title of *Pretty Maria*. A little later, and with all the vocal risks the interpretation implied, you burst into *Granada*, which you ended by putting between my fingers a flower of melancholy that no one, until then, had ever given me (a flower that was immediately absorbed by the sucking greed of my mouth that always smokes while waiting for men it doesn't really want to come).

I smoothed the lace at both wrists and noticed that my hands had begun to age. I twisted the ring under whose garnet stone I conceal a certain type of poison that I tend to pour into large papal goblets, and while I held your gaze of clear hypnotic designs, I arched an eyebrow as only I know how to do, after which I asked you—with that delicious crow's voice with which I have cawed in many movies that end with the same loneliness with which they began—that you sing for the rest of the night, but only and exclusively for me.

You were dumbfounded by my request: I felt it in the cracking of your shoulders and in the renewed passion with which you began to paw the keys (I calculate that at least three of them exploded within you).

The others—strange like you and me but not as strange as the two of us together—had ignored the music after realizing that it shut them out completely. My husband, entertained as he was in explaining the plan of the *summa* novel that he hopes to write soon, to the group of the disemboweled who, due to the effects of rum, displayed a condescending openness toward open structures and didn't even notice the tête-à-tête a few meters away in which I was a co protagonist (and if he did notice, he had no right to make me an object of a single objection, since there is little or nothing he can do in the face of those flashes of nymphomania that run through my hollowness, flashes whose duration I, and only I, determine).

I'm not maudlin, but when with a rapid glance I noticed that almost everyone, including my husband, had drifted away through the fissures of their origins, and that the painter we'd come to say goodbye to had also slipped furtively through a corner of the salon to go to bed so that he wouldn´t have to say goodbye to anyone, I started crying in a thoroughly objectionable way, with sobs that I had repressed for years. You were visibly upset: The three lines in your forehead began to zigzag and something on them derailed deafeningly.

In reality, my weeping could have been generated by two distinct motives: on the one hand, the indiscriminate mixture of liquors to which the host had subjected us (several rounds of margaritas alternating with tragic incursions by a devastating vodka with grapefruit juice); and, on the other—on the other hand—the fickle connection I managed to establish between my own life and the lyrics of that *pasillo* you had played at least five times (and that by the sixth had made me cry in the heartbreaking way I cry even today).

The *pasillo* talked about a river and about a nostalgia that had nowhere to flow. I let the confluence of the two fall toward the most distant perception I have of myself, and as I tend to get sad when I remember the day I lost my own way because some birds ate the crumbs I'd let fall for obvious reasons, I tried to console myself by bringing to my mouth the toothpicks with bits of cheese that some accommodating soul had discretely placed on the lid of the piano.

Just then you stood up to offer me your customary bit of consolation. The tension against your fly grabbed, suddenly, my attention: A red fig leaf grew there whose central point released—slowly but visibly—a drop of red wine that evaporated before reaching the floor. You menstruated, it was clear that you menstruated. I wanted an immediate confirmation of my suspicions, and thus I ran my inquiring gaze over your gypsy violin thorax, now, yes, revealingly feminine. In spite of the tightness of your flowered vest, your breasts struggled to come outside in open and desperate reprisal against those restrictions that you had imposed upon them for who knows how many years: maybe from the time you discovered that the great majority of men do not have the ability to love truly and intensely which is precisely what is needed by those women whose markedly virile melancholies can only be extinguished by intelligences that are beyond considerations limited to sex.

I'm attending a new social gathering, this time organized by the decorativist poets. I'm going dressed in burnt yellow. In lieu of smoke, I'm taking among the folds of my skirt ashes which in vain try to recall a fire no longer in effect in the least within what I have decided to call "an abject image of myself."

HUILO RUALES HUALCA

(Ibarra, 1947)

Huilo Ruales burst onto the Ecuadorian literary scene on receiving the Rodolfo Walsh Spanish American Literary Prize, awarded in Paris in 1983. In that same year, he won the national Aureliano Espinosa Pólit Prize for literature and, in 1984, first place in the *short story contest sponsored* by *Ultimas Noticias*, a Quito daily, for *Nuaycielo comuel dekito*, and the Joaquín Gallegos Lara Prize awarded by the city of Quito, in 1989.

The author´s published collections include *Y todo este rollo a mí también me jode* (1984), *Nuaycielo comuel dekito* (1985), *Loca para loca la loca* (1989), and fetiche y fantoche (1994). Ruales has also written a play entitled *Añicos* (1991). His stories have been translated into French and German, and included in a number of anthologies.

Ruales has co-founded literary groups, including La Pequeña Lulupa and Eskeletra, and has led literary workshops and promoted literary magazines. The writer lives in France.

Ruales has a fine ear for the colloquialisms of his generation which he successfully incorporates into his works, examples of new realism or, better yet, hyper-realism. So determined is he to reproduce the spoken word that he often resorts to phonetic rendering of language in his stories.

THE IMPORTANCE OF THE JUGULAR IN THIS MATTER OF LIFE*

Enriquito's death was one of the straws that broke the elephant's back. His concave, unwavering gaze was the hypnotic command that nudged us to the kiss, the caress, the ripping off of clothes, and the hands and mouths filled us with hungry dagger thrusts and my sex turning you into vagina from hair to the hiddenest of nails, plunged us into the madness of creating a new technique in a chair and on the roof, in the light and in the tongue, in saliva and in wine, trying to delay orgasm so that it would serve only for the crash, for total destruction, for the complete evaporating of our lives, and that apart from the labyrinth of clothes and the colloidal panting in the air, there remained only the empire of his crane-gaze storing away every element of our lascivious holocaust, storing it in his memory's strange stadium. He took with him so many things from our colors. Remember how he greeted me when I burst into your apartment its ceiling aslant? He knew how to defend you since before you learned the interminable train of the tear or fright and that's why, when

---

*From the collection *Y todo este rollo a mí también me jode,* 1984.

the first time in his presence we cut to the kiss that left us naked, I thought I felt your fingernails, but no, it was his jealousy signing my back lengthwise and crosswise, and then we had to make love buried in your blankets. So, the house was woven with precautions and we walked so that he would come around to my side, and even though I had to go about extorting him with small gifts, and to pretend to be ignored so as not to provoke his ire, life was made of clay and what was important was to tell you about how yogurt where I come from is a province of tiny white multiform animals who are so happy in the milk they live in that they quadruplicate from one day to the next, and even though you couldn't believe me because that seemed too tender, you lit up the bedroom, the kitchen, the bathroom with your laughter, or you told me, both sad and proud, that to celebrate his father's birthday, Franco had him shot by a firing squad in a plaza in Toledo, and I explained to you for hours that my typewriter was as human as Enriquito, or you tried to persuade me that just as you accepted all that stuff about literature I should understand the umbilical contract between you and him, because apart from my sporadic visits and your fifth-rate art school, you had nothing more in the world. I accepted him with pleasure and he conceded his stamp of approval, and so my typewriter took over the desk while you, seated in the lotus position on a cushion, worked at your sculptures or sketched my scowl which, you claimed, came to life when I wrote, or you gazed at the cassette rack to hear the music better, or brushed him as though it were worth the trouble, or invented some catastrophic dish, or wandered around the possibility of a kiss, and you got it, and promisquated until the papers, the typewriter, the chair, the desk, your spatulas, your apron, melted and our hands metamorphosed, from delicate spiders—ascending descending our bodies—convulsed octopuses, and the roof came down and the floor was an umbrella over our heads and your girl's body turned into a spirited mare and the screams wove into the jazz making a fabric that enveloped us like a uterine membrane, and he, from some corner, filming it all with a little spark in his retinas that looked a lot like resignation. Later, rested and still naked, we watched that butterfly-grandmother of sleep come, or when we emerged from it, with your heart finger you walked my profile until coming to my lips and carefully carved my silence, you turned into a girl marinating the fable of the father when he told you how the people of my country manage to tell time though light and verbal inflection are prohibited, and you were a mixture of mother-friend-heroine on touching the matter of my wife, my children; always perched in that exuberant pyramidal present of him and us, digging to find out something about us or having something to talk about in the orography of the past. During that time the autumn, which by mutual choice seemed a lot like us, became a thread running through the loops of the other seasons until with the next summer three matters merged: You switched to a school with earlier classes, my novel wanted to walk on its own two feet but they were crippled, and he turned into a taciturn ball of tangled wool. Then June came kicking at the windows, exile invented its toadstools, and one night as hot as molasses I found you with your pockets and your mouth blinded by demands: What would I do with my family, that I definitively forget the hotel and we wake every morning together, that we walk the streets licking ice cream cones like kids, that I suggest once in a while that you put on that particular dress, that we have dinner in some little Chinese diner to whisper that strange word called future, that I forget about writing for awhile to look at you in the sketches, in the circles under your eyes, in the tear, in the voice. Though I'd always expected that moment, I couldn't answer you or I answered you loving you as though I were covering you with ointment, that I couldn't, that my country, that missing not being able to be on its streets or in its jails or dead, that literature, that gangrene. A few days were sufficient to descend from sex to the shuddering discovery, grasped in our hands, that something had broken like an egg, or that maybe that something had never been, in spite of having managed to keep it upright as long as we didn't scratch identities or clocks, and that inexhaustible gray hemorrhage began, stuck in silence, in the reverted sob, in Enriquito's illness, in the trotting of my typewriter bolting in downpours, rats, scorpions from my childhood and from my country, until asphyxia had me doubled over, and without saying anything to you, I went on tiptoe to crash in my hotel room, in the café, in the cigarette, in the thin correspondence, I hurled my typewriter like a despicable hired mourner, and then I roamed the streets in order not to keep on measuring the importance of the jugular in this matter of life, and I filled up on bewildered parks of jobless Arabs and old homosexuals and, as though I would find the loose end of the ball of wool, I went back to the little plaza where, a year before, the drunk beggar was beaten by the police while you and I observed appalled from different sidewalks until, out of solidarity and impotence, we began to walk together, talking as though we already knew each other and, urged on by those same motivations, we ended that devastating Sunday making love on top of the crumbs, cigarette butts, records, papers that peopled the floor of my room.

At the little plaza fear came to meet me, and at top speed I watched myself climbing your street, that kind of question mark made with laziness and with no exit, dotted with garbage cans, fish shops, bars, old sailors anchored in drink; I got to your door, I found it decrepit, I rang, I imagined Enriquito announcing my arrival, nobody answered, I rang again and, at last, though I don't know why, your slippers were wearing away from the fifth floor. Now in your apartment and like a thief, I could see you: Even though you were more beautiful than ever in that Hindu robe, you had something so strongly of smoke, of ash about you, that you looked like a ghost, and when I noted his absence I thought overwhelmed that in you the two had fused. Only at dawn did you break the silence overtaken by poetry by Brel, and you told me that a few days before, knowing his death was coming, you had had the dignity to go to receive it someplace else. I couldn't add anything. The guttural chatting of the pigeons tossed the day on your mattress and I found you deeply asleep, I left the chair, I stretched my body at your feet and, with eyes open, I dreamed that he came back, he climbed up to your lap, he crawled under your skirt, and let me know that you were naked, and you drew me toward you, and you asked me to draw all the pain from your lips, your belly, your thighs, and you begged me to crucify you with your face to the wall, stretch-legged, panting, dripping with sweat, and you pleaded with me to burst your breasts with kisses, to squeeze you standing up, like a proper assassin, and that in an extension of defeat I go beyond the domestic limits of humiliation, that I liquefy you until I'd reduced you to a scream, a brown puddle, palpitating. On waking up in the middle of the day you handed me a cup of coffee and looking at the time you told me dryly that it was time I left, that that territory was now your future and that... I tried to propose one last cablecar: escape by gas behind closed doors, those little bottles of pills, the amazing multiplication of tiny yogurt animals as the most original of suicides, the adoption of another Enriquito so that he would emerge from your hair, your arms, your legs, your canvases, but everything, even that, was way too late.

At the corner bar thick with smoke and the hoarseness of pensioners, immigrants, and men mutilated in war, I fell on a bottle of black wine so inexhaustible that the night came out of it, and from the night a soothsaying whore with a flaccid jaw that she stuck in the wine went for my neck and in retrospect she even unmade-up her face to give me a better idea of her tragedy. And when the chairs were lifted to the tables upside-down, and the broom placed us in the door, she took my arm, taught me to hum hymns she learned in concentration camps, to break the squalor of the streets with the sharp point of a belly laugh, and when we were in her room packed with cushions, astrological signs, tarot cards, and climbing plants, she was honest enough take off her cloths and show me her wretched condition, and before inviting me into her high bronze bed, she put on a turban, took my hand, read my palm, and said to me: I see a dead cat here.

IVÁN OÑÁTE
(Ambato, 1948)

Poet and short story writer Iván Oñate is the author of four collections of poetry: *En la casa del ahorcada* (1970), *El ángel ajeno* (1983), *Anatomía del vacío* (1988), and *El fulgor de los desollados* (1992).

Several stories from his collection *El hacha enterrada* (1987) have been included in some of the finest anthologies of Ecuadorian short stories, and have been translated into English, German, and French.

Iván Oñate has a doctorate in communications from the University of Barcelona. He teaches semantics and literature at the Central University of Quito.

With poetic, and effective, prose, the action of Oñate´s tales, whether set in Ecuador, Spain, or Italy, is thoroughly credible. There is a human density in his stories: the reencounter with ancestors; the man offered as a sacrifice—in an arena, a parade, a celebration—to cruel gods who form the very tissue of society. Some of his works are among the loveliest penned by members of his generation.

THE FACE OF GLORY*

I

The night of February 3, the eve of the ceremony, once
again Justo Aníbal Suárez couldn't sleep. Discouraged,
because he knew even before he began that the effort
would be to no avail, he tried the breathing technique
his boss had recommended that afternoon for insomnia. It was useless. Something higher, viscous, struggled in him, forcing him to fail, to resign himself as best
he could in the face of the inevitable enemy. Desperate,
he wanted to go out, to drink something that would
save him from that hour. But when he heard the rustle
of his sleeping wife searching for him at his side, he
decided to stay there, lying very still, avoiding the possible and sleepless dialogue that generally establishes
itself in the arena of the marital bed in the middle of the
night: Are you sleeping? Are you thinking?
Whimpers, complaints disguised as whispers in the
loneliness of the shipwreck. Yes, that stillness, that
silence was better. On similar occasions, faces used to
come to mind, the shapes of a time he never shared,

*From the collection *El hacha enterrada*, 1987.

foreign splendors that in desperation he pulled out of the void.

There she was, for example, Doña Raquel: grand-daughter, daughter, and now wife of the small town's mayors, year after year, spreading a lovely mantilla on the balcony to watch the parade. Also, year after year, he went to love her secretly from the sidewalk across the street.

"Why always the same spot!" his wife protested, pale, dignified, encased in her little tailored suit.

"Because it's the best spot," he replied.

Delirious, and during his periods of insomnia, Suárez saw Doña Raquel arrive, perfect, even her fragrance jelling, little by little. He listened to her panting, bringing her hands to her chignon and letting the black, furious lasciviousness of her hair fall over her shoulders, her breasts. He watched her smile, arranging her lips as though she were sipping something, and finally open her arms, the same bare arms with which she had spread the mantilla, but now as though she were offering something. And so, drowning, he sank his hands into the vision to incorporate it into his night and found only the fragile body of his wife, her tiredness, her complaints.

"But tomorrow will be another day," Suárez said to himself and clenched his fists, gritted his teeth, and pressed his eyelids shut, searching for sleep.

In the darkness, barely sensing the nearness of his wife who now breathed heavily, Suárez still remembered her possessing a discrete beauty. He listened to her panting, struggling against something obstinate in her sleep. But he didn't wake her, didn't shake her to free her from the horror. Very still, he heard her sob.

Alone and pursued through the rooms of her nightmare.

At dawn, no doubt led astray by his lack of sleep, Suárez thought he heard the fluttering of angels who went after him with a pack of dogs.

"Good Lord," he exclaimed, sitting up. "I overslept."

He blindly felt around the night table and found his watch.

The light from the lamp hit him from the side.

"Five-ten," he sighed, relieved.

He blinked and lay down again. He stayed that way for a long moment, the lamp on. Mechanically and without the least awareness of what he was doing, Suárez put the watch on his wrist. He breathed deeply and when he had managed to calm the flow of his blood, he turned to switch the lamp off. But first, due purely to habit, he looked one last time at his watch. That was when he saw, with amazement and for the first time, the strange mark on his left hand.

It was a recent injury, still fresh on the bluish veins that spread across the back of his hand. At first glance, it seemed to be the quick clawing of a woman in the vertigo of love or rage. But under the steady light of the lamp, Suárez verified, astonished, the perfect bite, the secret marks of teeth that had penetrated his flesh. "It's the insomnia," he thought as he turned off the light and shook his head as though to banish doubt.

In the morning, paler than usual and with his hair uncombed, Suárez walked into the small dining room.

"Another sleepless night," his wife scolded as she set the table.

Suárez didn't answer. He ate the frugal breakfast in

the silence that had reigned over their childless marriage. A cup of black coffee and two slices of fried plantain.

"You should eat an egg today," she said, seeing him weak, insignificant in his convalescent's pajamas.

"You know I can't stand them!" he answered in anger. But immediately, in a sweet, conciliatory tone, he added, "A shower, a cold shower. That's what I need!"

"That might make you sick," she warned, "they say it's deadly after a bad night."

Suárez didn't comment. He simply gazed, for a long time, at a stain in the shape of a heart spread on the tablecloth printed with the scene of the Last Supper.

A few minutes later and contrary to his sacred habit of waiting for the weekend to go to a public bath, Suárez went out to the patio in his underwear. He connected the hose to the tap, hung the other end over a clothes line, and, standing next to the laundry tank, he bore the water's old blow that squeezed his head.

"Don't stay under there too long," his wife shouted to him from the house. But he didn't hear her now, enveloped in that delicious ice-cold spray.

Shivering under the almost perverse pleasantness of the water and knowing that he was on the threshold of the crowning ceremony of his life, Justo Aníbal Suárez gave himself over without rancor and for the first time to the memory of that distant afternoon when he was a child and everything began. Lost in tender thoughts, he remembered his parents preparing to take him to watch his first parade. He remembered his smiling mother buttoning his pants, straightening his bowtie, and combing his hair with pineapple juice. He remembered being anxious to get to the parade, a parade to which they arrived late for some reason. The teeming crowd at the intersection didn't let them pass to see the parade. Then the struggle, the shame that would lead him to this day. Over the pleas of his mother and the futile efforts of his father, he heard insults, he tried to breathe, he felt the fury of the mass crushing him. But then, when he was about to collapse, overcome by the lack of air, he felt his father pulling him off the ground and lifting him over the crowd and there, through his tears, he spied glory. The face of glory that at that very moment was kissing the right hand of a man and handing him a bouquet of flowers over the white carriage.

Enraptured, he held even tighter to his father's arms which were trembling with the effort, and he understood that the only way to save oneself from the overheated masses was by getting up there, into the white carriage that now moved on like a soap bubble in a fairy tale, floating away, pulled by gleaming black horses.

"It's time to come in," he heard his wife's voice, "you're going to catch a cold."

But Suárez didn't obey. He wanted to prolong the memory of that day.

His wife went to the tap, turned it off, and covered his back with a towel.

"Dry your feet before coming in," she said.

In the bedroom, Suárez found his clothes laid out on the bed. The shirt, the tie, and the suit his wife had cleaned with gasoline. The new shoes were too tight.

"Help me with this necklace," she said, seated at the dressing table, looking at him in the mirror.

Suárez tightened the lace on the right shoe and went

over to her. At her back, he took the ends of the collar and verified that the hook was broken.

"Try this," she said, handing him a bit of thread.

Suárez took it and patiently joined the ends of the string of white beads. Some of the pearls were chipped.

"There you are," Suárez exclaimed, and in a moment of uncharacteristic rapture, drew his lips near to kiss her on the neck. Then, an ice-cold tremor charged with vertigo stopped him: There it was, the mark. In the firm, tender flesh of that neck, tiny teeth had left the same bite that he had on his hand.

"What's wrong?" his wife asked, alarmed as she felt her husband's shaking fingers sink into her shoulders.

"Nothing, it's nothing," he said, easing the pressure from his hands. "Just a dizzy spell."

"Can I get you something?" she asked, looking at him in the mirror.

"No, it's already passed," he said. And, as proof that all was well, he kissed his wife. Exactly on those freckles that he had confused with a bite.

When it was time for the banquet, surrounded by the personages of the town, Justo Aníbal Suárez felt as though he were dying. While the mayor spoke, he was overcome, little by little, by a cold lassitude. "I'm going to faint," he thought and damned his wife's warning hours earlier. "It must be the excitement," he lied to himself and tried to reach for a glass of wine. But, horrified, he saw how it eluded his grasp and how the banquet table reeled together with all the diners. He looked at his wife, at the bishop, at the group of faces around the table, and he found them pale, disfigured, gesticulating with abominable mouths, and he thought he perceived in the fog of his eyes that the crème de la crème of the town had been stricken by the same fever.

"Go on," his wife pinched him. "The mayor has said that you should go on."

Ashen, trying not to vomit, Suárez felt an urgent need to rest his head on his wife's shoulder immediately and confide in her, slowly, the fact that hell was a cold place, and not hot, as was commonly believed.

"What's wrong with you!" his wife said, pushing him away. "The mayor has said to go on."

"I told you to wait a minute," Suárez begged. "Just a minute. I told you."

Red with embarrassment, his wife shook his arm.

"Don't be ridiculous!" she said. "We'll be the laughingstock of the town for the rest of our lives."

Suárez listened to his wife and, like a dog dripping wet, he shook his head. "No, not that!" he said, or thought he said, because now his memory was a whirl of images, of enemy faces ready to mock. With unexpected clarity, he heard the laughter of his classmates when, one afternoon in May, he said to a treacherous friend that he wouldn't forget to greet him from the carriage when thanks to his own efforts he was elected Man of the Year and received the medal from the town's mayor. He saw himself older, crying in the bathroom because of his colleagues' cruel jokes. He remembered his parents, exhausted, tread on by the mob, and in a leap he was on his feet. He freed himself with a shove from his wife's hands resting on his neck and walked very erect, twisting his body back as though he were drunk. He took three steps. With the forth he tripped. "Shit!" he said, grabbing the back of a chair. He looked to either side and immediately closed his eyes in fear. For reasons he didn't understand, the world had disappeared. "Clarita!" he thought of his wife. But immediately he reflected that his call had no object. Because he, better than anyone, knew that when it came to nightmares, nobody was allowed to interfere in another's horror. He was alone, paying the price of that ill-advised bath.

"Hurry up, Suárez!" the mayor scolded into the microphone. "Everyone's waiting for you outside!"

Suárez hadn't finished hearing the call when something more fearful than his illness knotted him to the bone. Suárez! On this, the most important day of his life, the mayor had called him Suárez. Just that, Suárez, after so much effort.

He jumped, like a boxer who throws himself at a biased referee, Suárez fought against the group of guests who, to help him, were holding on to him.

"Let me go!" he shouted and, with a slap, he rejected the fat woman who approached bringing a vial of perfume to his nose.

"What manners!" the fat woman protested, searching the floor for the stopper. "They should be more careful about who they select!"

"It's the excitement," someone said. "It´s understandable."

"Lean against me!" someone else said. "I'll take you to the stage." Freed from the row, Suárez got to the stage, alone and energetic. He pursed his lips as though waiting for the rebuke, but then the mayor looked at him and smiled. "Maybe I heard wrong," he said to himself and offered his chest, defiant.

"Such impatience, Suárez," the mayor said, pinning the medal to his lapel. "You should have waited until tonight to start drinking. After the carriage ride."

There was no doubt about it. If a moment ago Suárez looked for refuge in a mistake, now he knew that that stupid joke was the real speech, the reward for a lifetime of sacrifice. And so, Justo Aníbal Suárez, a citizen educated to fear God and man, who had never offended his fellow man—in thought, word, or deed— would have blasphemed for the first time in his life, had he not at that very moment discovered a mark exactly like his on the recently shaved neck of the mayor.

"Very well, Suárez!" the mayor exclaimed, slapping him on the back as though he were a tame ox. "The parade is waiting for you. Let's go!"

Suddenly agitated, unable to find the thread that connected the coincidences, Suárez let himself be led, like the sleepwalker he was, to the door.

"You see?" he recognized the voice of his wife who was waiting for him with the other guests. "You wouldn't listen to me. The bath made you ill."

"Clarita," he said, taking care that the curious guests surrounding them didn't overhear, "I need to tell you about what's happening to me."

She took him by the hand and led him to the corridor next to a little statue. "There are marks," Suárez began, but the fat woman with the perfume came between the couple.

"You're so pale!" the fat woman said, bringing the vial to his nose.

Instinctively, Suárez twisted his head away.

"Take a deep breath!" the fat woman ordered. "Take a deep breath! It will do you good."

In his desire to free himself immediately from the

intruder, Suárez inhaled the perfume until he felt that his brain was freezing.

"Now let's go!" the fat woman said quickly and took him by the arm. "Help me, señora! We'll take him to the carriage!"

II

A characteristic of traditions is that their origins get lost in the mists of passing years and men. Obedient or careless, generations add to or subtract from the splendor of their vestments but almost always ignorant of the meaning on which they were based in the beginning. Something like that had happened to this celebration. None of the townspeople remembered how it had got started. They had merely conserved it as a grand habit that made them forget the colorless, day-to-day routine of the species. The oldest frowned upon the luncheon rite, said it was an invention of a gluttonous mayor a few decades earlier. But nobody questioned that a select member of the town should be paraded in a carriage and finally rewarded with a kiss from the mayor's wife as he received a bouquet of roses. It would be well to remember that researcher Paulus Cuvidress Sánchez believes that the finale reflects a hypocritical and symbolic suppression of a more profound, more generous prize. Be that as it may, toward this parade and this kiss, Justo Aníbal Suárez had directed a lifetime of effort. But now, a few minutes before the parade was to begin, the guest of honor felt sick, beside himself, and in that state he absently stroked the carriage's red tapestry.

"Justo Aníbal!" he heard his wife call from the side of the carriage.

Suárez turned and saw her on the sidewalk, flanked by the fat woman and the other luncheon guests. Overjoyed, his wife waved goodbye with a little lace handkerchief. Suárez returned her smile. The pathetic smile of someone who is not smiling within.

"Gentlemen!" the mayor's voice came over the loudspeakers. "Let the parade begin!"

The carriage shook with the command. Over the music the band was playing, Suárez head the crack of the whip and the snorting of the horses as they backed up, indecisive. There was a moment of pressure, of metal grinding against wood, pushed to the limit by the sudden rush of forces. Holding tight to the handles, Suárez feared for a moment that the carriage would fly apart and that the lurching start would toss him into the air; but the din immediately gave way to the rhythmic swaying of a ship sailing with the current. Then, vaguely surprised, Suárez recognized the top hat and the black cape of the coachman. He was afraid. Unlike the coachmen normally hired for the festivities, this one seemed thinner, too tall in spite of being seated in the coach box. Fearfully, he tried to see the man's face. But suddenly he remembered that he, throughout his entire life, had eyes only for the face of the honored guest and that it was unlikely that he had noticed the anonymous face of the coachman. He leaned against the backrest and with the legitimate hesitancy of someone preparing himself for the unknown, he clenched his fists and pressed his eyelids shut and tensed his body. It was not illogical to think that after the unpleasant experience at the luncheon, the consequences of the sleepless night would continue during the parade.

From either side of the street sounded the first

bursts of applause. He opened his eyes and noticed that people smiled at him from balconies, doorways, crowded sidewalks, and that in addition to the clapping and the acclamation, he heard the firecrackers and the rockets that flew with a whistle from the elated hands of the boys. "What would it have cost him to call me Señor," Suárez said sadly to himself, as though the fiesta were not for him and were taking place at a good distance. As though the careless attitude of the mayor had yanked him, irremediably, from a dream from which he had not yet awakened.

"Señor Suárez! Señor Suárez!" He heard an agitated voice at the side of the carriage. "Please, my daughter!"

Surprised, Suárez looked that way and saw the fearless face of a girl who offered him a carnation.

"Do you remember me?" said the man who ran alongside the carriage, all the while holding the girl in his arms.

"Of course!" Suárez replied, with the shock of someone waking up. But in reality, that black face, straining with effort, meant nothing to him.

"Why yes," he reaffirmed, still looking at the man who for a moment looked like the treacherous friend who had made him an object of ridicule one afternoon when he was a boy. And so, to verify this fact, he wanted to mention his name, the indelible name that for years he had repeated before going to bed. But, maybe because of the bath, it didn't come to him now, remaining lost in the drawer where old resentments are kept.

"Congratulations," said the man, disappointed, putting the girl down.

"Of course I remember!" Suárez shook his head and,

as proof, he wanted to get out. To rest his head on the shoulder of the disloyal friend and confide in him that something wasn't right here. That all he wanted was to be alone and to sleep. To sleep, on the day of his triumph.

It was only after half a block, when the band had switched to another march, that the name of Pedro Méndez emerged from forgetting with a lightening bolt of hope. "Parrot Méndez," they'd called him, and repeating the name to himself, he turned around with delight to look. But now there were other faces on the sidewalk and other children held up in the arms of their parents, waving handkerchiefs and pennants, and with evident distress, he repeated, "Parrot Méndez," and moved his tongue to where the molar he lost as a boy had been. "It probably wasn't him," he consoled himself. Maybe just an acquaintance, just another classmate or colleague. In any event, forgetting had set in and he was just one more shadow on that troubled day of his triumph.

Disappointed, listening apathetically to the ovations of an audience increasingly more elegant and euphoric, Suárez thought that if they had allowed him to delay this moment and sleep for a few hours as he should have, on waking he would have been another. His blood would have been charged with the dignity necessary to receive the honor. He looked up at the sky and, given the architecture of the houses, he observed that they were approaching the neighborhoods of the center. "She should be on the balcony now," he thought about Doña Raquel and his hand mechanically went to his tie and to the hair that had fallen into his face. Just then, the carriage stopped suddenly throw-

ing him forward, against the shoulders of the coachman who leaned back, tightening the reins forcefully.
"Whoa, whoa!" he heard above the music and the
noise. He craned his neck and, over the coachman's
shoulder, Suárez saw two policemen struggling with a
group that had spilled into the street. The band fell
silent and immediately there was a shower of shouts,
whistles, orange rinds, the cries of children in their parents' arms trying to get air, a chaotic scene. "That's all
I needed," Suárez said to himself, fearing not so much
that the interruption would prolong his torture as the
possibility that people would besiege him with praise,
with their stupid questions about how it felt to be seated in glory. He closed his eyes and waited to get there.
But he felt only the wind that blew his hair into his face
again. He opened his eyes and realized that no one
was looking at him, that everyone was enjoying the
ruckus. Then he shuddered at something he hadn't
expected. He saw a woman who had fallen, with her
legs in the air. He saw a strange calligraphy near the
seam of one of her stockings. A line that climbed to the
skewed hats of the policemen, continued along the
black suit of the coachman, and jeered at his chest,
where they had pinned the ridiculous medal.

"Do something, man!" he ordered the coachman,
breathing with difficulty in that air of a bad joke.
"Hurry!"

But the coachman didn't move, and abandoned in
his seat, Suárez contemplated how easily those faces
were distracted. The grotesque spectacle that they had
exchanged him for. He sighed and longed for the days
before he had been touched by glory: Slowly, he saw
himself walking, year after year, dragging a chair and

his wife to watch the parade. "You're a maniac," his
wife would be saying to him now, protesting their
return to the same spot facing Doña Raquel's balcony.
"But woman," Suárez would say, "it's the only good
thing about the fiesta." Or maybe he wouldn't say anything. With the chair in his arms, he would simply look
for the best spot to begin his secret ceremony, to see
Doña Raquel come out to the balcony and spread the
mantilla, her arms moving languidly, her coquettish little fingers meticulously arched. He would see her
smile and with her bare arms respond to the applause
of the people. With unyielding voracity, he would
record in his memory the smallest details of her dress,
her hairdo, her earrings, her necklace, her bracelets,
and even the living sound of her stockings which he
would hear being removed, slowly, throughout the
entire year and in each of his secret nights. Biting his
lips, he would see her sit down, turn her face to someone's call, and, as though unaware, part her knees
slightly and lift her breasts and they would rise to the
neckline of a dress that he would carefully fold over a
chair in the happiest moment of the ritual.

He would be seeing all of that now, at this very
moment, if he hadn't been sitting in the carriage. With
what joy would he watch her rise and squint into the
distance, because the black gleam of the horses pulling
the carriage could be seen a block away. Then, standing
on the chair and steadying himself by leaning against
his wife's shoulders, Suárez would prepare himself for
the most exquisite pain of the celebration. With his heart
racing like a maddened animal, he would watch her disappear behind the red curtain on the balcony, he would
imagine her holding a mirror, touching up her makeup,

and a minute later he would watch her emerge, splendid, illuminating the darkness of the doorway with a bouquet of flowers in her arms. Slow and pagan, like a queen he learned to fear in catechism class, he would watch her climbing into the carriage and preparing to kiss his hand, he would see her present the flowers to the elect. Content with envy, his fingers digging into his wife's shoulders, he would remember yet again the firm promise he had made himself one afternoon when he was a boy: He would be in that carriage accepting the flowers from the hands of the goddess. And, above all, he would know at last the odor of that body. An odor he would cherish in his innermost being forever. But now (Suárez moved, uneasy, in the carriage), now he would no longer be surprised at the unfortunate attitude of the elect, he would no longer judge with disdain those clumsy gestures that did not correspond to one who had been kissed by luck, he would no longer repeat, tirelessly, to his wife that that Man of the Year was not cut out for glory: Because on remembering the lips of Doña Raquel approaching the hand of the individual whose turn it was to be honored (now he heard the shouts and the laughter of the ruckus), Suárez had discovered something that could only have been revealed on this, the precise day of his triumph. "No!" he exclaimed, "It can't be!" Because on Doña Raquel's face he found not the joyous and illuminated kiss with which the living are awarded, but repressed disgust, the fleeting but perverse grimace with which the dead are dispatched. "It's the sleepless night," he insisted, but now his memory was a crazy disjointed lantern, a rabid beam of light that unmasked the wan faces of the elect that had preceded him. With implacable clarity, he remembered the resignation in their eyes, the definitive sadness with which those kissed by Doña Raquel held the flowers to their chests and disappeared into the shadows at the end of the parade that immediately would begin preparing its funereal machinery for the following year. "Idiots!" he moaned, because the ray of light moved to the banquet table and vented its cruelty on the faces of the guests. He saw the mouths gesticulating in those floured faces; he saw the peach queen looking at him with a curious pity from the other end of the table, the judge, the bishop who hid their eyes over their guilty plates, and he no longer harbored even a shred of doubt: This year, he was the tribe's atavistic offering! The individual selected to entertain the jaws of death!

"Poor idiots!" He shook his head and looked at the people still following, entertained, the proceedings of the fight. Then he thought about flight, about cheating the lying retinue that paraded its prey through the town in the role of victim. He passed his hand over his face and put his right foot into the stirrup, he stopped. Suddenly he thought that if at the end of the parade the disgust of Doña Raquel awaited him, what he would find at the end of his flight was mockery, unforgettable collective laughter. He brought his foot inside and fell back into his seat, defeated. "Poor Clarita," he sobbed. In the trembling of his body, in the unbearable pressure on his chest, and in the furtive tears that wet his cheeks, he thought he recognized his wife's desperation when he left her alone, pursued in the labyrinths of the nightmare. "Except that I'm awake," he said to himself, and recognized that that small difference left him trapped forever in his own: Because there is no waking for those who have found The Dream.

III

It might be supposed that the story of Justo Aníbal Suárez would end here: with his docile acceptance of the facts, as happened with all those selected. But Suárez, winner on two occasions of the school oratory contest and with good grades in composition, resolved that in the row (the catcalls could be heard against the onslaught by police reinforcements), he'd won a stay, had been called to intervene energetically in his own destiny. It was not in vain, he said to himself, that he had achieved revelation, discovered the real motive behind the ceremony.

A ceremony that in truth no longer suggested torch-lit ebony warriors, nor high priests pulling the victim along to the final delights with the goddesses (in order to drag him off, handcuffed with flowers, to the sacrificial stone); nevertheless, the smell of multiple, ancestral terror was still in the air; of the drunken mob who waved their threatening fists toward a horizon planted with crosses.

Timidly, Suárez looked quickly over the shoulder of the coachman and hid his face in his hands. He no longer thought about flight. He thought about what he should do when Doña Raquel appeared in the doorway with the bouquet of flowers. "Now I'll show her," he said to himself and looked up. The carriage started to move again and the people to applaud. "Now I'll show her," he repeated, and on his face there shone the sad majesty of those who have just dried their tears.

Though he was concentrating on vengeance, when the parade was farther along the town's main street, Suárez had to admit that until now he had only moved along the edges of paradise. People received him with uncommon enthusiasm. As though in the pause, in the impatient leavening of the delay, a unanimous ferment had maddened them. With genuine surprise in his eyes, Suárez noticed that the most prudent women of the neighborhood, with the smiling approval of their husbands, moved their tongues over their lips and blew kisses to him from hands trembling with desire.

He lifted his gaze and saw the young women. Oh, God, leaning dangerously over the edges of the balconies, the loveliest of the town dropped insolent handkerchiefs impregnated with the furor of their bodies. Dumbfounded, Suárez caught one and, so great was the commotion the odor caused in the depths of his being, he wondered if it was worth rebelling. Maybe the wise course was to close his eyes and let himself be taken away, stunned, by that great uterus of delight. A drum roll brought his gaze forward, and above the coach he spied Doña Raquel, who from the balcony waved to the people. "I should do it!" he mumbled. "Damn, I should do it!" because his heart, deaf to the dictates of his head, was surily opposed within his chest. He estimated at a glance the distance and realized that he barely had time to gather up his courage. He closed his eyes and found that everything was ready: words, gestures, movements, and, above all, the final onslaught of his vengeance. He had only to wait until the carriage covered the block and, enveloped in acclamations, he entered the domains of the goddess. But then, as the first horses reached the corner a rocket whistled through the air, bounced on the ground, and got caught in the hooves of a horse that whinnied, surprised by the snake of sparks and smoke. "Whooooaaaa!" shouted the coachman, who was unable to control with the reins the fear of the rearing beasts. Behind the dense, fetid cloud of smoke, Suárez saw the bodies of two horses rising on their hind legs and the madness began: the screams of people fleeing, the violent jolt pulling them off the designated route and bolting, downhill, along a street that led to the river. "Stop, for the love of God, stop!" Suárez screamed, slamming into the sides of the coach, fearing the bottom of the precipice. To no effect. Given the clumsy movements of the coachman, Suárez understood that the man wasn't going to regain control over that chaos. "I have to jump," he thought and immediately got to his feet. Another jolt and he fell to the side, hitting his temple against the small door. Dizzy, he touched his forehead and saw blood on his fingers. Then, engulfed in pain and blood, Suárez observed the inexplicable: He saw the coachman lift the whip and bring it down on the horses, encouraging them in their mad race. "What are you doing!" he shouted. But the coachman, as though responding to a polite comment, turned toward Suárez and smiled, lifting his hat. "No!" Suárez exclaimed, and the hand with the bite marks quickly disappeared. That smile revealed the origin of the mark he had discovered that morning. "It can't be!" But the smile remained, implacable, when the coach left the edge of the cliff and began to float through the air.

"The kiss?" Suárez asked. "Shouldn't it be on the other hand?" But he immediately realized that his question had no purpose. That since that morning he had rushed for glory and that all the rest was mere spectacle, a formality invented for those who had yet to meet my face.

JORGE VELASCO MACKENZIE
(Guayaquil, 1949)

Jorge Velasco Mackenzie, a student of literature and traveler to Spain and Mexico, currently teaches at the university level.

The author's published story collections include *De vuelto al paraíso* (1975), *Como gato en tempestad* (1977), *Raymudo y la creación del mundo* (1979), *Músicos y amaneceres* (1986, Nacional José de la Cuadra Literary Prize, 1983), *Palabra de maromero* (1986), *Clown y otros cuentos* (1988), *Desde una oscura vigilia* (1992), and *No tanto como todos los cuentos* (collected stories, 1998).

Velasco Mackenzie has published four novels: *El rincón de los justos* (1983, prize for the best novel of the year, sponsored by the Society of Ecuadorian Writers, 1984). *Tambores para una canción perdida* (1986), *El ladrón de levita* (1990), and *En nombre de un amor imaginario* (1996, first prize in the Fourth Biannual Ecuadorian Novel Contest). Finally, he has written a play entitled *En esta casa de enfermos* (1991).

The writer's works have been included in anthologies in Ecuador and abroad, and translated into English, German, French, Italian, and Portuguese.

Velasco Mackenzie's works, through which runs the theme of exclusion, constitute an interesting probing into urban misery, especially that of Guayaquil. The best manifestation of this is found in his novel *El rincón de los justos*, a work of great vitality as well as sensuality at the textual level. One of Velasco's greatest virtues is his ear for the speech, and his eye for the surroundings, of his characters. His narrative has opened over time to more fictitious worlds, and he has even explored the genre of historical fiction.

RAYMUNDO AND THE CREATION
OF THE WORLD*

On the first day of creation, Raymundo looked at the earth, round and parceled like the shell of a turtle, set up a blue taffeta tent on the big hill, and sat down to watch. The fields were deserted, sunk in profound darkness. So Raymundo switched on the generator and there was light, white during the day and yellow at night, and nailed a large sign over the tent that said:

thE worLd. vAudEVille CiRcuS

and presented the first show. Zacarias Carpio and Sufragio Intriago came with their wives to see what was going on but nobody went to the show that day because Raymundo still hadn't built a bridge over the waters that separated the large hill from the rest of the planet. The bridge was built, and he called it El PaSo, a name he'd heard in other distant lands. The first fish jumped in the water, and they were waterprickers, strawhats, snorers, names new to those incredulous ears.

*From the collection *Raymundo y la creación del mundo*, 1979.

The women, impelled by the black wind of curiosity, asked their husbands for permission to go and have a look. Raymundo stopped them halfway across El PaSo and demanded two animals, female and male, as the price of admission. To everyone who paid he gave a red ticket on which his name was printed, and he put the animals in a corral so that they would reproduce, the hog with the sow, the dog with the bitch, the rooster with the hen, each one with its species, and presented the first show. He performed the somersault without a safety net, he was clown, juggler, and weightlifter. When he threw his head back to swallow the swords, he decided that he needed two assistants, a man and a woman, to present a complete show.

At dawn on the second day, he walked silently among the four dirt-poor houses in the area, he moved his white spats over the big hill and the little hill, he got to the town in no hurry. At the first corner, sleeping, off a binge, was Antúnez. Raymundo put him on his feet like a man of clay, blew in his face to rouse him, and, as he came to, said to him, starting today you will walk in the air, you will gather balloons that I will release over the heads of monkeys, and you will perform the strangest of acts. Antúnez managed to say yes, and allowed himself to be led by Raymundo who had already seen the wound in his ribs. Without asking about the cause, he left him sleeping under the blue tent and went to look for the hand that had left the mark on the ribs of his assistant.

Someone waved a right hand of painted nails at him, and when he followed with his eyes those fingers as slender as onion stalks, he found slim arms and a prominent bust, until, a little bit surprised, he looked at

Evelina and dragged her like a doll to his side and told her that beginning today you will take care that Antúnez doesn't break his noggin while he's walking in the air and you will make sure that the balloons don't burst over the heads of the monkeys and you will perform the strangest acts: the tiger leap, the legs on the shoulders, the taming of the colt. She said yes, and went with Raymundo to the tent, and lay down next to the assistant who slept dreaming about heaven on earth. When they woke up, they found themselves united, he to her and she to him, dressed in nakedness quicker than fever. The owner of the world gave them two new sets of clothes so that they could cover themselves and he set them to earning their keep with the sweat of their brows: They scrubbed the pigsties, cleaned the dog houses, hatched the hens' eggs, while Raymundo, resting in his hammock of *mocora* fiber, made plans for the third day of creation.

While the circus presented the evening show that was prolonged with Antúnez floating through the air on cables, Raymundo watched the Turks who came unannounced, situating themselves on the other side of the waters now tamed, opening trunks, and offering trinkets, earrings, and colored glass, papers that looked like bits of gold and fabric embroidered with flowers and parrots. Before going into the tent and leaving the animals in the hands of the owner of the World, his assistants bought those useless things. The women made themselves smart with the earrings, they wore the colored stones on their fingers, they dressed themselves in the fabric, with a bird on the shoulder or a flower on the chest, and made their men carry clay pots disguised with enamel paint, wooden spoons decorated with green ribbons, a quill with indelible ink that produced invisible writing. Behind the Turks the Chinese came with their delicacies from the Orient, and the inhabitants of the world ate under the big top, throwing the leftovers to the ground which little by little was covered with noodles and chicken legs, lettuce leaves and celery stalks, shrimp, tamarind seeds, hard-boiled eggs, all those tidbits spiced to excess that the Chinese prepared in great earthenware pans. Then the whores came, and the thieves, the women installed their brothels next to the diners, and the thieves got in lines to absent-mindedly slip their able fingers into the pockets of those who made up the clientele.

So Raymundo's circus was an exciting place, a tumult where strange languages were spoken, where phrases were pronounced in which the *p* was a *b* in the mouths of the Turks, and the *r* turned into an *l* under the blunt tongues of the Chinese. What's worse, said Evelina while she twisted herself into a ball of flesh before the respectable one, is that strange language of casseroles and thieves, where everything is heard backwards, as if when speaking they were reading what they say in a hand mirror.

Illusions, said Raymundo, when he saw the trinket sellers reflected in the dark quicksilver of his fury. It was true that the owner of the world didn't know how to read or write, that he didn't even know how to sign his name with two lines forming a cross, but he knew his powers. The monkeys refused to perform the act with the colored balloons and masturbated in front of him; so he canceled the nightly function and looked for a roll of barbed wire, crossed El PaSo with a firm step, and with Antúnez's help nailed the first post across from the stands of the Turks and the second beyond at the tables of the Chinese, and the last at the very door to the brothels, and then he stretched the wire and made a circle around the hill he considered his.

In spite of angry protests, the squatters saw their merchandise strewn over the ground, the Bucarams, the Adoums stood stiff with anger over their empty trunks. Old Chan Chan, an expert at fried shrimp and chicken with rice, felt the little white grains falling like rain over his bald head. Cast out of the World, the peddlers set up their stands beyond, marginalized, forgotten by the crowd, on the edge of bankruptcy, they formed a group and decided to open a great store, as high as the hill on which they stood. From there they looked at the circus growing, the blue big top decorated with hundreds of stars swelling, filled with more and more spectators. The Chinese, who were always the most enterprising, located themselves below, opened the shops named after their stews, wantag, chu lu, and put golden bells at their doors, and real sunflowers, and always the drawing of a jacaranda on the shiny windows. The Turks, not known for caution, made the next floor, where from the balconies they hoisted silks, linens, and percalines that continued mysteriously to arrive. The first Club de la Unión was also housed there, with its immense *U* fixed over the main window. Bamboo and poles continued to form the ToWEr, as it came to be known; the whores and the thieves took their places, other people were housed. Copulation spread like a vice among the sons of the Chinese and the prostitutes, among the Turkish women and the thieves who made love on top of the goods that life had provided.

And the town came again, uniting their purity with impurity, they learned other voices, knew other bodies, bought objects even more useless and ugly. Revolvers for personal offense, evening dresses for affairs, and tasted exotic delicacies, frogs' legs fried in oil, boiled opossum, they tried everything and made its acquaintance, while the circus of the World went under, the big top deflated, empty of crowds. Evelina and Antúnez fled, running from the fury of Raymundo who accused them of living in sin, the woman carried a nine-month ball in her belly, and the man, for the first time since they woke him from his binge, felt ashamed of all that had come to pass.

Raymundo, as lonely as on the first day of creation, his teeth clenched, said that the plagues would be snuffed out like a flame, the plagues and the World would end in a rain of ash as white as the passing years. With rapid step he crossed for the last time the bridge he had built with his own hands, came to the plain and crossed it in two strides. At the ToWEr, which at that hour slept the sleep of its greatest excesses, he extended his finger which was like a flame at the tip of his nail. What was at first a spark soon turned into a tongue of fire, long like the tongue of an anteater, and then it was an immense flame that embraced the building, consuming Chinese and delicacies, Turks and gabardines, whores and pimps, everything coming to an end until, with a sudden collapse, a spark from those fires jumped to the big top trying to flee the catastrophe, but the innocent little glow set the light blue fabric on fire and from one moment to the next it turned bright red with the flames, burning jerkins and masks, elephants with trunks extended spraying streams of fire instead of water, lions with singed manes and without fierceness. The fire, like evil, brought all to an end; of the circus there remained only a remnant of the great sign burned at the edges and then when the ash turned into a mist that spread throughout the place, Raymundo watched the monkeys leave the ruins unharmed, performing their act with colored balloons on burnt sticks, on the bones of animals burned to a crisp, after looking at his work destroyed he watched them head down into unknown valleys. The monkeys began another descent, clumsily imitating men, until there came the dark cloud that today covers the great Hill like a curse.

ELIÉCER CÁRDENAS
(Azogues, 1950)

Eliécer Cárdenas, born in the southern province of Cañar, achieved recognition in 1979 with his excellent novel *Polvo y ceniza* (winner of the national Casa de la Cultura Award, 1978) now in its sixth edition, two of which have been published abroad. His other novels include *Juego de mártires* (1976), *El ejercicio* (1978), *Del silencio profundo* (1980), *Háblanos Bolívar* (1984), *Las humanas certezas* (1989), *Los hombres de provecho* (1990), *Que te perdone el viento* (1993), *Una silla para Dios* (1997), and *El oscuro final del Porvenir* (2000).

The author has also published three story collections: *Hoy, al general* (1971), *Siempre se mira al cielo* (1995), and *La incompleta hermosura* (1996), and a play, *Morir en Vilcabamba* (1989).

Cárdenas is a journalist and has organized the Bi-annual International Art Exhibition in Cuenca. His stories have been translated into English, French, and German, and have been included in a number of Ecuadorian short story anthologies.

During a period of empty formal experimentation, Eliécer Cárdenas demonstrated an unusual gift for freshness, a steady hand, and brilliance in his narrative. Without a doubt, *Polvo y ceniza* is one of the best and most original manifestations of realism in the Ecuadorian novel. None of his other works, be they short stories or novels, has achieved the surprising vitality of this novel, a recreation, both romantic and realistic, of the life of a rural bandit.

THE SWEET STABBING*

*And so the inheritance came to me,
a poor hope, and also the small
object, and I went out into the world.*
NORMAN MAILER

He must have come late at night. After the last soap
opera that the radio apparatus tore to shreds with tears
and perverse cries in the room at the back, my parents'
room. That's when it must have been. Otherwise, I
would have heard pounding at the door, or at least a
whistle, the steps hurrying to open it, the dogs in the
entire neighborhood barking. I would have heard
everything from my bed. But at that age sleep comes
like a sweet stabbing in the temples and an overwhelming desire to forget everything: the exams coming up, standing in line in the school patio, the scold-
ings, mama's muffled voice when, with the morning
coffee, she made papa pray difficult prayers that would
help him in the world outside, she claimed, in the difficult world of work.

It was midnight, I'm sure of that. The words woke

---

*From the collection *Siempre se mira al cielo*, 1995.

me up when they must have already been stringing together the stilted conversation for some time, poisoned by bad memories, with allusions, calculated questions and answers, reticent. I'd never seen him before. One day they told me that he'd died in the jungle, another time that he was in bad shape, very bad, in some hospital they couldn't name. When he was mentioned, Papa shook his head in silence and mama sighed, saying, "poor thing." I imagined him to be very tall, the owner of mysterious suitcases in which everything fit, and leather boots split at the sides by the mud of terrible storms and the crushing force of the sun. He sat at the head of the table, tearing a piece of bread into small piece, while papa looked at the beams in the ceiling and mama said, sadly, if we had known you were coming we'd have had something more than bread and plain coffee. He looked at me; he left his bread in crumbs and pulled me toward his face, sweaty and smelling of a cigarette recently smoked. He was small, much smaller than papa, and he wore shoes with indigent tongues, filled with the white dust of highways, and he had a moustache that reminded me of the movies they showed in the park. He must have had a nice voice and played the guitar at least as well as papa, I thought during the embrace of that stranger who was my uncle Antonio: the one who was lost, the traveler, the one with the bad head, the man who took off with the family's entire stock of adventures. Maybe that's why papa was so sad, so coldly sedentary.

He brought a single suitcase. In fact, a little pile of hard canvas, with holes and dark stains. He and that suitcase, I found out from the bench I chose in the kitchen so that I could study him carefully and without any sympathy whatsoever, though filled with curiosity and shyness, came from Puerto Cabello. Where was that? Venezuela, where our first president was born, I remembered from the fourth grade teacher. He looked at his rough, thin hands, and he rubbed them together as though he were cold. He was working there in a factory where they made powerful poisons and breathing them in the warehouses had made him very ill. His teeth, when he smiled, were the same yellow color as the light bulb, like that ceramic bulb that adorned our monotonous meals from the center of the table. Papa coughed his smoker's cough and said that a while ago he had heard him say that he had come from the Amazon. That was before, uncle Antonio quickly corrected, accepting with a slight movement of his shoulders another steaming cup of coffee that mama offered. That in the Amazon a Shuar chief went after him with all of his naked warriors for refusing to take his daughter as his wife. He was so brave hunting alligators with his spear that the chief, impressed, wanted to make him a son-in-law, in other words, the future chief of the tribe. Papa coughed again. His tone was much colder and almost bitter: But in a letter in which the uncle asked for money, he had said that he was involved in a very dangerous mission at the border. Uncle Antonio looked to me for support, and to mama who, though her head was bowed, was listening to every word. Yes, said uncle Antonio, that before the matter with the Shuar chief he had been a spy on the border. General Zurita sent him on the highly risky, top-secret mission reserved for courageous civilians like him, downriver on the Curaray to study enemy fortifications, landing strips, arms, and the approximate number of troops. A platoon of Peruvians captured him. He was transferred as an enemy agent to Lima, but on the way he jumped from the plane and was saved, unharmed, because he landed in the crown of an immense *ishpingo* tree. Papa no longer dared to cough and said that uncle Antonio would sleep in my room, in the bed of my brother Roberto, who was a seminarian at the time. I couldn't object. I'd never heard the snores of a stranger, worse, those of an uncle I was just getting to know.

The walls of the room were yellow. He looked at them slowly as he entered; he went up to one, scratched with his fingernail at the paint which came off leaving a blue scar on the wall. Uncle Antonio smiled. "The room was blue, I clearly remember that," he said, and then he turned to the high ceiling, contemplating its chipped uneven surface with bamboo showing through like an old skeleton. Next, he asked me if we could move one of the beds into the opposite corner. Surprised, I told him yes, and we moved my brother Roberto's decrepit bedstead, leaving shiny marks on the wood floor. "Now we need a chair," he announced, "so that I can reach the ceiling." I went to the dining room for the highest chair and I must have made a lot of noise because, from his room, papa asked me what I was doing. It was odd seeing a man I didn't know in my room climbing a chair he'd put on the bed and reaching to pat the plaster ceiling. I didn't say anything. Papa had taught me that it's not good to ask adults questions whenever I felt like it. Uncle Antonio managed to stick his fingers into the biggest crack in the ceiling, the one completely festooned with old cobwebs, balancing himself on his feet so that he didn't fall to the floor. He nearly yelled when he said that yes, that it had been there all those years. He pulled a stiff, smudged piece of paper out of the crack. "This was the map to the treasure in the ceiling," he said as he care-fully unfolded the paper. "Your dad and I searched for it on moonlit nights." I also didn't want to ask if they'd found anything in the ceiling. His narrow face seemed happy then. I looked at the paper: The marks had faded.

That would have been the night, warmer than usual, that we stayed awake, lying there, making our beds creak until well after midnight when I heard him get up and look in his shirt for a cigarette. Lighting it, he began to talk to me, not like I was someone he'd just met but as though we were lifelong acquaintances. And as though he and I were the same age then. Uncle Antonio's voice broke the room's formless gloom into little pieces. And he told me that there were terrible women in the world, evil, sinners. That a man's secret for never getting drunk was to drink a good quarter bottle of oil before a party, and then to eat a large, spongy piece of bread. Then you could drink all you wanted. But if some woman, one of those evil ones, knew the man's secret, she'd go purring around the man, burning him with endless ardent glances, lan-guidly dropping a perfumed handkerchief, and when he bent to pick it up the unfortunate man would drop dead on the spot. "Because of the bread and the oil," he added as he threw the cigarette to the floor and its burning tip was a red anguish that glowed in the night. I swore to him that I would never pick up any woman's handkerchief. "That's best," he said to me and slept with satisfied snores, while dozens of perverse women with perfumed handkerchiefs attacked my dreams and left them naked in the living flesh of insomnia.

I didn't go to school the next day because of him. While we drank the insipid coffee that mama called "half-coffee with lima beans," he suggested that I go for a walk with him through town. "Missing a day of school isn't going to make a donkey out of you," he said, and his mouth opened like a dry fruit displaying uneven, white seeds. I carried my notebooks, though I didn't know what to do with them later. I felt ashamed, a sluggard in the town's hard-working streets, with their rows of ocher mud walls and chestnut guama trees whose blossoms burst open on tiled roofs. I followed him, that's all, without asking questions. In the park, we stopped at a stand with magazines for rent. We sat on adjoining benches and read two magazines that we later exchanged when the fat man in charge wasn't looking. He'd chosen one with true romances in which a man meets a married woman and dies in a flash of gunfire on a stormy night. "Love is the cruelest thing in life," he commented as he led me down a street to the stands made of sheets of tin in the market. "Do you know how to eat easy?" he asked walking past a pan of golden potato patties, a shiny, big-bellied pot where some sort of soup boiled that probably had revived drunks that morning, and truck drivers who worked nights. Innocent, I said yes. I'll never know the texture and flavor of that soup. All I remember is that the little table at the stand was indigo and worn, with uneven legs, that there were dead flies on the surface, and a glass of badly cut papers that served as napkins. He got up and told me to wait for a minute after he left. He walked solemnly, in no hurry, as though he were just going to urinate against the nearby wall.

With my heart pounding, agitated, producing thunder-claps loud enough to give us away, I bolted, knocking over the chair, carelessly forgetting my notebooks. He was waiting for me at a light post two blocks up the street, shaking with laughter. And we lost ourselves in the bitter, noisy labyrinth of the market. Later we walked to the station where the trucks were parked, impassive at that hour, their mudguards yellow with grime, their names, the funereal color of dust on their hoods, and their steering wheels motionless in the cabs.

The guy with the malicious face and kinky hair who recognized him must have come from the freshness of the crowd of trucks, from the darkness of the tarps covering their boxes. He took him by the arm to talk behind a truck. Uneasy, I watched from afar as they whispered, and then gesticulated, as though they were about to start fighting. Uncle Antonio returned with his head down, as though he had left his contentment in that man's kinky hair. I didn't ask him anything; but he told me that one day I would understand why the world is bad. Nothing could restore my happiness, not the breadfruit that he took from a stand in the market, pretending to bump against something, nor the sweet flowing juice when we ate them on a bench in the park, where I began to damn the hour I'd forgotten my note-books.

Uncle Antonio didn't talk much during lunch. Papa advised him, and he was eloquent, telling him that he ought to reform, settle down somewhere. "You're not a gypsy," he said to my uncle, "you're a Suárez, from the good side of the family." That was when I saw my uncle's last smile.

That afternoon, terrified about my lost notebooks,

depressed because the petty crimes I'd committed with him might be discovered, I invented a headache that my uncle helped me perfect, telling mama that it could be sunstroke: a very serious condition if one didn't stay in bed for at least two days. He knew all about it from the terrible sun in Salinas where he worked in the salt mines with only a linen cloth to protect his head.

Lying in bed with my invented illness, I heard Uncle Antonio's to-ings and fro-ings, his moving about in different rooms, his goings and comings from the patio and the bathroom. Mama must have been busy in the kitchen. At dusk, Uncle Antonio came to my room and sat on the edge of the bed. He told me, cruel, that mama was making a dreadful dish of angel hair noodles without salt. Then he was silent. He pressed my hand and left. I must have fallen asleep because the sounds from outside turned into a timeless moan, the peace of a lying-sick boy, almost a fugitive.

Mama shrieked, insulted papa, the entire family. "That swine took all the clothes, even the sheets," she sobbed, maybe from the dining room. When I woke up I couldn't figure out where her cries were coming from. Papa mumbled confusing replies. Then he went out, leaving us with an ominous slam of the door. I sat up. Uncle Antonio's canvas bag was on his unmade, sheetless bed, as though inviting me to pick it up. And another thing I hadn't noticed at first: There was something clutched in my right hand. Dizzy with mama's renewed cries, I unfolded the paper. And I managed to make out, very clearly, as though they had been printed the day before, the markings on the map to the treasure in the ceiling.

GILDA HOLST
(Guayaquil, 1952)

Gilda Holst Molestina studied literature in Guayaquil, where she also worked in Miguel Donoso Pareja's literary workshops. She has published two short story collections, *Más sin nombre que nunca* (1989) and *Una turba de signos*. Her stories have been published in numerous anthologies, including Julio Ortega's *El Nuevo cuento latinoamericano*. The writer has also written a novel, *Dar con ella* (2000).

Holst´s works constitute an ironic, humorous demystification of the way the world has been organized by men. Nevertheless, the worn routine of daily life is the reality that offers the greatest surprises, which the writer transmits in a fashion that is always subtle and fresh.

REUNION*

for Simone de Beauvoir

If it's precision we're after, we would have to take into account the reunion of my husband's former class-mates as the point of departure for the changes I've undergone. They hadn't seen one another for eight years. Most were professionals by then, with their respective roles to play: lawyers, engineers, pot heads, salesmen, psychologists, doctors, writers, and with their respective spouses or fiancées to introduce. The introductions came and went, the once-overs, the high school jokes, the nicknames, the "remember when…," the "whatever happened to…," the "I swear, man…" They left us women in a corner, looking at one another with neutral, bored faces, and with nothing to talk about, obviously. Little by little the "what a lovely dress, where did you get it?" began, while in the men's section they had already gone beyond the cars-acquired-and-cars-discussed stage and that of last Sunday's goals, and were at how to get laid most effec-

*From the collection *Más sin nombre que nunca*, 1989.

tively by women who were very good at it. But they always went back to high school, to the fag priest, that bastard Rodríguez, the arithmetic mean hanging on the blackboard, the laughs. In the women's section, they didn't talk, or even pretend to know anything, about subjects that had nothing to do with maids and children. I got up and walked over to the men. I probably should have stayed at the edge of the group, carrying a tray or doing something to cloak my presence, but I moved to the center. There was silence and I saw Roberto's face, undone, drop to the floor and end up deeply embarrassed among the shoes. The others, ill at ease, didn't know where to look and or what to do. From between my legs, the odor of sex began to filter and everybody noticed. Luckily, just then dinner was announced.

When we got home, Roberto said I was filthy and worse, and no matter how much I assured him that I'd bathed before going out and that I couldn't explain what had happened either, he didn't believe me.

The first few days after the incident, I didn't go out at all, constantly worried that the phenomenon would recur. I bathed three to five times a day and sprinkled myself with talcum power and cologne at least as often. Since it didn't happen again, I returned to my usual activities, though taking strict precautions without fail. Never, under any circumstances, did I go out without washing myself. I wore slacks and every two hours changed the scented sanitary napkin I used. I noted that Roberto seemed content because in those months I never had to say to him: "Wait, I'm going to wash myself."

Everything was fine, there wasn't the slightest hint

of what was to come. The room was small, a few people, faces without makeup, simple dress, beer, smoke, and from somewhere a song. After two hours, everyone was chatting together, but there was no doubt that Andrés was the center of attention. He surprised us with his observations, made us laugh with his jokes, listened when that was called for. He acknowledged all the women, reflected on politics, knew, with all due modesty, that he was superior, and he was happy. I also participated frequently, but within precise limits in order to maintain the flow of conversation: agreement with a nod of the head, occasional admiring glances, a number of discrete expressions of verbal support. Then a subject on which I was well versed came up for discussion. I wasn't aware of anything until I felt a mixture of surprise, disdain, and horror in the looks that came to rest on my person. My voice had been moderate and the argument I proposed simply another point of view. I tried to position myself in the last possible refuge and said to him: "It could be that you are right." But it was useless, Andrés kept moving away. They got up, covering their noses, and situated themselves in groups at the far end of the room. I've never turned so red in my entire life, nor felt so humiliated.

I covered my face with my hands and perceived that dreadful odor in my body. I left running, without waiting for Roberto, who also left after apologizing to everybody.

I didn't get a cab for fear that the taxi driver would smell me. I walked, I walked for a long time, and when I finally got home I ran in desperation to the bathroom and washed myself ten, fifteen, twenty times, to no end. The odor spread in waves, erupted from everything, impregnated the walls, filtered through doors and windows, I couldn't hide myself anywhere, the odor gave me away: My mouth, my gestures, my skin, even my words smelled. There was nothing to be done about it, the odor stayed, very still, forever present. Roberto didn't return.

I didn't go out, I couldn't stand myself. But then an odd thing happened: My sense of smell began to get used to it. I accepted the idea that I had to be like that. Becoming accustomed to having it forever, there were times when I didn't even remember it. On other occasions, I sought it out. It took on a life of its own, sometimes very strong, sometimes tenuous and sweet, sometimes strange and new. There are still a lot of people who can't stand me, but I don't care anymore, I like perceiving myself with my smells, and thinking that the end of the conversation was ridiculous, when Andrés said that I thought like that because I was a woman and I said that no, that I thought like that because I was right.

LILIANA MIRAGLIA
(Guayaquil, 1952)

Liliana Miraglia, an accomplished photographer, studied literature at the Catholic University in the port city of Guayaquil. She has published two story collections: *La vida que parece* (1989) and *Un close up prolongado* (1996). Her works have been used by Julio Ortega in his literature classes at Brown University (USA).

The writer is an artist in the field of photography. Her expertise in this respect is reflected in her subtle, ambiguous narrative. Miraglia's stories, based on the slightest of anecdotes, reveal the ambivalence and even the lie that flows from the evidence provided by the senses, particularly that of sight.

THE LIVING ROOM*

Thinking about having a dog again turned out to be one of the hardest decisions our family had ever dared to make, for reasons more or less serious, worth taking into account, but also, I believe, though this seem absurd, because we had just installed wall-to-wall carpeting in the living room. Actually, what we had carpeted wall-to-wall wasn't the living room as such but an area designated the living room, within a space that also contained the dining room and the entry way, the area papa preferred, where he spent the entire day because the fact is that back then papa spent the entire day there.

The carpeting of that bit of the house was a project delayed for a long time, because it was papa who wanted to do it and mama who was constantly opposed because she said that papa was the only one who used that part of the house and that afterwards cleaning was going to be a serious problem because one became a slave to the vacuum cleaner and the spot removers, and of course mama apologized later, papa couldn't get it that dirty, but that in any event the car-

*From the collection *Un close up prolongado*, 1996.

pet was going to limit our freedom and that what if at some point we decided to have a dog again, or something to that effect.

Papa didn't say anything at first, accepting in silence, from within his pale skin accentuated by the purplish color of his bathrobe, the fact that he had no argument, but then he didn't, later he started to protest. Weakly, at first, until one day, according to Adela, he stood firm and I can still see her lips move as she said the word firm, and asked, begged, that that part of the house be carpeted and so it was, they installed a carpet with long, soft pile that mama chose, brown speckled with little flecks of white and orange. I remember that papa sat on the sofa next to the record player and his feet in his slippers seemed to sink into the carpet's deep pile, as though they might disappear any minute now as soon as somebody forgot about them, like a sleeping dog, papa very quiet, with his music that at the time was becoming all that was left of him.

I would have known about the trouble I was getting myself into, even if Adela hadn't reminded me. Mama's comment about the carpet and the dog got me to thinking, and not because it was that important but because I'd always known mama like that, argumentative, obsessive, formidable, always wanting to have the last word about everything, and also always trying to blame others for her failures, her own failures, and there's no doubt that the matter of the last dog side by side with that of the carpet could be considered a failure in her life. Mama and her bad habit of competing, her need to be perfect. I remember that before that dog we had had others that hadn't been around for long, a little female pointer that Adela and I wanted to call

Alexandra and that mama wouldn't let us, worse, she was horrified and made it perfectly clear with reasons and all for why dogs should have dog names and all the better if these had only two syllables and she called her Luba and I stepped on Luba's paw, without meaning to, of course, one day when I was in a hurry to get to school and later I spent the entire day crying and nobody knew why, because I didn't want to say anything and at school I had to listen to the usual comments about how strange we were. Later it was a cocker spaniel that I don't want to remember, black and crazy, not very intelligent, which mama was never able, because it was always mama who was in charge of these things, to teach not to ruin in a fraction of a second whatever piece of paper he found in his path be it yesterday's newspaper or today's and what drove her craziest was that he wasn't a normal dog because he could never lift his leg to pee the way male dogs are supposed to. I truly believe that mama always thought that we looked ridiculous having a male dog that peed like a female and even worse with such basic imperfections.

So mama took Doggy, because again it was mama who got her way with the dog's name in spite of the fact that Adela and I used to call him Alberto when she couldn't hear us, in hand from the start and she didn't make a single mistake and it was shake and two cookies, and sit in English because it's shorter than *siéntate* and a piece of a biscuit, and the famous and stellar up, Doggy standing on his hind legs for a chicken breast, treats that once the lesson was learned he didn't get any more but that he continued to hope for because of that thing about reflexes. Doggy´s hygienic habits were also impressive, except for the fleas that would have proliferated if we had had a carpet then. He was an exemplary dog, mama didn't have to teach him to lift his leg to pee, he was a beautiful dog, the envy of the neighborhood, very different from the lap dogs our neighbors had, until the terrible day of the incident in the park, a four-legged incident like Doggy, white with a curled tail, who wrested the perfect Doggy from mama's hands with no remorse and took him who-knows-where which we never found out.

However, mama's perfections didn't matter much to me, I truly thought about having a dog again, even if it peed on the carpet and filled it with fleas, and I wanted one even more each time I saw papa's slippers next to the sofa, lying on the long pile of the carpet, just the way he left them.

AMINTA BUENAÑO
(Santa Lucía, 1958)

Aminta Buenaño, born in the coastal province of Guayaquil, has published two short story collections, *La mansión de los sueños* (1985) and *La otra piel* (1992). Her stories have won numerous prizes, both in Ecuador and in Spain, and appear in anthologies of contemporary Ecuadorian literature of the highest quality.

SPLENDOR IN THE DARK*

On my sad breast a wilted flower rests, like the one you gave me when we met. It was odd, yellow, the wild color of grand passions. You pressed it to my lips, brushing yours lightly against mine, and then, violently, as though it were a strange warrior rite, you snatched it away and looking deeply into my eyes, as though a decided thirst for vengeance were forcing you to defy me, you devoured it little by little, until only its dying stem danced between your lips, and then, just imagine, it seemed as if you were waiting for a final plea. For some odd reason, I though about a cat with a bird between its claws and, painfully, I turned my face to you.

It was April and there were birds and shadows among the trees and the cries of little boys chasing dogs, your smile opened, insolent, to the world, with the same metallic stridence of the menacing chains that hung from your hands so that people would be afraid of you. Your head shaved punk style, the many holes wisely opened in your faded jeans, the pointed slogans screaming from your t-shirts, and the incredible tattoo

*From the collection *Veintiún cuentistas ecuatorianos,* 1996.

of a quail with a bull's head that made me shudder a little, delighted, I even laughed with you when a couple of old men sunk in their dusty recall of old memories stopped their world for a moment to look at you in horror, and you deigned, from the imposing mass of your sarcastic biceps, to give them a pitying look that had something of disdain and a good deal of repulsion about it, and then, with a grimace, like someone sharing a regrettable confidence, you said in a low voice: "You've got to respect the old farts, I've got grandparents too." And, contradiction of contradictions, I felt more solidarity with you than with them, maybe because of that instinct that impels us more to life than to death. I remember that my ties date from that day, the miniskirt I never wore, the necklaces with the heart featuring John Lennon on one side and Hitler on the other, the buttons with the swastika and the hammer and sickle that functioned as safety pins on the frayed and dirty denim jacket that you loved and that, as proof of your love, you gave to me, four rock records that I could never like even though I tried hard and danced to them "like an expert," you said, with an enthusiastic thumbs-up, while you threw yourself onto the floor convulsively, strumming an imaginary guitar and I insisted upon imitating you, sinking in back pain and exhaustion.

The strange metamorphosis began that day in the park when I was someone else, and a cloud of dust like a cyclone producing seismic noises interrupted our date and nearly drowned us, and they were your friends from I don't know what gang, armed with their cycles and their dark helmets, surrounding us with their laughter and jokes, come to abduct you. You left me just like that, without a backward glance, calculating the precise gesture that would erase from their eyes love's weaknesses, and I went home with a feeling of foreboding, overwhelmed by a strange sensation of fatigue, as though I had run a great distance and was out of breath. That night I couldn't sleep, but not for the usual reasons, the house, the cooking, the interminable cleaning. That old bed where I'd given birth to my children began to spin like an ancient wheel of love that I had thought forgotten, I imagined you in different circumstances, outrageous, I rehearsed what I would say to you, I anticipated your replies, the pretty clothes I'd wear to impress you, I dreamed of understanding you, and silly me, see how love makes fools of us, I believed we were equals. I tossed and turned, nervous, suddenly everything was imbued with a supernatural reality and shone, yes, shone, with a new, blinding light. I felt a persistent fluttering of invisible butterflies attacking furiously from within, the incessant rain falling on the sidewalk, reminiscent of the footsteps of a despotic, stubborn God, the tick-tock of a sleepless clock on the table talked to me of a dual reality from which there emerged a cold sheet of metal as thin as a piece of paper, bent, and that was me and I wasn't me. Torrential forces, all out of proportion, heretofore unknown, shook me, cruelly mocked my will and my reasons, and I felt hopelessly attracted to them, trapped, like those nocturnal insects, suicidal lovers of light. I remember that my husband was restless. He´s a light sleeper and unusual noises wake him. He asked me several time, floating in that state between sleeping and waking, what was wrong. And I, like a child caught doing something she isn't supposed to, with guilt weighing insidiously, made things up, the children's uniforms, his wages that always fell short, and I kept him from sleeping in the end, as always. Doubly remorseful, I stroked his back, that large, docile back, and consoling ourselves we made the love we always made, and that was when I first made love to you.

Ah, what a fool I am. So many times I believed you, like a child delightedly sucking a piece of candy, I believed your flattery, I hung onto your pretty phrases, fascinated, the way a drowning person hangs onto the last board torn from the ship, and a week later, like a fifteen-year-old in need of sleep, I said all the things girls say when they are in love.

Yes, it's true that I'm not young, a point you hurled into my face the last time, as though that fact offended you. It's true that I have crowfeet around my eyes, a few lines in my forehead, and stretch marks from my pregnancies, but I'm not old yet. It's not true that I dye my hair, not yet, nor will I be seeing a plastic surgeon next month, as maliciously, a cigarette dangling from the corner of your mouth, you heartlessly advised from among our tangled white sheets. It's not true. I don't know what unfathomable impulse drove you to such lengths to make me suffer for no reason. Sometimes a long, mysterious poison emerged from your lips and you only wanted to hurt me and to see me cry and that made you feel good. It's strange, because you talked of love and how you wanted to change the world, and you preached an ideology that enflamed your friends. Getting old is repulsive, you said. Why does it frighten you so? Some day you won't have on your lips that mad, frenetic laugh that lures, the way light lures moths, nor that crazy drive that makes you think you can be whatever you choose, a general, a president, Che Guevara, you'll share my suffering then, and maybe you'll remember me with a compassionate smile, and then, for the first time, though apart, we will be at peace. This isn't a reproach, it's just a matter of time and of my feelings trampled like the butt of the cigarette I've just smoked.

But no, I know that's not true, the person who said those things wasn't the boy who was so adorable when he pretended to be mature, with whom I, fearful, anxious, tender, like someone who tries a piece of fruit knowing that it will make her ill, fell in love. That boy who brandished his youth like the most solid of calling cards, but who at times seemed to turn into an old philosopher, unusually serious, who then recognized me, and what was oddest of all is that that was when I blossomed, sending out the softest of petals, and my neck straightened like an open crown and in you there grew, unexpectedly, the years, and there was, at times, a touch of weariness in your words. Like the time you asked, a little innocent, a little perverse, how old I was, and I dodged the question, like a girl who hides, ashamed, a scar that mars her features, and you, sweetly mature, took my trembling hand and said that what really mattered was the heart, and we walked through the park, creating a scene, perhaps painful and ridiculous. People would think that I was your mother, and I filled with the secret pleasure that came from knowing that I was your lover. Like a girl, I hung on to your arm listening, fascinated, to your dreams, your projects for seeding the earth with love and making, finally, war on all wars. You were young, furiously young, and your leather jacket and your jeans tight at the hips displayed with pride your recently discovered manhood, and you were bursting with vanity. I'm the best man in the world, you said without thinking, as though asking for confirmation, and there was something like a volcano in your look; later, now seriously convinced, you repeated those words, and it seemed that the park, the trees, the birds, and the world that lived around you disappeared in the spell cast by your thirst for the absolute.

I thank you for your grand passions. That night I watched television and washed the dishes, and when my daughter told me about her adventures, it even seemed possible to tell her about what we had. I felt so close to her, as though we had met in school and shared the same desk.

And then the calls and me, waiting in line, running, upset, at each impudent ring, fighting with my children for the telephone, talking in code, making secret dates, discovering, surprised, that the days don't repeat themselves, that there are days and that there are nights when pleas are met only by silence. Knowing that among the clothes I had to wash, the endless repetition of plates on the table, the gentle, tolerant voice of my husband asking about the children, you were there, that other reality, undefined but certain, noisily full of mysteries, offering yourself long, naked, indecipherable.

Something broke that afternoon when, after love's caresses, with the same anxiety of the fiancé who hides the ring in his hand, you asked me, suddenly aged, that I leave everything, that I abandon my children, my house, that I flee that quiet, stable world that is called a home. You promised countless joys where we would discover that happiness can be eternal, a house where the most intense of passions would reign, and a love so sacred that not even God's name would be sufficient to name it. You spoke with such force, there was so much heat in your gaze that it seemed more like you were talking of a battle, of a strategy arduously calculated to disarm love rather than to make it. Inflamed, surprised by my lack of enthusiasm for a proposal that you had prepared with the finest cellophane paper, you held me tight, hurting me, my wrists shaking with strange forebodings. Inevitably furious, in the gravest of tones, you demanded again that I break with everything, that I damn all to hell, with the typical mercilessness displayed by those who have never suffered, those who have yet to live the beginnings of disillusion, those who have not measured the defeat of their dreams, nor learned to raise the white flag of surrender. I cried, I trembled, and I even believe that I tried to convince you that we should live that love without commitments, without those small, horrible miseries caused by punishing others with what we have, accepting the probabilities of love with the same insistence with which one waits for rain, without giving up to machines and numbers. I ended by begging for mercy for this love that had come a little late, and you, it was as though a stone had hit you between the eyes, your face contorted and you pulled away, repulsed, as though suddenly in your mind the precise conclusion of your feelings had been revealed, the precise turn of your doubts, the exact bridge that would cut off communication between us, and it was maybe there when, for the first time, scornful, irritated, like someone spitting venom, you called me old.

There has never been a woman who followed you with such anxiety. There has never been a woman who spied on your lost moments, greeted with the warmest of smiles your friends just so that they would tell you about it, waited for hours across from doors at the university to watch you coming out with the cap falling over your eyes, the books in your arm, kicking pebbles. No mother has ever watched you with so much love, nor has any lover waited for you with such impatience, when rooted inside the car, disguised with a Spanish shawl and dark glasses I tried, though from afar, to get a glimpse of your face, to discover in your transparent look the slightest worry or feeling coming into being.

In the chance moments you chose to see me you seemed to calculate with hard determination the most cutting remarks, the most painful ways to look at me and demonstrate to me my failings, the naked presence of my years, to mock my love and even—I found this out later—to boast that "you did me the favor" of being with me. You hoped that I would leave you, that I would give you up for the sake of my dignity, as though defying my very presence, that self respect that ought, clearly, to have been in me, and you even went so far as to ask me, with that smile that made your face sweetly perverse, why I stayed with you. If you want an explanation, there is only this: I clung to you. With you, the tepid, battered roots of my dreams came to life again, they stirred, stunned, as though wanting to live again, as though wanting to rise up, and for a time they hurt, until they became numb once more. You were so sumptuous, so lovely, so young, in you I saw my broken dreams, the train I wanted to build that would take men to the Moon at the speed of the old Apollo, the countries I hoped to visit and the important person I dreamed of becoming, little by little I resigned myself to being the self-sacrificing woman, the good mother who fulfilled, almost every Sunday, that old ritual of going to the market after mass, of discussing, with fearless energy, as though it were a battle in which the destiny of mankind would be determined, the unpredictable fluctuation of prices. The woman secretly resigned to the small defeats she inflicted.

There was something of my dreams in the stubbornness with which I arranged Luisito's hair, soaking it with tonic and embroidering the ringlets with the same tenacity of someone creating a masterpiece in gold, I wanted people to ask who had arranged those curls, Luisito, who gave you that marvelous hairdo and for everyone, amazed, to conclude that you had the best mother in the world. There was a little of heaven in that. My children carried on their heads and in their white shirts that had cost my hands so many callouses, a bit of my dreams of being important. If you want another explanation, there is only this: I wanted to take revenge on fate, defy it, jump on it and smash it to pieces.

You think that I'm dying, but the opposite is true.

I'm not so silly as to complain, to blame you or beg you, I anticipated this sadness a thousand times, I suspected it long before meeting you and submerging myself in the strange labyrinth of your arms.

It would have been so easy to close my eyes to reality and let myself be pulled by the furious storm of your dreams, but no, that was impossible; I can't die now that I've been born. And so, even though you are far away, maybe lounging, playing those guitar solos, maybe remembering some strange or painful episode from the time we were in love, talking to my daughter whom you've begun to see, or inventing ingenious arguments to blow up—cigarettes and music at hand—the spirit of doubt in your listener and creating in a single breath the discussions that reveal your personality so completely, I'm going to remember you forever. With the same spirit that's in your look now, with the same vitality that smashed stars and powerfully defied life and its mysteries, with your delirious way of making love and discovering love, every single day.

I will be here, each night, next to my bonsai, maybe I'll look at the moon or sing one of my children to sleep on my lap, and there will always be for you, whispered between my lips, a prayer, as though you were a familiar paean, though beyond my reach.

Rest assured that in my memory your image will never be marred by the battle of the years; nor, when the winds blow, will your dreams be snuffed; nothing will take from you your youthful essence. Everything is in place, my love. Everything the same and certain. Indescribably beautiful and filled with mystery, like a fleeting adventure that sowed in me that strange sign of life…

RAÚL VALLEJO CORRAL
(Manta, 1959)

Writer, journalist, and university professor Raúl Vallejo Corral completed his university studies in Guayaquil. He served the nation during Rodrigo Borja's administration (1988-1992) as national director of the Literacy Campaign and minister of Public Education.

Vallejo has published six short story collections: *Cuento a cuento cuento* (1976), *Daguerrotipo* (1978, winner of the national Pablo Palacio Literary Prize in 1977), *Máscaras para un concierto* (1986), *Solo de palabras* (1988), *Manía de contar (personal anthology*, 1976-1988), *Fiesta de solitarios* (1992, winner of the literary contest sponsored by El Universo, to celebrate the Guayaquil daily's 70th anniversary in 1991 and winner of the National Joaquín Gallegos Lara Literary Prize for the best work published in 1992).

He has also written two novels, Todo temblor, *toda illusión, and Acoso textual* (1999), and three book-length essays: *Emelec, cuando la luz es muerte* (1988), *Una utopía para el siglo XXI* (1995), and *Crónica mestiza del Nuevo Pachakútik. Ecuador: del levantamiento indígena de 1990 al Ministerio Étnico de 1996* (1996).

The author has also published two anthologies of contemporary Ecuadorian literature: *Una gota de inspiración, toneladas de transpiración* (anthology of the new Ecuadorian short story, 1990) and the indispensable *Cuento ecuatoriano de finales del siglo XX. Antología crítica* (1999).

Love and marginalization (social, sexual) are the two recurrent themes in this prolific writer's works. With time, his style has gone beyond the facile so characteristic of the narrative of his generation. Today he is one of the most audacious experimentalists among Ecuadorian writers. His novel *Acoso textual* is a fine example of the use of hypertext in narrative. Nevertheless, the stories structured in a more traditional fashion are perhaps more sincere and accomplished than his experimental works.

FLASHES IN THE SEA*

for my daughter Daniela

When I was small they sent me to Manta for vacations. Well, you know what it's like being small and being sent. But I'm not complaining because it wasn't bad. My grandfather had a huge two-story house with a ton of rooms, or at least that's how it looked to me at nine years of age. I don't know why—when you're small they never explain anything to you—but on the ground floor there was a state liquor store, with policemen.

A strong odor of tobacco and cane liquor reached the room right above, a kind of jail for the liquor store where they generally put drunks who fell asleep in doorways, *cholos* who were caught with cartons of American cigarettes and cases of whiskey they unloaded from the barges anchored on the beaches in Tarqui and hid in the saddlebags on their mules, and sometimes even naughty children.

There was a hammock in the room where I swung, back and forth, back and forth, while in the dining room next door, my grandmother, my aunts, and the

*From the collection *Fiesta de solitarios*, 1992.

maids gathered around the table to listen to *The Right to be Born* on the Zenith radio. When you have a hammock and you're swinging in it, imagine that you're floating on the sea in an inner tube.

One night, just when Albertico Limonta, the doctorcito in the soap opera found out I don't know what about his real mother, there was such a commotion downstairs, almost in the middle of the street, that radio and hammock were abandoned and the window was too narrow for all the faces eager to find out what was happening in the state liquor store.

I caught a glimpse of an older boy, held by two policemen, struggling worse than a striped mullet, yelling that they shouldn't put him in jail. A man at the wheel of a jeep was also yelling, but at the policemen, and he said something like they shouldn't stick their noses in something that was none of their business, that the matter was between him and the boy, and they replied that he better get out of there or they were going to shoot. I, who was scared of everything, left the window before my grandmother yelled, "Chechiul, get inside!" I left at a run and knelt in front of the Sacred Heart of Jesus who blessed the living room and promised to behave for the rest of my entire life so that they would never put me in jail.

Right after that, my grandfather came upstairs with the story. He took off his straw hat and hung it on a hook that he had put in the wall across from the dining room. He sat at the head of the table—all he needed to be king was a crown—the cooks went to prepare his coffee and a fried plantain ball and the rest of us settled around the table, dying of curiosity.

"You remember Don Artrides Mendoza, who had a

farm just beyond Montecristi? They killed him in an ambush over a land dispute that was never cleared up entirely; that was right before Chechiul was born. Where's the coffee, girls? They say that the man who ordered the killing was Don Trajano Intriago, who died a few months later, it seems he was stung by a hornet he crossed paths with on the road. Since then, because they couldn't kill the father to avenge the death, Don Artrides's sons have sworn vengeance against Don Trajano's sons. Don't forget the salt! The fellow in the jeep tonight was Temistocles Mendoza, the oldest son. He's a man now, and he was three sheets to the wind because, they say, he was drinking with the prostotitu-ties at Blancatatitie's cababaretete. The kid was Cristóbal Colón Intriago and I believe he's about four-teen. The guards at the liquor store locked him up so that Temistocles couldn't kill him. Poor kid, he has death written all over his face."

Just then the coffee and the plantain ball arrived; I felt like I had a piece of plantain stuck in my throat and, contrary to custom, I didn't get mad when my grand-father spoke in code, but instead got up saying excuse me and that I was tired, but instead of going to my room, I went to the room over the liquor store jail to peer through one of the enormous cracks in the wood-en floor and try to see the boy my grandfather had been talking about.

The boy paced back and forth, back and forth in the tiny cell; for cases like this one my grandmother had a saying: "That boy is just like a devil in a bottle." I heard him growl and I thought of the sea between the beach-es of Murcielago and Tarqui on nights when the tide rose and pounded, furious, against the enormous rocks of the seawall.

At some point, his eyes met mine; I moved in a flash from the crack and ran again to the living room, the way I ran from the cookie jar my grandmother keeps on the highest shelf in the cupboard when I heard her footsteps. You'll say I'm a coward, but show me somebody who can look death straight in the eye.

They were round eyes, as black as the trunk of a *pechiche*. They shown like the eyes of an enraged bull trying to get out of the barbed wire he's tangled up in. If, tomorrow or the next day, somebody were to look at you that way, it's for certain because misfortune is going to be at that person's side for life. In any event, and in spite of being scared, I went back to keep watch at the cracks in the floor over the room with the hammock.

"Is it true that they're going to kill you?" I asked him in the voice I use in school when I want the classmate sitting in front of me to whisper an answer to a question on an exam.

"It's not true. They think I'm still a kid," he said in the same tone, and I was alarmed by his reply.

"And when you grow up?"

"Only God knows."

"I've got goose bumps. You have the mark of death on your face."

He roared with laughter, and I was shocked. Imagine, I was as serious as I've ever been and there he was, acting like his own life was a trinket. After I got to know him better, I realized that he always laughed at things that worried everybody else and that he got serious about the things that amused other people. But just then I was really scared and there wasn't a joke in the world that would have seemed funny to me.

"You sound like the grown-ups. Who told you that?"

I felt like I'd been caught in a mistake. But even worse, I felt stupid. Especially because his laughter was genuine. Without saying another word, because at times like that you know there's nothing more to say, I went to brush my teeth and then to my room. There I slept like a dry log.

The next day I asked my grandmother for permission to go to the beach and you'll be thinking that she must have been distracted because she said fine and she also let me go alone, but the truth is, things are different in those towns. In Guayaquil, for example, even today, even though I'm grown up because I'm fifteen years old, my mother argues with me when I want to go to the movies alone. In Manta, on the other hand, I've always gone for walks along the seawall when I have nothing better to do, and on the beaches of Murcielago and Tarqui, just like I did that day.

Have you ever seen a canoe filled with fish coming in from the sea? It's a great sight. When the waves throw the canoe toward the beach, the *cholos* put down two or three logs and they put the canoe on them, moving it along until finally the canoe looks like it's falling, tired, on the sand. In the sky, the seagulls circle round and round, and the minute the fishermen's backs are turned, they grab a fish still flopping around in their beaks. People surround the canoe and shout, offering the lowest possible price, always wanting the biggest fish.

It was almost noon. I was walking on Tarqui beach and came to a pirogue loaded with striped mullet. The net was spread on the sand and a group of swimmers watched the mullet jump. Everybody seemed fascinated by the noise and the movements they made. Suddenly, somebody signaled toward some point in the net, indicating I don't know what to the man standing next to him, and they both started laughing. I watched the spectacle, hypnotized. A whisper in my ear brought me back to earth.

"Hi, I'm Cristóbal Colón Intriago. Remember me? You never told me your name but I know you're Don Abelardo Delgado's grandson."

"Excuse me. I'm César Paúl Delgado Zamora. They call me Chechiul."

I shook his hand and he seemed a lot bigger than he had the night before. It was strange, but in his eyes the entire midday sun seemed to be shining.

"What are you doing here?" he asked in an odd tone.

"Looking at the mullet," I said, stupidly.

"You mean watching the mullet die of asphyxiation."

I couldn't think of a reply and I let him put his hand on my shoulder and, without realizing it, he moved me away from the canoe and the people.

"I hate the way grown-ups come to watch fish jumping in the nets. Look, Chechiul, it's just like if we came to sit on the beach and watch a drowning person thrashing around."

Do you know how to catch those small crabs that live in the little holes that appear on the beach? Cristóbal Colón was an expert and, thanks to him, I'm an expert now, too. The day of our first meeting I watched, open-mouthed, how he did it. First you need a piece of string a little thicker than the kind you use with a top. At one end you make a sliding loop. This is fundamental; I mean that the loop be well made. You take the other end of the string between the thumb and the index finger, with the loop hanging down, and find a hole with the tracks of the crabs still visible at the opening. If the tracks are deeper on just one side of the entryway, it's because the crab is gone; if, on the other hand, there's a tiny mountain chain around the mouth of the hole, that's because the crab is still in the hole.

According to my grandmother, with patience you get to heaven. According to Cristóbal Colón, with patience you get crabs. You have to put the string into the hole very carefully and squat there, waiting like a statue, until you feel, in the fingers holding onto the other end, something moving around the loop. That can take an eternity and then cramps become your worst enemy. When you detect a weight tugging on the string, it's because a little crab has put a claw into the loop.

That's the key moment. Cristóbal Colón says that it's like when his namesake discovered America. You have to let the crab work up its confidence and tighten the noose, from above, millimeter by millimeter. We've all pulled out loose milk teeth when we were small, tying a piece of dental floss around them and pulling hard and with a single jerk, right? That's exactly what you have to do with the string for catching crabs. The crab hangs on, and you have to put the string down on the sand right away because it tends to climb and gives a tremendous scare to the open-mouthed.

"You can take it for a walk, like a dog," Cristóbal Colón took a step and the crab followed him in a mad race, "but that's not the point of all of this. What's the point of training a crab?" Sometimes he talked like a grown-up, but I thought it was wonderful: "The patient waiting, the ability to pull the string at the precise moment, to defeat fatigue, that's the key to success. Then you pick up the crab, squeezing the pincers you untie the loop, and you let it go." He paused for a long time and then, looking at the sea, he continued just like he was a priest saying mass, "We grow by overcoming obstacles."

It was only when I realized that the entire day had gone by without our noticing that I got worried and took off at a run to get home as fast as I could. It was a sissy thing to do, of course, running away like that without saying goodbye to my friend, but when you're nine years old you get worked up about everything. I rang the bell and it was my grandmother who, like never before, opened the door.

"Ay, Chechiul! Where have you been? You gave us a fright!" she hugged me and I realized that nobody in the house was mad at me.

"But, grandma, you said I could go."

"I know that, love," she kissed me again and, as she arranged me in her arms, she added, "What did you do all day?"

"I was with Cristóbal Colón Intri…"

Before I finished, she let me go as though, suddenly, I had changed into a duckling. The maids, who'd been eavesdropping, standing straight up and close together under the little statue of the Sacred Heart of Jesus, opened their eyes wide and made the Sign of the Cross. My grandmother put her hands on her head, paced the living room several times, and came back to where I stood, very quiet, not saying a word.

"Listen to me, Chechiul, I don't want you to spend time with that boy again."

"But…why not, grandma…he's a good person and with me…"

"You aren't going out again, Chechiul… They're going to kill that boy and I don't want you to be with him when that happens, it's very dangerous. I don't want to hear another word about it. Go wash your hands and come to the table for dinner, the fried plantain patties are getting cold."

But on that occasion I had no intention of being a good little boy. I wanted to be good with myself, so the next day, without telling anybody, I went to the beach again. Except that this time I didn't go to Tarqui Beach but to Murcielago. I stopped in the street, at La Caleta, and I cracked all the knuckles of my left hand. I couldn't do the thumb and that was a bad sign but the sun was frying the people who rubbed Coca Cola on their bodies so that they'd turn the color of black coffee in a teaspoon, the sand was shining like the silverware my grandmother gets out for holidays, and the sea, though there were some whitecaps, was blue-green and filled with flashes of light, that is, ready for a little car.

Since to grow up you have to test yourself every step of the way, I took off my beach shoes and moved with skips and hops over the sand that burned until I got to the edge of the sea and could cool my parboiled little feet. I heard applause at my back; on turning around, I saw that it was Cristóbal Colón who had discovered me.

It seemed like a good time to impress him, so after secretly making the Sign of the Cross, I threw myself into the waves. I dove and grabbed about five waves with no problem so I decided to swim farther out and then I stopped and turned on my back. You don't think of anything when you're floating, you just let yourself go. Right then, I felt like the sea and the sky were all mine.

When I wanted to get back to the beach, it seemed like I stayed in the same place no matter how much I swam. I told myself not to panic, but I was panicking. Listen, you don't know what it's like, wanting to get back to shore and seeing that you're not getting any closer, no matter how hard you try. In spite of that, I kept swimming; I wasn't going to just up and die, either.

I swam a million furious strokes and, even though I was little and everything, I cussed. What made me madder than anything just then, I swear, was imagining that if anything happened, people would say that it was because I'd been bad, going out without permission, and for disobeying, for being with somebody I wasn't supposed to be with.

I started getting cramps in my toes and thrashing about so that I swallowed water and more water. I prayed to myself, angel of God my guardian dear, don't leave my side by day or by night, and an arm circled my neck and pulled me real fast to the beach. I got to the sand and threw myself on my back, gasping and with my face wetter with tears than with seawater. A little later, Cristóbal Colón hugged me and I hiccupped.

"It's ok, Chechiul, it's ok, and nothing happened. I'm always going to take care of you but don't do dumb things."

It was nice, curled up there, like at night next to a

bonfire that keeps the mosquitoes away, or like an afternoon waiting under the eaves of a house someplace for a storm to pass so that you can get on your bicycle again, definitively, we were going to be straight with one another.

"Promise that they're not going to kill you," I begged.

"I've already told you that as long as I'm a kid they're not going to kill me…"

"Promise!"

He laughed, but not too loud, and shook his head back and forth like grown-ups do when they think that kids have said something clever.

"I can't promise because it's not up to me; it's up to Don Artrides Mendoza's sons…"

"Then why did you promise that you'll always protect me?"

"Listen, Chechiul, sooner or later they're going to kill me, and that's why I can't let myself die before that happens. The Mendozas already want me and my brothers to live under lock and key, scared to death. It shouldn't matter to you if they kill me or not. I'll always be here when you need me. You just have to look out there, by day or by night, in the flashes in the sea, that's where I'll be."

During those vacations, and the next three, I sneaked out to be with him a lot without my grandparents noticing. I learned to ride the waves, to build sand castles, to dive head first from the deck of a boat, to fish with a line sitting on the stones of the breakwater, to sail a canoe and to walk in its belly without falling down, to use a casting net without getting it tied in knots, to spread the nets, to scale fish without cutting myself with the knife or the fins, to make sea bass ceviches, to throw a top and make it spin from the ground onto the palm of my hand, to play teetotum. I think that I learned just about everything anybody needs to grow up. Well, the truth is, the one thing I didn't learn was how to drink beer because I didn't like the bitter taste.

I remember the last conversation we had last year, when my vacation was almost over.

"You know what? I think I'll go to Guayaquil pretty soon."

"That's great, man!"

"Not so great, Chechiul. It turns out that at my house they're saying that I'm too old to be running around like a turkey."

"They've been wanting to kill you ever since I was small."

"That's what I say, but they still want to send me to your city. Give me your telephone number."

"Three four six three four seven."

"Hey, you have two telephones?"

For the first time since we met, I saw him stumble. I realized that I had to be careful not to hurt him even a little with my answer. It was also the first time that I spoke with no intonation.

"No, the thing is, in Guayaquil the telephones have six numbers."

Cristóbal Colón was serious for a while, then he put his hands on my shoulders and looking me straight in the eyes as if he were trying to hypnotize me, though he looked more scared than anything, he said to me with that sermon voice he used when what he was going to say was really important:

"You're going to have to teach me a lot of things about your city."

Now that I'm telling you this, I'm not sure that I've grown up enough. Let's balance the books, as the accounting prof would say. Credit column: I feel my lips puckered up and my eyes swollen, which means I'm going to cry; subtract a point from being grown-up. Debit column: I'm at La Caleta, drinking a glass of beer, not bothered at all by the bitterness; this compensates for the previous point. Balance column: Temistocles Mendoza killed Cistóbal Colón, in the early morning hours of November 4 at Blanquita's cabaret, and I've just found out.

I drink the beer down in one gulp. I pay and go to walk along the shore. As I approach the breakwater, the sea covers my feet and I hear the spattering of the foam disappearing. I feel my pants pocket for the string for catching crabs. I burst into tears and it's like I'm going to explode. My heart beats worse than an old car, and then I calm down, just like that, because all of a sudden I'm certain that he's here, with me, and that he'll be with me not only until I grow up but until I grow old. It's like the time when I saw the entire midday sun shining in his eyes.

CAROLINA ANDRADE
(Guayaquil, 1962)

Carolina Andrade is a student of literature at the Catholic University of Guayaquil, and has lived for some years in Mexico where she attended literary workshops offered by the General Society of Mexican Writers (SOGEM). She has published two volumes of short stories, *Detrás de sí* (1994) and *De luto* (1999).

Raúl Vallejo writes: "With her second book, *De luto*, Carolina Andrade presents readers with a text of tremendous maturity and sustained narrative proposals. Her writing is temperate, polished, a discursive organization that, in her dissection of the theme of death and the act of mourning, offers evidence of the wisdom she brings to the craft."

THE DEATH OF FAUSTO*

For the past seven days, Fausto has appeared in all my dreams to tell me that things haven't been going well at all since he died. Not even in those painful circumstances has he lost the ability to be charming, always young and even a little cheerful.

"What happened, Elena?"

"They say you committed suicide."

It's true, Fausto's death was said to be a suicide. I read about it in the newspapers: "Young student takes his life. The body of twenty-year-old Fausto Briones was found in the early morning hours…," in the bathroom of a hotel room, hanging from the shower, with his own belt around his neck. My husband asked me to read the reports while he expressed his sorrow about the misfortune.

It's still hard for me to accept having had a lover. Our relationship wasn't premeditated, at least it wasn't for me and I don't think for Fausto, either. He was the son of my husband's partner; his father took him to

*From the collection *Detrás de sí*, 1994.

work in the business and my husband invited him to dinner at our home on several occasions. My twenty-year-old daughter was so impressed with him that she never stopped talking about how marvelous he was, and, as always, she eventually convinced me. Fausto, for his part, went to great lengths to make me feel like the perfect woman. Everything led me to accept the fact that we would make a wonderful couple. In fact, he was beautiful. I remember how much fun sex was, and Fausto learned a lot from me. We laughed at how lovely it was, the boy was crazy. To die like that.

Fausto liked to experiment with everything, he was daring and reckless. Maybe, being a mature woman, I should have counseled him, but when I was with him I didn't feel like being an adult. One of his crazy ideas was the one about the journeys, and it's precisely that that has him so misplaced since he died. My dear Fausto used to run himself ragged, what with the university, his job, and me; this, according to those who know about these things, can become an element in the spirit's rejection of the body. Ecstatic, he told me about his first experience:

"It was incredible, Elena, I was lying in bed, dead tired, but with my eyes wide open, and suddenly it was as though I had left myself and were seeing my body from above, as though I were on the ceiling, do you understand what I'm saying?"

I understood the first time around, but that didn't stop him from explaining it to me, time and again.

"This time I scared myself and all I wanted to do was get back to my body, but next time I'm going to try to control myself."

The following occasion was not a success.

"It was terrible, Elena, and I was scared."

Fausto read a stack of book about those journeys and decided that he was going to ignore the fear. Finally, with great tenacity and a good deal of time, he managed, fully conscious and at will, to be in two places at once. It was all a game to him; in fact, he enjoyed leaving his body just about anywhere and wandering in spirit wherever he fancied going... Until the day of his death. On the night of June thirteenth, we met at the usual hotel. As a joke, or maybe to impress me, he left me several times making love just to his body; it was uncomfortable, it reminded me of my husband. Fausto laughed a lot at my anger; later, while I was getting dressed, he said that he was sorry, several times.

"I promise not to do it again."

"I hope not," I told him. "I don't like it when you laugh at me."

"Don't be mad at me. It won't happen again, I promise, it was a joke... Will you come tomorrow?"

"Yes."

That was the last time we saw each other. Fausto is also very aware of our last meeting and goes over it with me every night in my dreams.

"I didn't commit suicide, Elena. Do you think I did?"

"I find that impossible to believe."

"After you left, I decided to leave my body lying on the bed and to go into other rooms to see if there was anybody there I knew..."

"That wasn't very discrete!"

"Don't scold me. When I got back to our room, my body wasn't on the bed. I looked around for it and found it in the shower, dead. I can't get back into it. The first thing I thought about was to look for you and you told me about the suicide. It's enough to drive a person mad."

"To drive a person dead."

"Elena, please, find out what happened, so that I can be at peace. Please, Elena, please."

I have a dead man asking me for explanations every night. I don't know what to do. I can't clear up his death; I can't talk about Fausto with anyone. I don't have anyone I can talk about Fausto with. It would be unfair to deny how important he was to me, I loved him so much, he comes to me because he knows that. I don't have the heart to hurt him, it would be so painful to admit that I killed him. Besides, he would never understand.

LEONARDO VALENCIA
(Guayaquil, 1969)

Writer Leonardo Valencia has lived in Guayaquil, as well as in Lima, and in Barcelona, where he currently resides. Julio Ortega has included a story by Valencia in his anthology *Cuento hispanoamericano del siglo XXI*.

Valencia came to the attention of readers and writers with the publication of his collection *La luna nómada* (1995). Debate, a publishing house in Madrid, has brought out his first novel, *El desterrado* (2000).

The author's essays and translations have appeared in magazines in Barcelona, Madrid, and Mexico.

In each of his stories, Valencia remains faithful to a world peopled with cultural references, talismans, signs that speak to the reader of different cultures. Whether the action unfolds in Cuba, Italy, Spain, or China, his stories are metaphors for uprootedness and for the relation between human beings and their signs. His works are rigorously structured, his style meticulous, elegant, and tempered. Valencia is not a simply promising writer, but already an accomplished artist, one of the great story-tellers of contemporary Ecuador.

THE EYE OF THE CYCLOPS*

Every Sunday, for twenty-five years, Victoriano Masdéu closed himself up in the secret room of an old house with a caissoned ceiling on Trocadero Street. That part of the Cuban capital is known as Old Havana. For others, it's no more than the ancient city within a city, the city of shadows.

The room measures no more than ten square meters. A narrow skylight serves as a window, and though it provides little light, at least it ventilates the room. The walls are rough, unfinished, but wisely shield against the suffocating tropical heat, and from them hang candelabras with twisted hooks and thick tallow candles. For three generations, the room was a secret passed on exclusively from father to son. Then, finally, they told the rest of the family. They could know about it because the fears of corsairs which led to its creation had long since become no more than a dusty memory: The island was a peaceful, promising tourist emporium. Thus revealed to all, no longer a secret, the room gradually disappeared again. It was only when the

*From the collection *La luna nómada,* 1995.

first revolutionary movements came into being and the country became uncertain, that Victoriano Masdéu warned his family and his friends that they must not talk about the room to anyone. It was a secret shouted from the rooftops with a degree of faithful complicity, but it never left the intimate circle of which Victoriano became the center.

One night, Victoriano invited his former classmates from San Bernardino High School to celebrate another reunion. But Carlos Cowley, guest and friend, didn't share in the spirit of the festivities. He knew about the hiding place and he was restless. When dinner was over, he took Victoriano aside and pulled from his pocket a tiny object wrapped in a handkerchief and handed it to him.

"Hide it where they won't find it," he said to Victoriano. "It's very valuable. Anita, my wife, doesn't know that I have it. It could be of use to her when she needs money to leave the island. I'm going tomorrow."

Surprised, Victoriano didn't mention it to anyone that night. He decided to hide it in the room which no longer had any other use. Three days later, Carlos Cowley's flight was the talk of Havana. On the fourth day, closed up in the room and alone, Victoriano opened the handkerchief. He found a pocket watch with a gold watch chain, a Breguet, mounted in a case of gold inlaid with onyx and diamonds. The watch was a jewel, both because of the materials used and because of the artisan who had fashioned it and the man who had been its initial owner, according to the inscription, dated 1790: *faite par Breguet pour m. le duc d'Orléans*. But Victoriano wasn't aware of the value of the object in his care until he mentioned it to his neighbor, who was also his best friend and one of the most cultured men on the island. And so it was that on the fifth day after Cowley's flight, the poet Luis Leoncio Luna entered the room in the Masdéu house.

"Breguet watches," explained Leoncio Luna with his labored asthmatic breathing, "were already being forged on a regular basis in his day. For that reason, most genuine Breguets have, apart from the normal signature, a particular sign drawn according to a secret process and only recognizable under a certain light, and, in addition, there is almost always a registration number."

They verified the matter. In effect, on placing the watch at an angle and with the aid of the candles, they found the seal.

"I fear, Victoriano," Leoncio Luna pronounced, "that you have the singular fortune to possess one of the objects most coveted, one which incites the greatest rivalry, among international collectors today. However, somewhat apart from the piece, the conjunction of onyx and diamond bothers me. They are stones with opposing virtues. The first inspires fear in the individual who possesses it, the second confers value. It's a strange Zoroastrian balance." Victoriano, paying little attention to the unassailable disquisitions of Luis Leoncio Luna, told him how the watch had come into his hands and asked that he not say anything about it to anyone. The poet agreed with a smile.

But the Breguet was only the beginning. Later, a tiny Pi-Hsieh dragon arrived, an archaic amulet of reddish jade from the Han dynasty which, according to Chinese belief, frightened off demonic spirits. The Pi-

Hsieh was no more than thirteen centimeters high, but it came in a marble box five times that, which served as the amulet's temple. Its owner, another of Victoriano's friends, warned him that the amulet and the box were not to be separated. As he could not take it with him, he asked that Victoriano keep it for him until he returned to the island. The collector agreed. But he did so with no joy: Two of his best friends had left at almost the same time. Something told him that he would never see them again.

And so, more objects of all sizes and types began to arrive, and more than one for every friend or individual recommended, who knew about that faithful and secure depository on Trocadero Street. A prie-dieu and a Fischer cane rocker made in Bohemia arrived, three small Egyptian Shawabti carvings of cedar with finishing touches of gold, a bush with vivacious little birds made of brilliant, colorful glass from Murano, a Mexican prie-dieu with hidden joints that had belonged to Malinche, twenty-seven crystal goblets by Mosser, a flawless shining tea set of Peruvian silver, a marble Hindu jug with two handles, each in the shape of an elephant's head, a portfolio of articles that José Martí had written in his study in New York, a clock on a pedestal inscribed with the words *Tempus Fugis*, three frightening knives... There was no end to the rare objects that arrived, one after another. None was rejected, save for two or three very large exceptions, like the Pleyel grand piano with alabaster keys that a musician brought. He must have thought that the secret room was blessed with infinite space.

In was at that time that Victoriano Masdéu and Luis Leoncio Luna began to compare every detail, every novelty, the history of each of the growing number of objects in what was turning into a museum, to the amazement of the collector and the delight of the poet. Amazement because Victoriano had never imagined that his friends and acquaintances could possess objects of such a varied and costly nature. How had a watch belonging to the Duke of Orléans and an amulet from the Han dynasty come to Cuba? Who had brought them? While Victoriano immersed himself in these questions and in nostalgia for his friends, for Leoncio Luna there was no greater satisfaction that that of receiving the surprise invitations to decipher the details of each new object delivered. He refined his bookish curiosity, shedding prodigious rays of light on each of the pieces in the room, so that his erudite speech rendered them transparent and dazzled the ignorance of the collector. And so it was that the meetings took place, ritually, every Sunday. Victoriano cleaned with the satisfaction of a numismatist and repeated the odd data gleaned from his friend's casual teachings. Leoncio Luna contemplated with pleasure the antiques and recalled others that belonged to his own family. From time to time, they freely spun stories about whatever piece Victoriano was dusting and shining, as they impregnated the few square meters of the room with their cigar smoke.

Cuba became more isolated, time stopped at its long splendid coasts. Luis Leoncio Luna became famous throughout the continent for his books, but it was a sad fame. The collector raised to ten thousand the number of objects in the crowded room in which it was almost impossible to walk. Victoriano's nostalgia also grew, though in a measure without any real reference. As the private museum's collection increased and he received no news from his friends scattered throughout the United States, Mexico, and Europe, he believed that a reunion was impossible. He even thought about leaving the island. More than his family, he was anchored by the responsibility of the objects his friends had left in his charge. Luis noted Victoriano's state, though he never asked him about it. Both were condemned to never leave Cuba, the collector to see his friends, the poet to conquer his reserve with the fascination of other landscapes and the joy of fame coming late in life.

"We can't leave Cuba," Luis announced. The Anankee, destiny, is here with the fixed eye of the Cyclops."

And it was true. Luis Leoncio Luna, friend and neighbor and great baroque poet, died two years later of a cardiac deficiency. A week before, he had given Victoriano the manuscripts of a number of books of poetry, published and unpublished. The collector was as surprised as he had been on the first occasion, with Carlos Cowley. He asked, ingenuously, if he would be leaving the country. Luis responded with the smile of a Mandarin but without the exalted spirit of former times:

"I'm going to the Ultimate Thule, my dear Victoriano."

As always, Victoriano didn't understand at first his friend's erudite reference. But when he heard the gloomy hubbub in the house next door, the death rattle of the poet, a sudden, inclement grief tormented him until translating for him, fuzzy, certain, the resonances of the meaning of the Ultimate Thule.

Increasingly alone, the collector continued to close

himself up, ritually, every Sunday. He cleaned the jewelry, preserved the relics, and wandered about his
memories, putting everything in a hidden heap which
helped him to hold fast in a haphazard way to a world
ciphered in the past. We'll never know how he felt in
the face of his memories of those who had put the
objects in his hands. He believed in heirs and sudden
widows who would come to thank him for his faithful-
ness. That gesture would have been enough to com-
pensate for the years of risky silence shared with his
friend. But only Anita Cowley went to get the Breguet,
in a hurry and without reminiscences.

TABLE OF CONTENTS

LA CANTIDAD HECHIZADA
NARRATIVE: